32 DEGREES

Cover concept by Raymond Beauchemin
Cover design by Richard Nantel, Pica Productions

Digitally typeset in Adobe Garamond by Marc Elias.

Printed and bound in Canada by Hignell Printing Ltd.

Legal Deposit / Dépôt légal, Bibliothèque nationale du Québec and the National Library of Canada, 3rd trimester, 1993.

Editor's note: Thanks are extended to the following for their support of this book:

Patrick Kenniff, *Rector, Concordia University*
Martin Kusy, *Dean, School of Graduate Studies*
Brian Counihan, *Dean of Students*
Gail Valaskakis, *Dean, Faculty of Arts and Science*
Graduate Students' Association
English Graduate Students' Association
Howard Fink, *Acting Chairman, Department of English*
Benoit Pelland, *President, Alumni Association*
Gary Geddes, *Professor of Creative Writing*
Ken Whittingham, *Director, Public Relations Department, Concordia University*

Canadian Cataloguing-in-Publication Data
Main entry under title:
32 Degrees: an anthology of poetry, prose poetry, fiction and drama
ISBN 0-919688-36-5 (bound).—
ISBN 0-919688-38-1 (pbk.)

  1. Canadian literature (English)—20th Century
I. Beauchemin, Raymond, 1962–
II. Title: Thirty-two degrees.

PS8521.T34 1993   C810.8'0054   C93-090609-8
PR9194.9.T44 1993

DC Books, Box 662, Montréal, Québec, H4L 4V9

DEGREES

Prose, Poetry and Drama
from Concordia University's
Creative Writing Program

edited by
Raymond Beauchemin

LIVRES
DC
BOOKS

DC BOOKS
MONTREAL, QUEBEC
1993

AN EDITOR'S NOTE

The best way I can explain what this book means to me is to say something about myself.

My parents were born in the Montérégie region of Quebec, near Drummondville and the Rivière St. François. Separately, (my father at eighteen; my mother at sixteen), they went to Holyoke, Massachusetts, a paper mill city whose heyday was long past. Like other French-Canadian immigrants there, they settled in the same quarter, attended the same church, continued to speak their mother tongue and tried to pass the linked values of language and faith on to their children.

I spoke French until I entered kindergarten, in a school run by a French-Canadian order of Sisters. I can't say when I began to think in English because sometimes even now I don't. Some distinction existed, however—my French was an oral experience, English was how I expressed myself on paper. And writing was the way I succeeded in school.

I wrote poetry through high school and college, won a couple of local writing contests/awards, but gave it up for a career as a journalist. After seven years of reporting and editing, however, I began to write short fiction again—awful, anecdotal pieces.

At the same time, I wanted to get back in touch with my French roots, with my parents' families that are here. I left my editing job at the *Boston Herald* and came to study Creative Writing, through the English Department at Concordia University. Coming to Montreal meant submitting to the voice calling me "home," to my parentage, to fiction.

I did not know who to expect as classmates; I was hoping not to find callow and pimply youths writing bad poetry, and I didn't. I found dedicated writers like myself, with experiences that made discussions in the workshop and tavern lively and inspiring.

Among the writers in my first-year workshop were: a playwright who, while scorning governmental bodies such as the CBC harbored a yearning to be heard by them, and who moonlighted as a carpenter; a former Arctic helicopter pilot whose tales to his young daughter went long-distance to her over the phone before making it to the page; a graduate of the Banff Centre for the Arts summer program who'd spent summers as a wilderness-camp cook and who transformed semi-auto-biographical stories into prose-poems; and a world-wise traveler who punctuated her prose with images from real and imagined lands.

There were others, too, whom I met in the literature courses that also make up the master's degree. It is in celebration of the homing instinct and because of my fellow students and our professors that I commenced this project. It is to them I dedicate the book.

Had I the time and space I would have included them all in this collection. But that could not be. There are nearly one hundred graduates of the Master's program in Creative Writing, which dates to 1972. My intention was not to exclude any one writer or thesis, merely to showcase a few—some of whom are recognized and others not. Perhaps there is another anthology out there that could capture another 32 degrees.

It is a tribute to the writers, and to the program as well, that those excerpted here have donated their royalties to the Irving Layton Fund at Concordia, which pays for the Irving Layton awards for fiction and poetry, awarded annually to the finest in undergraduate writing. My time was donated, too.

My deep thanks to the writers who agreed to participate; to Mansel Robinson, who was there when it began; to Professor Terry Byrnes, Coordinator of the English Department's Creative Writing Program, who took on one more in an infinite number of projects; to Professors Robert Allen, Henry Beissel, Gary Geddes, Mary di Michele and Richard Sommer for their advice; to Howard Fink and the Department of English for their support; to Susan Brown, graduate program secretary, for her support and patience; and to Denise Roig, whose own idea for the title, *The Master's Voice,* is, I believe, as well-suited for this collection as *32 Degrees.*

The writings selected here were culled from the collection of theses available in the R. Howard Webster Library of Concordia University. Every attempt was made to remain faithful to the original thesis.

Raymond Beauchemin
Montreal, August 1993

CONTENTS

Ray Smith
from *Family*, 1985

The Princess,
The Boeing and
The Hot Pastrami Sandwich

IAN KNEW HE WAS PERHAPS SENTIMENTAL, even silly, but he was moved by landscape and the air in it. I live in the world and this is the world, he thought, as he broke down out of the cloud into the clear air and floated to a stop in the powder snow just below the avalanche platform. This Austrian valley stretching off to the right and left was deep—he could not see the valley floor from here—and steep-walled, the sides dark with rock faces and precarious evergreens picked out by the snow: a dramatic and gloomy scene. But what moved him most was the mist clinging to the mountains across and below, the mist woven through the trees, seeming still. He thought that the people who, over the centuries, lived in these valleys and who spent the long winters looking up at such mist, who climbed up through the dark woods and into the mist, would naturally come to believe in strange beings dwelling here: werewolves, goblins, trolls. Yet I don't feel gloomy because of the mist; rather, I feel…peaceful, mildly exhilarated, privileged to see the mist, because…because it is below me. And he turned and skied down into the forest, the mist.

Stephanie did not share this interest in landscape: hers was a social bent. At midday, eating wurst and dark rye in the mid-mountain restaurant, she talked of the people around them.

"You'd think the British government had imposed currency controls," she remarked. "This is the third day in a row that couple has been brown-bagging it."

She knew they were English because their outfits were at least fifteen years out of date and the woman had watery blue eyes. "And only an English woman could have that colour hair; I think it's some sort of old-fashioned rinse they buy at Boots or Marks and Spencer where it is stocked not for profit but as a tradition."

Stephanie could go on for hours like this: acute, perhaps cutting, but rarely cruel and never nasty. She was entranced by the hand movements of the English woman, the precise, almost prissy way she would select a triangle of sandwich from its waxed paper wrapper and insert it between her teeth with her lips withdrawn slightly so as not to get soiled; how, nevertheless, after chewing each piece of sandwich, the English woman cleansed her lips with a paper napkin, making sure the few crumbs were carried back to the wax paper. Sometimes a crumb fell to the table; methodically she plucked it up and placed it with the others while lifting her watery blue eyes and sweeping her gaze across the windows.

"It's absolutely, quintessentially middle-class English. I bet they're chewing each mouthful a set number of times. And contrast her with either of the Stuttgart women over there. ..." They had parked next to the two German couples at the lift base and had noted the Stuttgart license plates.

Ian looked and followed the argument: she was right, of course. But he was more interested in the window beside their table, the two walls of windows and the mid-mountain view of the valley and of the wisps of mist which suddenly evoked in his mind a passage played on the oboe, something, he thought, by Schubert.

"...while the hair on *his* hands is...inappropriate: it seems almost obscene..."

Stephanie was talking now about the English man's hands, neat, plump and offensive.

The oboe line took a turn which caused a wave of melancholy to surge through him; with difficulty Ian controlled the tears, turning away from the streamers of mist and examining the fall of Stephanie's hair, straight and brown with a henna tint; beautiful hair. And the glint and vivacity of her blue eyes, how lively; he loved the sparkle of her life, like the sun on the blue waters of Penobscot Bay last summer. They had been in Maine visiting Stephanie's Aunt Ethel and Uncle Edgar who had a house on the water in Searsport. Every day Ian stole an hour or two of reading on the lawn, but read little, for the light on the water, the light glistening in the clear air above the bay, ravished him.

How clear-headed must people be who live with this light before them, with this air around them. Twenty or thirty miles away, the cumulus-humilis clouds floated white and benign over the ocean, clearly visible; overhead, on its weathered pole, the Stars and Stripes snapped in the breeze. Every spring Uncle Edgar retired the old flag and raised a new one, the red, white and blue strong and assertive, the new cloth heavy as sailcloth. Once New England had been powerful among the United States because of clear-headed, vigorous people; but it was powerful no longer. He must read some American history to find out what had happened; had the clarity failed, or had a different Texan or Californian clarity bested it, made it irrelevant?

But the clear air was most like Stephanie's mind and he loved her for the clarity, the vigour and the agility of her mind sparkling before him. She was the business manager of their union, paid the bills, reorganized the mortgage from time to time, booked their hotels and flights, wheedled window seats for Ian. From a Qantas window seat, while she slept beside him, Ian watched moonlight shining on towering clouds over the South Pacific, stared down into the depths between the clouds and pondered the immensity of the Pacific, wondered at the idea of lazy happiness the Pacific evoked in him, so different from the brutal menace of the North Atlantic. He remembered a line in a book, something like: "*The USS Bashful* chugged slowly between the islands of Apathy and Tedium with an occasional side-trip to Monotony." The names suggested the boredom of the sailors in the irrelevant backwater of World War II, but for Ian the important thing was the immensity of the ocean under the hot blue sky decorated with towering but harmless clouds. He thought of a television series about the war in which the Pacific had seemed so, and the goings-on across the Gilberts, Marshalls, Carolines and Marianas seemed, however gigantic in human terms, somehow small and insignificant in oceanic terms. Surely more important was that Gauguin and Stevenson had come here seeking peace rather than adventure. Was there something about these skies that granted a comforting humility? Not a humility which suggested the vanity of human desires, the futility of action, but the proper scale of man's state in the universe. And just as the North Atlantic could be peaceful in reality (as on Penobscot Bay) so the Pacific could be brutal; and somehow this was all connected with the *Enola Gay* in a sky of towering clouds; and the fireball and the towering cloud that sunny Sunday morning.

And presently Ian was able to watch the glow of dawn grow over the

Tasman Sea, lighting the depths between the clouds, dispelling the moonlight mystery and revealing, at last, the blue waters, green growing luxuriance and red tiled roofs of Sydney under the sun.

Ian and Stephanie had one child, Elizabeth, who shared qualities from both of them. Her hair, blond in infancy like Ian's, darkened like Stephanie's and she had Stephanie's quick, chatty sanity. Yet she could lie quiet in her father's lap while he read to her about the princess with the golden cup and the silver cup and the tin cup and the wicked stepmother who tried to steal them.

"Am I a princess, Daddy?"

"You're my princess, Lisa."

"But maybe you're not my real father and Mummy's not my real mother and my real Mummy and Daddy are a king and queen in a faraway land and they're hiding me from the wicked stepmother. Couldn't that be, Daddy?"

"It *could* be, I suppose, but then someday a herald from the king and queen would come and take you back to be a princess and you wouldn't see Mummy and Daddy any more."

"Oh yes I would, because I would be a princess and I would give commands and you and Mummy would get on a Boeing 747 and fly to the faraway land and visit me in the palace all 'spenses paid."

She was six years old when the herald came to her disguised as a drunk in a late model car; as far as is known, she did not become a princess in a faraway land; nor were commands given in regard to Boeing 747 flights; and her light faded from their lives ever so gradually, like the fading light of a northern summer sunset; and all their lives her memory glowed like the sun on the horizon.

Sunsets, though, were too easy, too obvious, like the beauty of Rio de Janeiro: Ian had decided that cityscapes were a form of landscape, and took a perverse pleasure in strolling about Edinburgh in the chill drizzles of January.

"By the Water of Leith, we sat down and wept," he murmured. Stephanie, with a more sensible attitude toward gestures, hustled him off to a talky pub on Rose Street and a pint of Leith Heavy for each of them, pun intended. She did not mention Elizabeth—what was the point?—but talked instead of the bright Celtic humour in the Scottish eyes, the languid curl of humour in the voices which caressed and piqued the words. "There is a generosity about the Scots which is most appealing. The Irish have sharper tongues, I think, they're more interested in pinching you into a reaction. It's easy to see why the Irish have a greater reputation for charm and laughter than the Scots, because they make jokes for an audience, they always have one eye on the listeners, looking for reaction, approval, a conspiracy of wit. The Scots, on the other hand, make a joke just for the friend and give it privately as a gift; theirs is a domestic friendship, warm and cozy. The Irish are performers on public display, and are therefore like actors, always a bit false and a bit disreputable. Now look at the group of three by the window, the girl with the green scarf and the two men. For some reason, which I can't guess for sure, although she is with the tall guy, she is trying to flatter the one in the blue sweater. Why she is doing it is not important—perhaps he's had a fight with his girlfriend; anyway, I don't mean she's trying to promote an affair with him—but she is definitely making up to him, but is doing it without making anyone, especially the tall one, uncomfortable. That touch on the sleeve, see, and the way she leans forward slightly when she laughs: those are inclusive gestures when we see that her other elbow is always near the tall one and her eyes go to the tall one quickly and with change *during* the laugh. She is flirting, of course, but openly and innocently, to promote the unity and warmth of friendship, not the division and…guile of an affair."

But while she went shopping along Princes Street, he walked in the drizzle through the squares and crescents of New Town, a section of cityscape remarkable, perhaps unique in the world, for its civilized unity and warmth, its lack of division and guile. In the late afternoon gloom, he stood in Charlotte Square swept by winds and sheets of rain and considered the admirable Adams' proportions about him. Here one could well imagine Hume's clarity, sanity and especially his good cheer (even though Hume had surely been dead before the square was built); here one could accept the notion of a semi-barbaric people bootstrapping themselves into a moral, intellectual and scientific force in the world; here one could look from the deepening darkness at the warmth of the windows of gold light and the people within, warm and chatty. He stood in Charlotte Square for some time gazing at the windows while the wet wind harried him; and so he mourned his daughter.

Stephanie had always been alert to his moods, but had thought it wise to leave him to "moon on his own." His suggestions about a trip to Greenland enraged her, for Elizabeth had been her daughter, too. She took him instead to Cortina where, yes, he was entranced by the Dolomites changing colour through the day, a shimmer of colours: rose, rose pink, pink, dark pink, red, red gold, gold, pale gold, ochre, buff, sand, pale orange, salmon, salmon pink, and so to pink again; a useless list of words, he said to Stephanie, because the colours of the mountains were too delicate, too evanescent for words.

Too evanescent indeed, said Stephanie to herself, and tried to interest him in people; though Cortina is an international resort, everyone becomes Italian to a degree, enamoured of display, of pose, of excess, of opera.

"Italians are, of course, the most transparent and the most opaque of Europeans, for their motivations are all operative: simple and childishly obvious. At the same time, however, we have to suspect that behind all the shouting and laughter and waving of hands there might be real human beings who think and feel just as we do; who, could they be cornered and somehow forced to stop acting, would admit to the ordinary muddle of ambiguous and obscure emotions. 'Yes, it is true, we Italians are basically human beings like the rest of you. Heavens, I suppose we're no different from the Swiss. Imagine! But I think perhaps our centuries of political instability—an accident of history more than an expression of character—have forced us in upon our families and the privacy of our own souls. When public life is always false, when it always means something other than what it pretends, then we adapt by becoming performers: actors and singers. Our deep affinity for opera is, as you have pointed out, Signora Stephanie, obvious enough to the point of cliché, but it is nonetheless real. But inside, yes, we Italians are just like everyone else, even the Swiss.' "

"He didn't say that to you."

"He did."

"I wish I'd been here to hear it. He certainly didn't look very reflective."

Ian had, on a pretext, snuck out to look at the mountains under the moonlight to see if they changed colour (they did) and Stephanie had filled in the time talking at the bar with Emilio whom they had met when he and his rather plain young wife had been seated with them at dinner. Emilio, as Ian had suggested, was handsome, even beautiful, the classic tall, dark Italian with delicate yet masculine features, a voice like the caress of true love (heartbreakingly beautiful with an undertone of poignant sadness) and gestures which displayed, with pellucid clarity, a remarkable range of simple, obvious, direct emotions utterly devoid of obscurity or ambiguity. Or, as Stephanie had put it, "Pretty but boring."

Now she said: "Ah, but he was reflective."

"What do you mean, 'was'?"

"Well, as soon as he said Italians were like the Swiss—said it the second time, I mean, at the conclusion—his face began to change, rather as if he had choked on his drink, which he may well have done. His eyes began to bulge out, his cheeks took on a red flush and his lips began to tremble. He staggered to his feet and had to hold on to the bar with one hand while the other rested, palm outwards, on his brow. His eyes looked up to heaven in supplication, his eyelids fluttered, then gradually he seemed to regain control. When his legs were steady, he let go of the bar, held one hand to his heart, flourished the other in the air and began to sing some aria by, I think, Donizetti. But before he was two lines into it his body was racked by spasms and he began another one, this time sad, so that he went down on one knee, clasped his hands before him in prayer and began to weep. Two lines into that one his body froze for a few seconds, then he leapt to his feet and gave a scornful 'Ha!' and began the derisive song of a young hero defying tyranny. He went through half a dozen of these changes, the variety remarkable, the clarity perfect, but they began to come faster, one beginning before the other was quite over. Gradually he was moving toward the balcony door over there. By this time, of course, he had the attention of the room. With the door open, he grabbed the red cape of the woman—you remember, the one in black who was sitting on the beige couch—wrapped himself in it, paused, then vaulted out, up to the railing, turning to sing snatches from ten arias, then leaped off."

"But it's thirty feet to the ground there!"

"Not to worry: he disappeared in a flash of light and a puff of smoke. Opera, you must remember, is an essentially harmless entertainment."

But while Ian enjoyed the felicity of her wit, he was thinking of the white wastes of Greenland and less than a year later, in storms of argument, they separated, he not to Greenland, but to Arabia; she, after considering London and Paris, to New York. Of course, he was seeking some sort of cleansing purity under the sun, craving the simplicity of a stark land under blue sky; but he found government regulations about travel, he found jovial and shark-like businessmen in his hotel: a computer programmer, a construction engineer, a stock consultant, a hotel architect, a highway contractor, a perfume manufacturer, a pipeline surveyor, a salesman of executive jets; and he found money; and air conditioning. Thus, when Stephanie called and suggested he visit her in New York, he accepted with rather more enthusiasm than he let on.

They were both beaten by the frustration of their grief for Elizabeth and by their separation and wanted a way back, not so much to what had been, but to something like it, something they could live through together. Ian recognized that she was the wiser of the two and put himself in her hands. Indeed, by coming to New York he was admitting he could not live without her and she was right. He worried that perhaps she would talk to him endlessly about people and how people must get on and talk and deal with one another and he was prepared to endure this, but she did not do it. Instead, after a certain amount of hesitation— a day or two while he talked of the loathsome hotel life of Riyadh—she came to a decision and showed him:

a one-armed man who smiled,

an aged, reclusive actress buying oranges,

Berman the tailor who joked as he smoked and coughed his lungs out,

three child prostitutes joking with a cop,

an off-duty cop who bought them many drinks and, in the small hours, wept for all the lost people of his city,

a little old lady from Dubuque,

a struggling actress from Sandusky,

Berman the deli owner who claimed he made the best hot pastrami sandwich in New York ("by which, of course, I mean the woild"), and who certainly made a great one,

the body of a heroin addict, black, about fourteen,

three fat ladies squinching up their eyes with delight as they bit into pastries,

a famous writer-actor-director playing clarinet rather warily in a club,

two chess players in the park, both from one of the Baltic republics, one small, neat and quiet, the other large, dishevelled and talkative,

a man who danced with his wife, repeatedly, and obviously loved it,

a young woman on a street corner who seemed not to have enough hands for her briefcase, portfolio, shopping bag, suit jacket, wallet and lunchbag, and who smiled with all her teeth when a truck driver whistled at her, but did not whistle back,

a young woman studying viola at a famous music school who laughed brightly but nevertheless committed suicide a few weeks later,

a flight attendant who said, "Memphis? No, we don't have a base in Memphis, but I wish we did: no more Memphis layovers!"

an insurance executive who wrote fine poetry,

a well-known movie actor, a specialist in villains, who bowed graciously as he held open the door of a shop for a young woman he did not know and who did not recognize him,

a pickpocket getting caught and shrugging,

a man in a business suit standing in the middle of traffic with tears running down his cheeks,

a man whose clothes were held together with safety pins and who claimed the earth is crystalline and will shatter if we all get together and hum the right note,

a man who said, "The fish import business? What I don't know about the fish import business you could roll into a ball and stuff up a mosquito's nose and still have room for my wife's left bazoom and let me tell you, my wife is built, ya know what I mean?"

a roomful of people having sexual intercourse with strangers,

two smashing transvestites who, for two and a half hours, explained Monteverdi's place in the history of Western music, nay, of Western civilization,

ten lords a-leaping,

eleven pipers piping,

twelve drummers (one the leader of his own band) drumming,

and old Uncle Tom Cobbleigh and all,

and Ian had to admit to Stephanie's victory so that, although she loved him more than ever and conceded that their next trip should be down the storybook, castellated Rhine from Mainz to Cologne, he had to concede that it should be on a boat filled with people drinking and singing and dancing,

and so it was,
and they lived fairly happily for quite a while afterwards.

❡

Julie H.P. Keith
from *The Healthy and Happy Garden*, 1989

Falling

THE BOWL OF FLOWERS sits slightly askew on a pile of magazines. As though someone has abandoned it there, guesses Lil, and some time ago, too. The petals of the daffodils have frayed into brown shreds. The crimson tulips are definitely overblown. But they have spread themselves wide to reveal surprisingly opulent centers—the purple so dark it looks almost black—and the contrast is arresting. Beautiful really. Only not like tulips, Lil decides. Not what you'd expect.

She has spent the quarter of an hour since she and Edward arrived in just this manner, trying to keep her focus on inanimate objects—to avoid, that is, the faces of the people around her. Especially the face of Edward's first wife. Joanna's dislike sits like a stone in Lil's stomach. Trying to ignore the weight of it, she has been staring earnestly around the room. By turns she has taken in the walls, the furniture, the curtains, compared their various shades of beige and cream and palest yellow, imagined how the room would look if someone straightened it up, and generally managed not to hear more than a few words of the men's conversation. Phrases like "sheer expediency" and "the next election or else" have occasionally reached her. But her mind is bouncing crazily around. It's awful to be hated, she thinks now, for perhaps the third time, glancing again at the ravelled edges of the daffodils. Awful. If only someone had cleared those dead ones out, just left the tulips, added water....If only this...if only that...You'll have to stop it, she tells herself.

A comfortable duet of male laughter signals the success of the conversation, and Lil casts an involuntary glance at their host, Colin. He has kind eyes, she decides. And his curly brown beard gives him the look of a minister. Quite unlike Edward's fierce, clean-shaven jaw. Colin, in fact, looks altogether a gentler sort of animal. And, really, doesn't this make sense after all? For Joanna would surely have chosen a softer, more contemplative character as her second husband. At least this seems reasonable—why would anyone risk getting hurt a second time—and Lil rather hopes it is so. She feels the need of a sympathetic type in the room. She wants Colin—as indeed she would want any man—just a little bit on her side. And yet…isn't there something about him that does remind her the tiniest bit of Edward? Her eyes flick to Edward and then back to Colin. No, they really don't look alike. Something in the quick, positive way they both speak then? Is it possible that Colin, like Edward, prefers at any given time to run the show? He does have kind eyes though….

"Sounds like a double-edged sword to me!"

Colin's remark startles Lil out of her reverie. What does he mean? But then she realizes that it's only a response to some statement of Edward. And now, as if he is resting on this particular contribution, Colin has leaned back in his chair and is taking a large swallow from his glass. The wine represents his newest find at the liquor commission…a Sauvignon blanc if Lil got it right.

Colin explained all this about the wine in the first cavernous moments of the visit. Australian, he informed them, while pouring out four big goblets, each so full he seemed to be making some further assertion. He was positive they would like it.

"Exactly," Edward is replying. "It won't matter what reason they give. The deed is done." The two men nod knowledgeably at each other, and then Edward, too, takes a large swallow of wine. In fact, thinks Lil, they seem to have adopted a common tone altogether. It's as if they've arrived at precisely the same opinion as to how this or any situation ought to be handled…and she, therefore, should just relax.

Easier said than done though. Daring to glance at their hostess, Lil sees that her eyes are flickering ominously. Whether from boredom or emotion would be difficult to say. Joanna is not easy to read as her eyes travel from the genial Colin, gently pompous in spite of his good intentions, to Edward's vigorous features, and then slowly drop away. She gets up and moves out toward the kitchen.

It's almost, Lil thinks, observing Joanna's heavy, swaying walk, as if she can't stand Edward's presence. Or maybe it's their collective presence. Not one more instant of the wicked couple.

But no. For a moment later Joanna is back with a tray of cheese and bunches of fresh, dripping watercress. She steps around a pile of newspapers and carefully places her burden on the coffee table. At no time do her eyes lift to glance at Lil, who is seated directly facing the tray. The effect of this is to galvanize Lil.

"What beautiful watercress," she cries as if jabbed. "Oh, cheese! Oh, I'm so hungry!" Sitting up straight she snatches a nugget of cheese and pops it into her mouth.

Joanna says merely in her soft, slow voice, "It grows here." She crosses the room and sits again. Lil slumps back. She will be stuck here in Joanna's living room forever.

"No crackers?" complains Colin, putting down his wine and peering over at the coffee table.

"We're out of them," Joanna says.

"Well, then what about that pumpernickel I bought the other day?" he asks. Joanna shrugs and then nods her assent.

Colin turns his head and draws in a breath. "Teddy," he calls. "Teddy! Will you come in here a minute?"

The boy appears almost immediately in the doorway. He is nearly ten, cheerful, slightly impatient and, thinks Lil, in much the same state of disorder as this depressing room. She smiles quickly at him and then glances at Edward. He too is smiling at Teddy. Something brown has smeared the boy's cheek—peanut butter perhaps, or chocolate. The tail of his shirt hangs well below his sweater. Nonetheless he is perfectly at ease, the only person present who is. Colin instructs him to bring the package of bread. "On a cutting board. Don't forget the knife...."

"And hold the knife point down," adds Joanna. "If you fall..."

The boy looks amused at their fussing. "I will, I will," he interrupts.

They can hear his running footsteps, the banging of drawers or cabinets, and then a moment later he is back. He slides the board with bread and knife on it in between the cheese tray and the precarious bowl of flowers. "OK?" he challenges them and stands back.

Edward, who has been watching this entire effort, lifts his hand abruptly. "Come here," he orders. The boy smiles as though this is some special joke.

As he sidles near, Edward reaches out and makes a grab for him. The boy dances back, then comes forward again suddenly to thrust his arms around the man's neck. In turn, big tweed arms enfold almost the whole of the boy's narrow body. And for what seems a long moment, the two hug. Then Edward's arms drop down. Meticulously he tucks in the errant shirt tail. He pats the boy's rear and then, as if inspecting his person, turns him full around, still in the circle of his arms. "Now then…" He grips the boy between his knees, takes out a handkerchief and rubs off the brown smear.

"There," he says, and grins at the boy. "I can see your face."

"OK, Daddy. OK, OK," says Teddy, ducking his head. He squirms in the vise of his father's knees, but he too is grinning. Released a moment later, he remains standing by Edward's chair, one hand on the arm. His eyes, skipping from one grown-up to another, taking in every move, are as eager as his father's. His mouth turns up at the corners with the same optimistic curve.

Lil has to remind herself that he is not merely a small, elfin Edward. He has been easy for her to love on this account—he resembles his father so greatly—but, of course, he has other traits as well. Different traits. Oh, my, she thinks suddenly. Teddy's soft, pale hair must certainly come from Joanna. His wide forehead, too, now that she thinks of it. And what else? Many things no doubt. Oh, what a price, Lil says to herself, really feeling it. Poor Edward…what an awful price. And leaning forward, by reflex almost, she takes a piece of the bread and holds it up for a moment in front of her face, as if somehow to hide the glimmer of triumph she cannot help but feel.

¶

Colin, who has decided at this point that all is going rather well, gets up and crosses to the coffee table. Smiling benevolently at Lil, he proceeds to arrange the cheese and bread into miniature sandwiches which he then offers around the group, with varying results.

Lil bounces slightly in her seat. "Oh, thank you," she cries. "I mean…no, thank you. I have some…. I can reach it if I want…." and she sinks down again into the sofa cushions. Teddy wrinkles his nose as the tray passes. Edward takes a piece of cheese only, leaving the bare slice of bread abandoned on the tray. Joanna, with the merest shake of her head, closes her eyes as the tray approaches. It's all too much, her expression implies.

His duty done, Colin replaces the tray on the coffee table,

appropriates two of the sandwiches for himself, and returns to his chair. Now that the guests have been supplied, he happily eats a sandwich. For one thing, he is hungry, and besides, he loves a sharp cheddar—nothing better, except that it does sting his tongue. He has told Joanna this many times—that for him the taste of cheese is too strong without the alleviating blandness of crackers or bread—but she forgets. Not that she means to be indifferent, he has decided. It's simply that individual tastes do not seem important to her.

Now, settling the second sandwich on the arm of his chair, he takes a large swallow of the wine. Definitely full-bodied. Even with the cheese. He nods to himself, but does not say anything for fear of sounding pompous. (He knows he can easily overdo this sort of thing.) He does however like to serve good wine. Full-bodied if possible. And he really is generous. He does like to take care of people. Throughout the visit, in fact, he has been keeping an eye on Joanna, a somewhat solicitous eye, for it is he who has urged her to take this step, a sort of normalization of relations. Also, he admits to himself now, he is guilty of a certain amount of curiosity. The former husband, Edward, appears at the house from time to time, collecting or delivering Teddy. But the second wife, this Lil, has remained offstage, an outline merely, an unseen and therefore oft-imagined character in the drama. Until now. And now he is surprised. This second wife, the vamp, the villainess of many tales, is ordinary looking. Long of body, dark and unkempt of hair, no more than pretty, she sprawls on the sofa, her legs jammed awkwardly under the coffee table. She is plucking crumbs of the bread off her sweater with angular fingers. If asked, Colin would say she looks pleasant enough, but not glamorous certainly. And no poise either...none of Joanna's pleasing languor, the stillness that hovers about her person. For Colin, wherever Joanna sits, wherever she stands, seems always the quietest place in the room. By contrast, Lil's corner of the sofa is positively aquiver. Of course, the girl is probably a little ill at ease. At any rate she has barely spoken except to produce the burst of compliments about the cheese, which she has hardly touched since.

So where then, thinks Colin, munching his way through the second sandwich, where is the Cleopatra he has been awaiting? The scene-stealer par excellence? For the implication has always been that the theft of Edward was accomplished by means of a physical attraction no less than magical. And yet, he does not doubt the truth of Joanna's perception. The image of "the other woman," the stories of betrayal and suffering through the long affair, have dominated too many late-night conversations for Colin not to believe in the history of treachery, in the reality of the pain endured by his wife. They jerked her around. That's the sort of thing she says when the memory takes hold of her. Edward was there, but he wasn't, and she, Joanna, never figured it out. She just worried. She kept thinking if she got pregnant again.... Whenever she reaches this point, her voice slows and she stares straight ahead. Colin knows then to put his arms around her.

He glances over at her now and nods to himself. The need is still there. For isn't it true that in the small, light eyes of his wife, in the blueish tint of her eyelids and soft bruised look of her mouth, which is not now smiling, the suggestion of martyrdom remains?

She is replying to some remark of Edward's. At the same time, Colin sees that Lil is dragging herself up into a more presentable position. Her corner of the sofa seems to provide no leg room, and the coffee table with its burden of magazines, breadboard, flowers, and cheese is still jammed up against her knees. But at least, thinks Colin (who likes his women to be womanly), she can no longer be described as sprawling, and she does have one elbow neatly propped on the pillow beside her.

¶

Lil has decided, in fact, that it's time she make another foray into the conversation. For, whatever the larger truth, she has no call to take on the role of guilty party within this gathering. Besides I'm much younger, she reassures herself. As though guilt can accrue only with age.

The cheese and watercress topic having been exhausted, she considers asking either about Teddy's school—isn't there some soccer game or school play in the offing?—or about Joanna's garden. However, the flowers are too decrepit to be discussed, and the topic of Teddy is likewise fraught with danger. Is there anything safe to offer? She glances around without taking in much—at best she could certify that no one is either weeping or snarling, that the sounds issuing from the various mouths fall into normal range—and is tempted suddenly to announce that this whole visit is a bloody farce. She blows in this manner from time to time. Such unpredictable behaviour is one of the things that attracted Edward in the first place. Lil's lean, girlish body, her explosive reactions and energetic triumphs, even her downfalls excite him still. And Lil is not above making a scene to attract his attention. She knows well enough what he likes. It is only consideration of the consequences for him here that makes her pause. Edward has, now and seemingly for all time, a precious hostage in the enemy camp.

"Such lovely flowers!" The high-pitched declaration startles them all. Lil as much as anyone else. She has heard her own voice with genuine surprise. The bravery of it enchants her. She hopes that Edward has taken notice. "I saw the garden coming in," she adds by way of explanation and makes a gesture that nearly knocks over her goblet. "I mean outside…you grow them?" She addresses this last to Joanna, who tips her head slowly to one side as though she is regarding someone demented. "I mean…" Lil chokes back a sharp desire to laugh. "I mean," she says carefully, "are you the one who does the gardening?"

Joanna consents to nod. "The soil here is good," she says quietly. "And spring flowers are easy of course. Later on…" She shrugs. "Working, I don't have much time…." Her voice is dead calm. Colin stiffens in his chair. The "working" remark must be meant for Edward. But Joanna is going on. "Teddy helps me," she says.

"That's nice," says Lil. She looks over at Teddy and then at Edward, who does not immediately see her glance. His eyes appear to be fixed somewhere well above Joanna's head. Lil's eyes move to the painting that hangs on the wall behind Joanna. And abruptly she remembers. It must be the one he has described, the one he chose for its colours—deep stormy blue, slashes of red—the one Joanna wouldn't give back. From time to time he still conjures up anger over the refusal. The painting was his, and indeed, thinks Lil, it does seem out of place in this pallid room. Too rich, too strident. She glances back at Edward hoping to catch his attention. Did he imagine back then the same thing she is imagining now? Yes, she decides, of course. The simile seems so obvious…that here in Joanna's house, the painting is like an escape route. No less. It is like a window through the pale wall.

❡

Colin glances at Lil glancing at Edward and decides that there is no question—his own wife is definitely the more attractive. Edward must have been out of his mind. Joanna's dove colouring, the slowness of her movements compared to this jerky boy-woman....He sees Lil drain her glass and realizes that his own and Edward's glasses are nearly empty as well. His caretaking, host's nature twitches. However, he has made a promise to Joanna. He will not offer refills. Enough tolerance and civilized behaviour being enough. She does not, quite naturally, want them there all afternoon, and since Colin is the sort who hates to let his guests go, he has been made to promise.

But still he feels chagrined as Edward and Lil lock eyes. Do they sense the hospitality withdrawn? Probably. At any rate they are agreeing with little nods that the time has come. They must go. Rising, Edward places his hand on Teddy's head as though he is memorizing the shape of the crown. Lil gets uncertainly to her feet. She glances around, searching for her purse, wondering evidently if she should clear away any of the glasses or anything else. Once or twice she shifts her weight. Her movements seem unstable, unpredictable even, especially compared with Joanna's smooth rolling walk as she leads Edward and Teddy out of the room.

Only Colin is left watching a moment later when Lil abruptly pivots, her mind made up, her face fresh with relief, and grabs up her purse. And it is then, at this moment so nearly at the end of the visit, that he sees the sudden grace of her. Like a running animal, he thinks, staring at the unfolding body. She seems to be moving too quickly as she crosses the room. Out of control nearly. Her knee has jarred the coffee table, her shoulder smacked hard against the doorframe. There is a sense that she may carom off the face of the earth. As she swings around into the hall, he feels a hunter's urge to chase her, to corner her and make the confrontation last. Eye to eye he would face her down. Her fear, if it is fear, would make him strong.

And yet in the moment he takes to catch up to her, the illusion of flight has disappeared. She is uttering a too effusive thank-you, then fumbling her way out the door after the others, putting one hand on the stair railing to steady herself, starting down the stairs. As he is watching this performance, she suddenly turns her head and glances back, and he is totally unprepared for the smile that streaks across her face. A brilliant, almost hysterical smile. He can hear the ring of laughter behind that smile. And the look she flings at him now, a look clearly meant for him alone, is both so full of guilt and so confident of his forgiveness that he thinks she would be able literally to get away with murder.

He is still standing there stunned when she misses her footing at the bottom of the flagstone steps and stumbles into his wife's border of daffodils. And without warning the whole of his heart rushes out to her. He wants to leap down the stairs and help her, to right with his own hands that long, kneeling body. And standing there in the wake of his wife's pained cry and Edward's exclamation, forbidding himself to move a muscle, he imagines with absolute clarity just exactly how it would be to fall in love with her.

¶

Jennifer Clark
from *raspberry vinegar*, 1985

this is a story

we first met in absentia he was in hospital having
very serious surgery and they put me in his office
which was so permeated with his presence I felt
almost calm which was hard in those days there was
an old drafting table covered with cigarette burns
my favourite and coloured markers all over the place
mostly dried up because their lids had been left
off and low dusty shelves with stuff dating back
20 years there was a scraggly collection of plants
and a wooden swivel chair which had lost its swivel
but not its tilt on the walls were bits and pieces
of things which weren't necessarily important to
him but got tacked up anyway to avoid getting thrown
away by the cleaning lady and had stayed on the
wall maybe 5 10 years and yellowed there there was
a small window with a radiator you could adjust till
the room was just about like an oven they gave me a
typewriter and I cleaned up a spot to put it on but
I always waited till the last minute to do things I
liked to keep the office door almost shut and sit
in his chair or look out the window somehow it just
felt reassuring not to do anything just to be I
could have gone up to the hospital to see him but
things got mixed up and I helped them choose a book
for him instead the secretary came back and reported
that his hands were so tiny and dry with tubes in
them

this is a story 2

when he came back we became friends almost right
away I wanted to be around him all the time I was
never afraid of having nothing to say or saying
something stupid it all came out like the funny
lettering that comes out of the mouths of saul
steinberg characters we laughed all the time
there was a man who had been his partner and
liked him too and he was very angry with us
though he never took it out on him he took it
out on me he would slam his door in my face
but we just kept getting closer and closer

this is a story 3

people were always in his office mostly women they
just loved talking to him there was something edible
about him you just couldn't get enough like thick
peanut butter sandwiches or dipping your fingers in
the honey jar he was a listener women told him their
stories about their boyfriends and their lack of
boyfriends and while they talked he smoked or he
drew always one or the other and then he'd get up
and butt his cigarette into a plant pot and everybody
would exclaim uggggh and he'd light another he
could talk and work at the same time he'd rip the
finished sheets off his layout pad and they'd come
in and take them away I wondered how he could
listen so much and never say even a little bit about
himself never even the tiniest me or myself it was
control like iron bands or all those padlocks
houdini used to work with once the company tried to
get rid of him but he survived and nobody knew that
at home he rebuilt his concrete steps and as he smashed
at the concrete he fought them all it was a privilege
to be told these things

this is a story 4

I knew he cared for me but every now and then the
bottom would fall out of it all and I would wonder
if he was just friendly to me like everybody else
I thought I saw something which other people didn't
see while they were telling him things while
he was listening and everybody loved him he was really
far far away he was a sea shelf and they were the sea
which just came and went and didn't make any difference
when you don't need anybody everybody needs you
I was never jealous of him except once when we got
a new department secretary and she discovered him
like everybody else I started off liking her a lot
but things went wrong she was tall and she wore
brownish lipstick always kind of fresh and wet and
she obviously spent a lot of time ironing her clothes
and polishing her shoes I wondered if she ever got
depressed and just didn't feel like putting a lace
camisole under an ironed blouse she talked about
her boyfriend phil all the time and how they made
love all night once he told me she came in with
her hair kind of matted and looking sort of cross-
eyed because she and phil had been on another marathon
he liked hearing about it because he liked talking
about sex then she got pregnant by phil my little
phil she would say she wanted to pose for him because
he was talking about drawing classes at the time
but the classes never happened so one day she just
lifted up her dress and showed him her stomach
I imagine it was brown like the rest of her

this is a story 5

if you love someone I guess you want to share things
with them maybe you share a bed a trip to europe many
years a child we shared escape from everything sitting
on our two chairs playing possum with everyone around
us I want to go to the arctic he said I'll go with
you I said it's not such a bad life except soon it's
all over and something's kept you from doing things
everyone always kept asking him for drawings I rescued
one from the garbage and got it mounted it is a perfect
little square of rows and rows of women's faces looking
up which is unusual because his drawings were
women's torsos and occasionally watercolour trees so
beautiful they looked just like a tear splashed on the page
and burst into bloom the people you really love go
away

this is a story 6

if I lose my mind I hope they let me keep a
few fragments I wouldn't need much because
moments with him were like a lifetime lived fully
and well I would ask for the memory of late
afternoon when he would draw and I would think
of words and I would place my feet through the bars
of his chair under his side I would ask for
the memory of the day he asked me to his
daughter's wedding

this is a story 7

one day the company folded most companies go
bankrupt slowly but this company died so fast
people's coffee cups were still full on their
desks we packed up our things and there was
something we couldn't share his feelings about
a long hard life in the company while I packed
up my things effortlessly he stared at his
markers and table and drawings like burn wounds
we could have been in a wheat field with the
wind whipping the shafts furiously we got in somebody's
car and drove first to his home and left his things
on the front steps and then to my home and left
my things in my apartment lobby years have passed
we have reorganized our lives we had photos taken
of us in front of a church the church wasn't intentional
but was suggested by the photographer who was a man
we liked a lot at the company we sat on the grass
in late autumn and we were laughing a lot and in
the middle of the session a young man came up to us
and said this was the exact spot he was supposed to
meet his brother whom he hadn't seen for years
after saying it he didn't really interrupt us just
stood quietly while the photographer took more
photos there we were very close in black and white
stuck side by side unless somebody loses the photos but
that doesn't erase the fact they were taken but
what is most amazing is the foliage behind us it
is like a theatre backdrop was it an accident or
was the photographer so perceptive to see we once
made leaves together

¶

Ruth Taylor
from *The Dragon Papers,* 1991

I know you.

I read the blistered braille
my breath has traced into your thighs.

I feel the stars stab
and drag at your tidal hair.

I see you clawing out the open dark.

Raw honey flows in your spine
and charges your discs.

I know where you lie, pearled and foamed,
in moony filigree with river hair undone
and oh, like a falling bloom
my Andromeda, the shortwave of your sigh
the lithe eternity of your postures
the too-perfect solitude of your skin, silence
your only infidelity.

I am dressed as a bride
at the mouth of your cave.
I am strapped to a jagged rock
the waves crashing around me.
Impale me quickly
on your monstrous tooth
wind your sinews into me
bind me in your Python's grip
burst the blood from me
that our bloods may commingle.

Fill me with the heads and tails
of your code, let
our mutual blood fall into the foam.
Rise, rise, my monstrum, my own.
Bathe me in blood's seed,
let me grip you in gentle tiger's paws, shed
my bridal skin, seethe myself
in my own milk, become
alabaster, submerged in the gulfs
of your groans.

Show me
your peacock's colours, render me
iris of your image in a rain
of living gold. Cleave me
from this rock, this morbid stone.
I am dehydrated as a crone.
Come, water me,
water me.

From the beginning it has been only this you've wanted—
simple images, a clear voice, an authoritative tone. You've wanted
the ins and outs of dragons, rain rushing down hard and fast,
burning of belladonna, sculpting of mandrakes into women and
men. How can I convince you meditation is its own reward?

Yes, rain falls, snow flies, kettle boils and dishes are stacked in
the sink. Yes, this is the brink of exhaustion where I curl up and
rock to my heart's slow metronome. Nevertheless, I am here, now,
some kind of maniac, neurasthenic, giggling at etymologies,
cackling at word and wyrd, drawing the moon down into this
vast agglomeration.

And the soul? It is, like yours, finally, more at home at the spa
than in lonesome dilatations. I, too, see the crows zoom in and out
of fog, know dreams' ludicrous diction, try to score more than the
machine, dare the ghost within, yearn to be haunted.

¶

P. Scott Lawrence
from *The Malory Arms Stories*, 1984

When the Elections Came to Town

I N NO UNCERTAIN TERMS, as was her wont, Mary McWhinnie spoke her mind: "If this promotion doesn't come through, I will be very unhappy."

Three months before the Elections came to this town, Horace and Mary McWhinnie were living behind a harness racing park in southern Saskatchewan. Horace worked for a manufacturer of glues and adhesives, and at that time was confident his fortunes were on the rise: the shop foreman was retiring, and Horace, because of his 22 years of seniority, believed he had an inside track on the position. He'd planned to celebrate by taking a trip to the Calgary Stampede.

"Pack your spurs, Mary," Horace said. "We're as good as on our way."

Mary wasn't so sure.

"My heel itches," she warned. Since childhood Mary's left heel had itched whenever something she didn't expect was about to happen. The first time, when she was six, her brother was born.

Horace was optimistic by nature.

"Let's hope it itches for the better," he said.

But Mary's instincts were correct. A new employee, John Roeneke, got the job.

Roeneke had been a jockey until, in his mid-twenties, he discovered he had an abnormal thyroid. His hands and feet had grown out of all proportion, and he came to blame the whole world for his condition. Beneath his quick whip, Horace, normally a friendly man with a high-pitched laugh that accentuated his rather prominent front teeth, soon began to fade.

As luck would have it, however, the day Roeneke was promoted Mary received a letter from her brother Martin. He wrote to say he'd been felled by arthritis, and desperately needed someone to help him run the family business, Mullins Hardware Supply. Would Horace be interested?

Mary had her doubts, and didn't immediately tell Horace about the letter. She remembered how it felt to move away from home. And they'd both heard and read about the political problems in Martin's part of the country. Mary knew Horace didn't wish to get involved in all that.

"There's something wrong with Easterners, Mary," he'd once said, only half in jest, while watching a television report concerning the kidnapping and subsequent murder of a provincial government official. "Maybe they're too close to Europe."

But Horace seemed beaten. He'd started walking with a stoop, and Mary missed his shrill laugh. Finally, as he peeled his workshirt from his bowed back one night, Horace confessed:

"I can't brook the man, Mary. I'm getting saddle sores."

"Enough is enough, Horace," Mary said. She showed him the letter. Horace didn't even bother to read it all the way through. The next morning he and Mary gave up the lease on their house in southern Saskatchewan and turned to the east, towards the province, and the town, that Mary had grown up in.

Two months before the Elections came to town, Mary's brother found them a home at the Malory Arms.

"This building was considered charming, once," Mary told Horace. Their apartment was on the first floor, in the centre block, and their front window looked out on a courtyard, the focal point of which was a cement obelisk. The neighbours they saw said hello.

The week they moved in Mary went to mail a postcard only to find that the mailbox she had seen there the day before had disappeared. When she inquired at the post office, a clerk shrugged and explained it had been blown up in the night.

Mary told Horace what the postal clerk had said, but Horace didn't seem to think it was very important. He was very excited about their new life. After half a lifetime in a factory, he saw the opportunity to prove himself a man of vision. He'd secretly fancied himself something of an innovator ever since he'd won a $25 prize for devising a whimsical slogan—"We'd like to teach the world to cling"— that the glue company back in Saskatchewan adopted for their letterhead. Three days into his job at the hardware store, he discovered the brochures sent out by hardware wholesalers. He took to them like a child to a Christmas catalogue, and would work the pages until they were as soft and pliable as flannel, always on the lookout for a new item. The ink from the paper blackened the whorls of Horace's thumbs.

"You look like you've just been fingerprinted," Mary said.

For her part, in order that she might better serve the majority of their customers at the hardware store, Mary began taking French lessons at a nearby high school. One night, when classes were cancelled because of a march by some day students who protested the arrest of a colleague suspected of sabotaging federal government property, she walked home with a Mrs. Dunphy, who lived three buildings down the street with her twenty-year-old son. Both Mary and Mrs. Dunphy were having a difficult time conjugating the future tense, so they quickly became friends. Mrs. Dunphy was separated, and she loved to tell stories about how her husband couldn't get along without her. "*Il reviendra,*" she'd say.

Mrs. Dunphy encouraged Mary to join the Sew and So Club at the Anglican Church. Most of the girls Mary had grown up with had left town when they married, so she was grateful for the chance to join the community. Back in Saskatchewan she'd had trouble making friends, and had never felt as if she'd fit in.

At that first meeting, however, Mary caused an uproar. When she found out that the church was sponsoring a lottery, with a trip to Florida as the first prize, she got up out of her seat and said that she couldn't condone such an enterprise.

"You did the right thing," Horace would later tell her.

But the other women thought Mary, being a newcomer, had no business passing judgment, and one called her impertinent. Mary stuck to her guns, and everyone grew more upset by the minute. Mrs. Dunphy finally suggested that Mary leave. That was the last time they spoke to each other.

Mary was very hurt.

"All things considered, outside work hours maybe it would be best if we kept to ourselves," she said.

Horace, on the other hand, was an immediate success. Claiming to be inspired by the details of everyday life, he introduced plastic plumbing pipe and washerless faucets into the town. When he painted their spare bedroom, and encountered an unusual number of dust balls, he went through his catalogues and discovered a paint brush that cleaned the strip of wall in the path of its bristles. Horace was particularly amazed by this device. All someone had done was put two good ideas together. The first shipment sold out in a week.

"All it takes is a little imagination," Horace said.

After her falling out with the women of the Sew and So Club, Mary needed something to keep her busy. She worked out a deal with the trust company that administered the Malory Arms. In exchange for tending the courtyard—the manager of the trust company mentioned that he'd like to see the obelisk taken away—and replacing burnt out light bulbs in the stairwells and hallways, the McWhinnies' rent was reduced.

"If nothing else, I want control over my own corner of the world," she explained.

Mary was particularly concerned with the courtyard.

"We'll be staying home a lot now, so I want it looking nice," she told Horace. "That's what the owners of the Malory Arms pay us to do."

She had never liked the cement obelisk that decorated the courtyard of the Malory Arms; at one time it had even given her nightmares. It was painted lime green, and what looked like a wooden leg projected from its peak.

Over the years the wooden leg had decomposed. The thigh area was riddled with holes and crawling with fat black ants, and someone had carved the initials of a local radical organization into the shin.

"This will never do," Mary said.

"Agreed," Horace replied.

"It's a question of taste," Mary concluded.

The next day Horace brought two Mountie Stetsons home from the hardware store.

"No need to fear going outside, Mary," he explained. "Here we've got all-weather headgear that will keep us protected from both rain and shine."

Horace and Mary put their Stetsons on, pulled the drawstrings taut, and went out to the courtyard. Covering the obelisk with a sheet of polyethylene, Horace and Mary went at it with sledgehammers, and pounded everything but the leg, which Mary dared not touch, into the earth.

"Now what?" Mary asked.

"I'm afraid I'm stumped," Horace said.

Hats in hand, Horace and Mary gazed down at the rubble for a long time. Mary picked up a handful of cement dust.

"A temporary failure of our imaginations, Horace," she said.

It was Horace's fascination with hardware catalogues that solved the problem of the courtyard.

One May morning, while he was at work, Mary's heel itched terribly. While she soaked it in salts a catalogue from a hardware notions manufacturer in Bangor, Maine, was delivered to the apartment. Mary flipped through the pages.

As she reached page 113, the itching suddenly ceased.

Mary phoned Horace and told him to come home right away.

When he arrived Mary was pacing the halls. She'd torn the page from the catalogue, and held it up to Horace's eyes.

"They're perfect," Mary said.

"Do you think so?" Horace asked. He picked up the telephone.

"Yes," Mary said. "Oh yes."

One month before the Elections came to town, Horace dialed Bangor.

The lawn ornaments arrived in a single crate, which had to be picked up at the customs office. If she'd had her way, Mary would have opened it right there. When they got home Horace lugged the crate into the courtyard. Before he even had a chance to straighten up Mary was prying off the lid.

She was even more pleased with the real thing than she was with the pictures in the hardware catalogue. Lying atop a bed of shredded newspaper, huddled in each others arms, were Jack & Jill. They were sold as a unit, joined as they were by flesh coloured cord that passed through eyelets in their wrists.

"It's all right," Mary cooed, "the worst is over."

The figures were expensive, but extremely life-like. Jack & Jill had blue glass eyes and held, he with the fingers of his left hand, she in the palm of her right, a yellow plastic bucket. The material with which they were made was elastic and tepid to the touch, like genuine skin. According to Horace's calculations, at twenty-five paces it took a keener eye than his to tell them apart from the real thing.

It took Horace and Mary almost an hour to set them up in the court-yard. Jack & Jill were smiling and Horace arranged them so they faced the street. Mary filled Jack & Jill's pail with water because she was afraid it might be flipped in a breeze. Then, sitting in their living room behind a partially drawn blind, Horace and Mary waited to see the neighbours' reactions. When Bauer came home he dropped a penny in the bucket and made a wish. Mrs. Hamilton patted Jack's head. Her friend Miss Shufelt stopped to talk.

They watched Jack & Jill from their living room window until well after midnight. More people passed through the courtyard, and most stopped to look. In the moonlight the figures were even more realistic. From time to time Mary believed she saw one or the other move. Horace couldn't disagree.

After Horace and Mary went to bed there were thunderstorms. Mary wanted to go out to check on Jack & Jill, but Horace assured her that they'd be all right. As soon as the sun rose the next morning, however, Mary's fears were confirmed.

Jack & Jill's clothes were ruined, the bucket had blown out of their hands, and Jill's hair was knotted right down to the roots.

"At least they're both still standing," Horace said.

Mary noticed that Jack's baby finger was stretched across the exposed knuckles of Jill's right hand.

"Look at that," she said.

"He's protecting her," Horace laughed. "In case they should fall."

Three weeks before the Elections came to town, debates raged. Both political parties claimed to know best what the God-given rights of the people should be, and each political party's list of God-given rights was different. Many people in town began to align themselves with one side or the other. The *News Leader* kept a running tab.

Horace and Mary put together a care kit for Jack & Jill.

Each morning they put on their hats and took a knapsack into the courtyard. Mary would ask Jack & Jill if they'd spent a pleasant evening, and fill them in on the news of the day.

"Another mailbox bombed," she would say. "And because of the Elections the Queen's visit has been postponed indefinitely."

Horace would laugh and ask Mary if she'd be surprised if one day they answered her. He bought Jack & Jill red flannel shirts and clear plastic raincoats which, when not needed, were tucked away in the bib pockets of their denim overalls. He also invented a device with which he pulled the dirt and dust from their clothes, affixing Scotch tape, sticky side up, to a paint roller. With damp blue terry cloths Mary would wipe Jack and Jill's faces, and with comb and brush she'd tease Jill's curly hair. The sun bleached it so white that it looked like a dandelion about to burst. Horace worried about hitting one of them with the lawn mower, so Mary added a pair of cloth-cutting shears to the kit, and clipped the grass that grew around and between their rubber feet. With the shears she also made Jack & Jill miniature felt versions of the Mountie Stetsons she and Horace wore.

"I think they give the lawn real character," Horace said. He'd decided to order some to put up for sale in the store.

"And a certain *je ne sais quoi*, too," Mary added, putting her French lessons to good use.

One morning Horace spoke to Jack & Jill first.

"We're in for a bit of excitement," he told them.

A headline in the *News Leader* quoted the leadership candidate of the party favoured to win the province as stating: "We'll be bringing the Elections to your town." According to the paper, he was planning a walk-past along the road by the river's edge so he could formally announce his intention, once elected, to replace the river with the kind of sewer system that better befit a technologically advanced people. The promise, if made official, seemed sure to win over the town.

Over the next few days, because so many local organizations wanted to get involved, it became clear that the walk-past would have to be a parade.

The parade was scheduled to pass right in front of the Malory Arms. The day before the Elections came to town a platform was set up at the water's edge, in full view of Horace and Mary's front steps. A city works crew assembled refreshment booths, and technicians laid microphone cables and hung loudspeakers in the trees surrounding the platform. Media from all over the province were scheduled to attend. It was going to be like a carnival.

That night Horace and Mary McWhinnie watched *Nitely News*. The producers had included a shot of the Malory Arms, and there in the courtyard were Jack & Jill. As soon as the broadcast was over, Horace and Mary went to bed, wanting to miss none of the next day's activities.

All through the night Mary's left heel itched and she had terrible nightmares. She would wonder later why she hadn't immediately realized that something was wrong.

Just after ten on Saturday morning, with a brass band and majorette escort, the future premier's motorcade drew up to the stage. The mayor, in his Chevrolet, followed close behind. A large crowd had already gathered, many with lunch bags and folding chairs, and as the premier and his platform party seated themselves, they watched a marching band from a high school in the next town and a float carrying a man in a canoe pass by. From their front steps Horace and Mary, binoculars raised, looked over the heads of the crowd, and waited for the speeches to begin. Some of their neighbours were out too, even Bauer and his wife, who were dressed to go sailing, in nylon windbreakers and canvas topsiders.

"Something is missing," Mary whispered.

"They'll begin soon," Horace replied.

After the mayor gave his opening remarks, the leader of the party began his speech. He said it was the God-given right of a people to be the masters in their own house. Then he added, with a grin, that he was sure his wife, Yvette, wouldn't mind. Many people laughed at his joke.

A group of schoolchildren waving baby blue banners marched up to the reviewing stand as the man who would be premier spoke of throwing off the yokes of oppression and taking control of one's destiny.

"We have a chance to take the future by the throat," he said. Someone in the crowd had a trumpet, and blew a fanfare normally heard only at hockey games.

"But something is missing," Mary repeated.

"I don't know about that," Horace said. "He sure seems able to stir up this crowd."

The schoolchildren waved their banners higher. The future leader then stated what most people had come to hear: rivers were meant for swimming, boating, and fishing, not for depositing raw sewage in.

"It can't be," Mary whispered.

As the crowd cheered she grabbed Horace's arm and pulled him into the courtyard. Jack & Jill's pail had been filled with fresh manure. Someone had torn the buttons from Jill's shirt and drawn a picture of a hand cupping the rounded nubs of her breasts. And there were two yellowed footprints in the grass where Jack had once stood.

The celebrations by the river continued until dusk. Mary washed Jill and mended her blouse; Horace cleaned and bleached her pail.

"I can't believe it," Mary said over and over again. "I can't believe it."

"It's just a prank, Mary," Horace said.

Horace was willing to forget the incident, and had almost convinced Mary to do the same. But the next morning, when he opened the front door to get his paper, he found a package.

A note inside the package warned that they had better keep the rest of their *famille* out of sight: she was an eyesore, represented imported culture, and was an example of the worst kind of cultural imperialism. The note was stapled to one of Jack's fingers. *Comité Contre la Colonialisme*, it was signed.

Horace phoned Mary's brother and told him he wouldn't be going in to the store.

"This is scaring the Dickens out of Mary," Horace told him.

Horace brought Jill inside the house and closed her in the spare room, away from the window. Then he telephoned the police, who came over and filled out a report. When Horace pressed, they admitted that the crime seemed like a kidnapping, but didn't take any of it very seriously.

Mary scribbled in a crossword puzzle book, and didn't say a single word all day.

"Funny things are happening around here," Horace told Martin. "If you care to look at them that way, anyways."

That night Mary broke her silence. She began to cry, and she cried for so long that, the next morning, she woke up hoarse.

On the second day following what Horace and Mary were calling an abduction, they received a box filled with Jack's hair. This time the kidnappers warned them not to contact the police.

"That'll be the last time we open our front door to get a look at an election parade," Horace said.

On the third day, one of Jack's ears arrived by courier. There was no note.

"It's not safe to go outside any more, in this town," Horace said.

Mary insisted that Horace hide Jill in the closet of the spare room. Then she took to her bed. Twice Horace looked in on her. Both times her eyes were wide open, but she didn't respond to his voice.

"She just lay there, on her stomach, all spread out across the bed," Horace told Mary's brother. "As if she'd been hit on the head with a stick."

The Elections were held and, as the media had foreseen, the candidate that had come to this town won. For three days, cars filled with supporters drove up and down the town's streets, horns blaring, celebrating the event. And for three nights, some of them stopped outside the Malory Arms and flashed their headlights at Horace and Mary's front window. Horace and Mary sat behind their drawn blinds, and jumped every time a shaft of light pierced the darkness of the room.

The ear was the last they heard from the kidnappers. But word of the kidnapping had spread. A magazine in the province's capital, *La Vie en Nord*, offered a reward if the perpetrators of the abduction would come forward. The editors were convinced that their struggle, and the action they saw fit to take, would make an interesting feature story. Within a week the reward was collected.

Two weeks after the Elections left town a full colour picture of the smiling kidnappers appeared on *La Vie En Nord*'s cover, below the bold caption: *Les Jeunes Croises*. The kidnappers claimed they were out on the night before the Elections came to town only to encourage people to make their houses present a pleasant face to the street. But when they saw the lawn ornaments in the courtyard of the Malory Arms, "a lightbulb was opened in our heads."

What upset Horace and Mary the most was the fact that the journalists had interviewed the neighbours, and the neighbours had agreed to speak.

"I kept expecting to look out my window one morning and find they'd been joined in the courtyard by a little black jockey, or a flock of pink flamingoes," commented Lambert, a young man in the next block of the Malory Arms.

The new leader of the province was also interviewed. He wished to assure the population that his party could not officially condone such an unkind act. It was essentially inelegant, he said, but added that the lawn ornaments had to be seen, it was unavoidable, as cultural irritants.

"They are like a piece of glass in our eyes," he explained, "and can anyone reasonable deny it is the God-given right of a people to try to take that glass out?"

One of the kidnappers regretted that the McWhinnies were upset so much by it all.

"But it was just a joke," he said. "After all, they weren't real. They aren't humans."

Horace read the article aloud to Mary.

"As far as I'm concerned, I'd just as soon be anything but a human," Mary said. "I'm ashamed to be a human."

After the celebrations died down and the town returned to normal, the trust company that managed the Malory Arms contacted the McWhinnies by mail. They said they regretted the incident, and promised to look into the possibility of compensation as soon as possible. They also told Horace and Mary they thought a flower bed, perhaps filled with fleurs-de-lys, would do nicely in the newly vacated space.

Horace thought it would be best if they simply tried to forget everything that had happened.

"The worst is over," he said.

Mary felt as if she'd been personally assaulted, but was willing to admit that, in all the commotion surrounding the Elections, perhaps she'd lost her perspective, perhaps things had been blown out of all proportion.

Nevertheless, she kept Jill hidden inside the spare room closet.

Mary was working in the courtyard one afternoon, preparing the earth for a flower bed, and she heard a crash. When she got inside the apartment she saw there was glass all over the floor of the spare room. A Mountie Stetson lay up against the closet door, balanced on its brim. Someone had thrown it through the window. It was brand new; whoever had thrown it hadn't removed the price sticker, which bore the logo of Mullins Hardware Supply.

Horace and Mary quit their responsibilities at the Malory Arms and took over the apartment above the hardware store. It was tiny and they had to either store or throw out many of their possessions, but it overlooked the parking lot, which was generally well-lit. Horace believed that, should a situation arise, it could be easily defended.

On moving day Mary decided to take Jill with them. She and Horace went to the closet in the spare room.

He opened the door. At first he thought Jill wasn't there. He switched on the light. The instant Horace and Mary spotted her they thought they saw the expression on Jill's face change. She crouched in the corner, her hands white at the knuckles, tightly wrapped around the handle of her pail. She appeared absolutely terrified, her mouth and eyes as wide as the moon.

"Oh my God," Mary said, "she looks as though she expects to be shot."

"Come, Mary," Horace said.

He slammed the door shut and locked it. Mary took his arm. As they turned away, they heard Jill's yellow plastic bucket clatter to the floor. It was a long time before they were able to convince themselves that they had just been imagining things.

¶

Elisabeth Harvor
from *Hospitals and Night*, 1986

A Sweetheart

ON THE WAY OVER ON THE FERRY, Kathryn wondered if she should warn Alec about her mother. They were sitting in the old black Plymouth Alec had bought for himself two weeks after coming out to Canada from England. They were the front car in a row of farmers' battered cars and trucks and so had a ringside view out over the water. The only barrier between them and the river was a long low-slung length of rusty old chain threaded through arched openings in the squat posts that had been nailed to the splintered front deck of the boat. Probably better not to warn him, she decided; once when she'd tried to warn a girlfriend about her mother, the girlfriend had reproached her later and called her mother a sweetheart and a living doll. So she only said, "My mother is English too."

When he didn't respond she added, "She loves to sing." Has a lousy voice though, she longed to tell him. But she did not. Instead she cleared her throat and said in an uneasy low voice, "She's crazy about the songs from *My Fair Lady*, so tonight we'll probably have a sing-song."

Alec said that that sounded like fun.

She threw him a distrustful, appraising look. She said warningly, "She'll probably make quite a fuss over you."

Alec said he never objected to having a woman make a fuss over him.

"Too right," said Kathryn, giving him a light punch in the arm. It ended with their getting into a mock-wrestle; they didn't stop until Kathryn, sneezing violently, collapsed against his shoulder. Then, as if they were tired, they gazed out over the dark autumn river. Kathryn said, "I think I might be coming down with the flu."

Alec said he knew a good cure for the flu.

"What's that?"

"Get you drunk. Get you plastered."

"Is that what they recommend back in the mother country?"

The mother country—he smiled to hear it called that.

Kathryn said that when she was small she'd thought the mother country was a country where only mothers lived. Mothers manned the streetcars. Mothers delivered the mail.

Alec smiled down at her with an expression of almost sappy affection. It made her want to squirm away from him in embarrassment. He stroked back her hair; said he wished he'd known her back then. *patronized*

Kathryn had quickly to list some things—about herself, to herself—that she didn't approve of, in order to keep from feeling guilty for being so critical of him. She was too shy; she was sexually inexperienced; she was too critical; the top part of her body was too matronly but her legs were too short and too fat, like a fat toddler's legs. Sometimes when she stood naked in front of her full-length mirror she felt like the top part of her body was mother to her legs.

Alec, still smoothing down her hair, drew her head to his shoulder. She ordered herself to calm down, and after a few minutes of listening to him talk about his work she was able to relax and even to feel somewhat bored. It was because of his voice; he had a knack for making it go incredibly dead. Which in a way was appropriate, since "dead" was a favourite word of his. But then with the British, everything was dead this and dead that. There were a lot of things he was dead keen on; for example he was dead keen on going out to see her parents' reclaimed nineteenth-century house. And then there were some things he found dead boring. Just so long as she didn't turn into one of them, she thought, feeling some embarrassment about her job at the bank. She stole a covert look at his profile—the hooked nose; the lank dark hair; the way he was staring out over the water as if it was making him angry. He was really incredibly handsome although some of the other tellers at the bank found him too stocky and short. It was true that when he came in at lunchtimes to visit her, and she was wearing her high-heeled sandals, she did seem to tower above him, but today, since they were both wearing sneakers, they were the same height.

Alec was saying he didn't think he always wanted to be an engineer and build bridges. He was considering going back to school to study architecture, he said. In his soothing drone, he told her that his great interest was in the restoration of old houses.

Kathryn said she didn't always plan to work at the bank either. She referred to it as "the boring old bank." She said she might go on to university someday herself. Last year, the year she had graduated from high school, she told him, was the year her parents had bought their old house. The renovations had eaten up all their cash. "Anyway," she continued, in a voice she did not entirely recognize as her own, "I don't mind working at the bank all that much. And I guess the boredom won't kill me." Only make me very tired, she thought; and she *was* feeling very drowsy by the time the ferry rounded the bluff at Cape Stedman. The smell of the Plymouth's upholstery brought back memories of trips in the family car years ago; the smell of hard-boiled eggs and bananas. But the sight of her parents' house high up in the trees made her sit up. "There's the house," she said. "But you can only see the top part of it."

Above a high bluff of maple and cedar trees they could glimpse the four chimneys and the black roof with its four gables and the top storey with its eight tall casement windows set in stone. There was the first touch of fall on the bluff's foliage and the deep river, near the island's rocky cliffs and small shale beaches, was a clear polar green. *wah "(*
The house's top windows, blank and bright with the afternoon light, seemed to be sending signals back out to the people on the boat. We rule this wood, we rule this water.

Alec and Kathryn got out of the car. The sun was shining down on the small distant house up in its high bluff of trees. They walked to the railing and then stood pressed tight up against it, looking southeast and up, toward the house. The sun burned their faces but the wind was cold—nipped their noses, fingers. Kathryn, who'd drawn her sun-streaked fine hair up into an untidy windblown bun, was feeling small and pleased and desirable. She felt held in the excitement of living in a cold clear-aired northern country. She felt in love with the little islands with the spruce and birch trees on them. She loved the wind-bitten headlands. Her short legs were hidden by her black corduroy trousers. Her big breasts looked smaller beneath her navy nylon windbreaker. She was glad Alec was so handsome, she was glad he was standing with his arm tight around her, she hoped the men who ran the ferry were looking down on them, from their glassed-in wheelhouse, up above the cars and trucks and roped-on lifeboats. She breathed in deeply, and, breathing in, was sure she could smell the golden decay of autumn in the trees of some of the nearby little islands that bobbed by the ferry. Out here in the middle of the bay the water was darker, an intense dark blue—almost black—in its windblown central channel. The ferry's engines sounded different too, in the fall—more heavily chugging, more insistent, a deep mechanical throbbing behind a sound like the constant flushing of six toilets on both sides of the boat.

"Your house is disappearing," said Alec. And it was; now only its chimneys were visible above the big bluff of trees.

"Going, going, gone," said Kathryn, and by the time the house had disappeared completely—the bluff seemed to have bobbed up and down until it had bobbed itself up to cover the house utterly—it had lost all its power. It seemed like a summer house then, lost up in the woods—a place belonging to people who lived somewhere like Massachusetts; old people; old crippled rich people; people who hadn't come north for ten, fifteen years; an abandoned house, forgotten, gone to seed in the woods. From here you couldn't believe that there was a road in to it or that it was only a six-minute drive from the village of Point Castile.

Ten minutes later, the ferry was starting to swing in a wide arc, starting to churn and tread water, preparing for its advance between the weathered grey breakwaters of the Cape Stedman landing. The breakwaters looked spectral, like two halves of a burnt-out flooded church. Between their windward and leeward grey walls they were piled high with grey boulders. Their nave was an aisle of still water. The ferry came flushing and churning in between the breakwaters, shaking up the wharf-images and creating a commotion among the gulls. The deck hand—a freckled, complaisant boy Kathryn recognized from weekend crossings on the ferry—sprang forward to throw a heavy rope out to lasso the nearest post of the pier; then, looking obsessed, began his impressive high-speed spooling of the rope around its sister-post on the prow of the boat. There were the little squeaks and adjustments of a watercraft being berthed at a pier. The deck hand spiked the ramp of the wharf with a long, finned spear that looked to Kathryn like a harpoon, to guide it into a better alignment with the ferry.

Alec's car was the first car up over the ramp. Being a passenger in the first car made Kathryn feel awkward. She waved a shy wave to the perspiring deck hand as the car eased past him but he only stared back at her as if he had never laid eyes on her before in his life.

Then they were on the road to Bellwood Beach, a road that climbed and clung to the wooded coast for nearly a mile. From the plateau of the first long hill they glanced back and saw the ferry, small down in the bay below them; a little white sled with a glass box on top of it, already starting to sled its way back to Port Charlotte across the cobalt-blue water.

As they got closer to the house Kathryn started to feel the old familiar knot in her stomach. It was the old coming-home knot; it made her feel restless and apprehensive, as if she might need to throw up. She could feel her legs getting damp inside her black corduroy pants. A briny female odour was coming up to her from between her corduroyed sun-warmed thighs.

Coniferous trees—dark pines and spruces—were growing close up to the south side of the highway. They were part of the bluff they'd looked up to from back down in the bay. But to the north of the road there were long sunlit pastures, sloping far back to small low-lying farms and grazing cattle. After ten minutes of driving they had to swing south, into the woods, sharp right onto a private gravel road for the final tree-shaded part of the journey to the stone house.

And then it came into view, looking like a manor house in some country where a chilled aristocratic northness was distilled in the air—Sweden, say, or Scotland. Alec swung the car up the gravel crescent of driveway, brought it to a stop just west of the formal front entrance. As he and Kathryn disembarked in the strong fall sunlight, Kathryn found herself feeling a little groggy and disoriented, like a tourist about to pay her respects at a shrine. The air, even this far inland, smelled of the fine invigorating salt sting of the Bay of Fundy, seemed to carry some memory of the foggy morning still in it—into the sad clear-aired afternoon.

The house was flanked on both sides by small groves of pines and blue spruces, and by formal mounds of blue lupines and delphiniums.

The sun was giving a haze of importance to all of it—above all to the speared flowers and spruces.

As she opened the front door to them, Kathryn's mother seemed to be totally caught in the grip of the painful brightness of welcome. She clasped Alec's offered hand in both her hands. Kathryn, hanging back, felt embarrassed by the intensity of her mother's greeting of Alec; thought, He will think I've never brought a man home before in my life. This was the case, but it caused her some pain to have it so clearly announced. It seemed to her that she was forever vowing to act womanly when she was with her mother, but that it only took two seconds for her mother to do something that would make her start to act resentful. At the same time she was feeling oddly proud of her mother—of her petite, freckled fairness; of the pearls in her pierced ears; of the way she was immaculately dressed—tailored white shirt tucked into new-looking tan dirndl skirt. Only her white ballet slippers looked grubby. Her feet looked veined and blue from the cold in them.

In the sunny living room Kathryn's mother linked arms with Alec and squired him over to the glass doors at the back so he could look down over the long lawns and gardens. Kathryn, tucking her shirt into her black trousers, followed behind.

It was a different sunlight back here; it felt like a different season. There was a breeze spinning the round yellow leaves of the young leafy trees; the air seemed more balmy. Kathryn's father was down on his knees in the garden, pulling weeds from one of the flowerbeds. When he looked up and saw them he rose, wiping his hands on his canvas gardening pants. Then he came walking up the garden path, a greeting that was more like a question than a greeting in his thoughtful grey eyes. He stepped inside. Shook hands with Alec; affectionately embraced his daughter.

Kathryn asked him if he'd been out working down on the boats; she said she'd seen one of the dories pulled up on the beach when the ferry had sailed by the bluff.

He said no, he'd been working up on the roof. "Come out to the front and I'll show you what I've been up to." And leaving Alec and Kathryn's mother still standing looking out over the back garden, Kathryn and her father crossed the sun-blocked front hallway and walked down the shaded stone steps and out into the bracing sunlight at the front of the house. They turned and peered up at the patched part of the roof. While they were studying his morning's work, Kathryn's father asked her if she'd known Alec long.

"A couple of weeks. He keeps his money at the bank. He always stands in the line for my cage. That's how we got to know each other." Remembering how she'd first seen Alec, hesitating beyond the roped-off section of the bank's lobby and then picking her out from a whole row of tellers, made Kathryn throw her father a quick anxious look. She loved her father and wanted him to like Alec, and so it puzzled her that she should at the same time be longing for him to say something disapproving.

They had their tea out in the back garden. Kathryn's mother fixed all her attention on Alec; asked him endless questions about England and his work. Alec said he'd been talking to some of the engineers down in Port Charlotte and that they'd told him there were big expansion plans for the land beyond the townships west of the harbour. "Shopping malls," he said. "A new hospital. But most of that won't be built for years down the road yet. For some of the developments they're projecting as far ahead as the nineteen-eighties."

Kathryn sat gazing out over the garden, trying to imagine what life would be like in the nineteen-eighties. In 1983 she would be the same age as her mother was now. It was hard for her to picture it. She could imagine herself in the future easily enough, but she could not imagine herself being older in it. She saw herself sitting out on a bleak modern terrace. She was seated on a streamlined white modern chair while she entertained a circle of people at a futuristic round white table; a robot holding a square metal tray was pouring tea for her blank-faced modern guests from a pot with a short utilitarian spout.

The garden, meanwhile, had cooled down. The afternoon was casting long shadows across the long lawn and grave-like mounds of the flowerbeds. Presently they had to go into the house to fetch jackets and sweaters. "We're nearly three miles in from the ocean." Kathryn's mother said to Alec, and she linked her arm through his. "But we still get our share of chilly sea breezes."

When the supper was over, Kathryn's mother announced the sing-song. Sitting on the white painted piano bench, Kathryn's father sorrowfully, skillfully played; Kathryn's mother, a pearl-buttoned cardigan caped over her shoulders, sang "The Rain In Spain" and "All I Want Is A Room Somewhere." Kathryn, her fair hair combed and still darkly damp from a pre-supper dip in the river, sang a quavering low version of "The Skye Boat Song" and then, in a surer voice, "The Red River Valley"; Alec sang a sexy slow Cockney version of "The Ballad Of Mack The Knife" in the professionally wistful voice Kathryn associated with British popular singers. Together they all sang marching songs and sea shanties.

When it was over, Kathryn's mother laid a tanned hand on Kathryn's bare arm and said in a poised low voice, "Come out to the kitchen and help me get the coffee."

But out in the kitchen her mother's eyes scanned Kathryn's face with a perplexed diagnostic sorrow, apparently very disturbed by what they were finding there. Her mother could be an intensely earnest person but it was earnestness in the service of false things, in Kathryn's opinion. Etiquette, for example. About the real disasters, although she could publicly be as horrified as the next person, Kathryn suspected she was secretly cavalier. But she was not cavalier about the disaster she apparently hoped to avert at this moment and so Kathryn understood that it must be a disaster of etiquette. At the same time, there was something so stern and, in the weirdest way, so heartfelt about her mother's earnestness, that Kathryn could not stand within the range of its searching gaze long without feeling that she might soon be obliged—and very much against her own better judgment—to totally alter her concept of good and evil.

Her mother was saying to her, "He's a lovely man, your Alec. A real darling."

Kathryn did not want to respond to this and so she only stared moodily out at her mother. She feared that almost anything her mother might say to her now might make her start to cry—that the only thing protecting her from it was the fact that she was keeping herself alert with distrust.

She watched her mother turn on both the hot and cold taps and then rinse her hands under the mixed blast of water. She watched her shake the droplets of water from her fingers and then dry her hands, finger by ringed finger, on an embroidered white cloth. She watched her turn to look at her. Her pale blue eyes seemed to have absorbed some of the cold of the September evening. "You wouldn't want to lose a man like that. Not a man of that calibre," she said. Kathryn felt distaste for the *calibre*—for the calibre of this conversation *too*—but, cornered, answered, "I guess not."

"I should think not," said her mother. "But you will, if you act vulgar. The way you were swinging your hips when you were singing! You have to try to be worthy of a man like Alec. You wouldn't want him to have to be ashamed of you."

"I don't believe he's ashamed of me."

"Believe me, dear little Kathryn, I only want to help you." Her mother was still staring at her with her terrible, earnest gaze. "Men are more fastidious than women, you have to understand that. Now that you have…a sweetheart…you will have to take care not to act crude."

Kathryn despised the word sweetheart. Having had it said to her, she felt the need to be alone and ran up the stairs to the bathroom. In the company of tall glass flasks stocked with eggs of beige soap and stacks of snowy towels that smelled like they'd been laundered in a subtle French scent, she peered at herself in the mirror, used the toilet. After she'd flushed it she could hear an echoing flushing down in the bay—the ferry making its final trip across the river for the evening. She crossed the hall to her bedroom window to look out.

Down in the black bay the ferry was making an odd spectacle in the night. No part of it seemed to be connected to any other. The wheelhouse was a lighted guardhouse looking down over a darkened fast-moving prison; below it the lifeboats, illuminated by powerful hooded lights, were white wooden hammocks hung from chains; below the lifeboats the paddle wheel, also lit up by a visored light, was a water-washed antique mill wheel for tourists. She stood watching the whole show sail past the point where she and Alec had got out of the car to look back up at the house. She recalled herself looking up—small and happy in the bright light. It made her feel spooky, as if back down on the boat she'd also looked puzzled, trying to catch sight of herself up here at her own bedroom window. Running back down the stairs she met Alec, on his way up. They swung hands, kissed lightly. "We better make plans to get away from here tomorrow night, or we'll end up spending the evening playing Scrabble."

Alec, squeezing her hand tight, whispered, "Too right."

All the way through the clam chowder the next night at supper Kathryn kept waiting for Alec to make his announcement that they'd have to go out for the evening. But he didn't. Judiciously breaking his French bread into careful chunks, he talked about former wars—World War I, Korea; said World War I was a farce.

Kathryn's mother looked startled. But she was quickly able to convert her shock into awe. "You know a lot about politics, don't you?"

Now, thought Kathryn, He'd better say it now. But her mother was leaving the table to go fetch the dessert. When she came back into the dining room with it—a heaving hot apple pie on a china tray—Alec said, "That looks sensational—doesn't it, Kath?"

Kathryn glanced at it and then quickly up at her mother. "Alec and I have to go out tonight. We've been invited to visit some friends of his over at Brewer Creek."

Her mother sat down. She was holding her silver pie-trowel upright in her right hand, like a bibbed King Henry the Eighth holding his meat-knife clenched in his fist. Her eyes were as blank and sun-struck as a gardener's. "Friends?" she asked. "What friends?"

"Friends from his office," said Kathryn.

The rest of the meal, under the constraint of Kathryn's mother's unhappiness, they talked about music. Kathryn said that her favourite song was the Bobby Darin song "The Ballad Of Mack The Knife."

Alec smiled at her. "That's not really a Bobby Darin song, you know. In point of fact, Bobby Darin stole that song. From Bertolt Brecht." The way he pronounced Bertolt Brecht sounded exaggeratedly German. "From *The Threepenny Opera*," he said. "From *Dreigroschenoper*."

It seemed to Kathryn that it restored her mother, to see her daughter being put in her place. She won't mind my going out so much *now*, she thought.

But now Alec was looking impassive—not there, almost—and Kathryn started to feel frightened that he wouldn't be able to get up and leave, once the supper was over. She was worried that if they didn't make their getaway fast, her mother would invite herself along for the ride. Or that she would detain them for so long with coffee and conversation that there'd finally be no point in going.

Her mother did suggest coffee. They took it out on the terrace. Alec and Kathryn stayed standing, drained their cups in a minute. But then Kathryn's mother asked Alec for some professional advice about an extension she was hoping to build on the back of the house. She guided him by an elbow to the western part of the garden. Kathryn followed behind. Her mother was still wearing her tan dirndl skirt but had changed her shirt for a pale-blue nylon blouse with a scoop neck. Kathryn could see the back of her white lace-edged slip through it and when her mother turned to Alec, to point out one of the mouldings on the west side of the house and then stood hugging herself against the cool of the evening, her breasts were very evident as well—hugged as they were into a high freckled fullness. Kathryn, sensing Alec was making an effort not to stare at her mother's breasts, hung a hand on the back of his shoulder, like a girl supporting herself while hopping on one foot to shake a stone out of the toe of her shoe. Then she started to tell her mother about how Alec was always making the other tellers down at the bank laugh, with his wild Cockney talk. She mocked him, in a flirty way; entertained him with an imitation of his own accent. But the fact that she had some success at this and was even able to provoke him into turning to smile into her eyes and say to her, "You're a daft one, you are," only seemed to make her feel more depressed, as if they'd had something together but lost it.

After Alec had helped her with the dishes, Kathryn slipped out into the pantry for her blazer. It was starting to rain. She could hear it drumming on the tin roof of the old shed out at the back. On the panelled east wall, where a pair of deer's antlers had been nailed up for windbreakers and jackets, a transparent plastic raincoat was hooked on one of the antler's horned twigs of bone. Next to it a forgotten sleeveless dress was hanging by an armhole from a porcelain peg. The dress was jade green with a mandarin collar. She had worn it in high school. She remembered standing out in the foggy May mornings in it, waiting for the school bus to come. Her books pressed tight to her breasts. Her nipples tightened and stiff from the chilled morning mist. Shaved bare legs and bare feet freezing in her high-heeled sandals. She wondered whatever had happened to the green dress's bolero. She could picture it all balled up in a corner, smelling of turpentine or Varsol. Or maybe it had been used as a rag to clean out cupboards and toilets. Above her, she could hear her mother traipsing around up in her bedroom. She could hear her creak back and forth between her bed and her dresser. What was she *doing* up there? She could imagine her twisting her hair up so she could spray the nape of her neck with her Tigress cologne, then leaning in low toward her mirror and applying her makeup with severe skillful strokes. On her way back into the living room she didn't even stop off in the bathroom, she was so terrified that her mother, by now dressed in her cream-coloured slacks and black rain poncho, would come running down the stairs calling out, "Darlings! I've decided to come along with you!"

"Let's go, let's go," she hissed to Alec when she came back into the living room in her blazer. She gripped the suede-backed lapels of his grey tweed jacket and, walking backwards, tried to pull him after her.

But he batted her down sharply from his lapels. "Will you for Christ's sake stop behaving like a child?"

She obediently dropped her hands and looked away from him, her eyes gleaming. She could feel a pin-prick of tearful resentment in her throat. She thought, All I want is to be alone with him. And what do I get? I get punished for wanting it.

Out in the wallpapered gloom of the high-ceilinged Victorian kitchen the phone started to ring. Kathryn's father went out to answer it. "It's for you, Peg!" Kathryn could hear him calling up the stairs. "Can you take it up there?"

Oh God, she thought, it'll be some old crony of Mother's, inviting us over for the evening, and Mother will say we all have to go. In the hallway above her, she could hear her mother pick up the phone and say hello. She could hear her father out in the kitchen, running a long blast of water. She seized Alec by the wrist—*now* he was willing to go, now when no one was looking!—and they slipped out the side door and together pounded their way across the driveway's crescent of gravel to his car. It was raining very hard by this time, and as the car took off, the rain beat its comforting enclosing tattoo on the windshield. Kathryn could picture her mother, stunned by the ripping sound of Alec's tires spitting gravel, racing down the stairs to try to stop them. The front door flung open to the rainy night; the car's dying drone. The scent of tire-gashed earth. The immense post-drone silence.

They seemed to carry the echo of that silence along in the car with them. They drove past stands of sapling birches and alders and long groves of quaking aspens whose round leaves were being needled and jiggled by the rain. Kathryn flicked something non-existent off Alec's tweed collar as a pretext for letting her hand rest there, on his shoulder. His eyes on the rain-attacked road, he ducked to give her a quick kiss on her fingers. She blushed, and a moment later slipped off her blazer and moved in close beside him.

They passed through Wolf River, Bellwood Beach, Bramley. They drove through North Dover, with its shack-like grocery store and romantic graveyard. On the outskirts of North Dover, they caught sight, in the distance, of a long rain-damp grey covered bridge. Someone had painted the last third of it blue. They emerged into farming country and passed by a white horse, thoughtfully appraising them over its barn-grey Dutch door. There were daggers of damp in the door's dried grey wood. The half-door made Kathryn think of the bank, and especially of her supervisor, whose office was behind a teak Dutch door. She could often be seen there, a slim pale-eyed woman in a sleeveless blouse and straight black skirt with metallic threads in it, halved and huddled, talking in a conspiratorial way into the phone.

West of Point Keenleyside they drove along a high ridge that looked down into a deep valley whose orchards and grey farms were brooding greenly in the rain. Then straight ahead for long but pleasantly tedious miles into a plain of dark pine trees. When they dipped again into leafy wet woods Kathryn whispered, "Could we stop somewhere soon? I have to go to the bathroom." Right away she hated herself for the childish way she had asked this question but she couldn't think of how else to put it. In this part of the country there were no gas stations; no human habitations or even shacks; no farms for miles and miles. The terrain had changed absolutely; now the road was up and down, up and down, making her feel seasick. Leafy banks of alders were crowding it like hedges. Then came a gap; a small field of tall grass. In it sat an abandoned country schoolhouse, once-white and peeling, a squat Tudor steeple at its front. It looked unspeakably forlorn—lost in time, lost in the woods. Lupine flowers were overrunning its grounds; their regal-looking pouched spears could blurrily be seen through the fogged, runnelly windows: pink on one side, blue on the other, flanking the steps of the deck-like front porch, which had a raw look—as if a quick-witted carpenter, only a half hour before, had slipped out of the woods to hammer it into place when no one was looking. The jolt of Alec's stopping the car seemed to bring back a memory of something unpleasant. Getting blamed for something. Kathryn got out, feeling car-sticky, disoriented; started to wade through the high faded grass that never got green, not even in this country that turned into a jungle in the rain, made her way round to the back. Then squatted there, in the old school's eerie shelter, the trees crying their creaky tree-cries in the dark woods behind her. She got such an old sad sense of long-ago feuds and secrets here. School! The foolish old word almost thrilled her. She dumped her lipstick and compact out on a flat wet rock behind her. Her lipstick was called Pretty Pink. She drew some of it on and wet her lips. She combed her hair. She pulled out her bottle of Ambush Cologne and sprayed some of it between her thighs and behind her knees. Then she aimed the atomizer at each nipple and sprayed her dress with it. Her dress was spotted with rain anyway: you couldn't tell what spots were Ambush and what spots were rain. But then she thought, What have I done? What if he kisses me there? What if he tastes the perfume? What if he wants to suck them? Last night, after her parents were asleep, he had sucked one of her nipples through the nose-cone of her bra and her peach nylon blouse. In the lamplight of her bedroom his eyes had had a sated milky look that had almost repelled her. She wanted him to do it though. She loved it. It made her feel so abundant. And so she unbuttoned her dress and shook herself out of the top part of it and unhooked her bra and pulled it off and stuffed it into her shoulder-bag, bedding it down carefully under sunglasses and Kleenex. Then she buttoned it up again, but not quite all the way, and finally started her self-conscious trek back to the car.

As she edged along the side of the schoolhouse she gathered her dress into a high bunch at the front to keep it free of the timothy grass that had a pollen of mist on it. She shivered a little too, the grass's wetness making her think of pee, not rain. She passed by the school's side door. A faded red, it was dried-out and hairy with age but this evening had a haze of mist on it. She shoved it open and cautiously stepped inside, glancing quickly to right and left. The desks looked very small to her, very small and obedient, all facing front. Everything else had been carted away—blackboards; globe; teacher's desk. She had been a good student; the lingering fragrance of pencil shavings reminded her. But she had an unsettling memory of herself back then, having to take her turn standing at the front of the class to recite "The Lord Is My Shepherd" in French. She remembered standing with her head bowed—out of shyness, not piety. She recalled her childish fear of making a mistake.

She walked back to the door, stepped out again into the rainy twilight.

When she climbed back into the car, she smiled up at Alec, her eyes anxious. "I went into the schoolhouse."

Alec said he'd been thinking of going in to have a look too, but had decided not to get himself wet. "You got yourself wet," he said. "Your nose is wet." He kissed the tip of it.

"Nothing left in there now but the desks."

"No beds?" he asked her.

The question made her feel as shy as she had felt as a child when she was the butt of some adult's affectionate teasing.

"No beds," she said.

Alec drew her head to his shoulder and sang with a Cockney accent into her hair:

>All we want is a room somewhere
>Far away from the cold night air…

Kathryn, looking up at him with nervous affection, pulled a cigarette out of her package of Player's and asked in a small voice, "Could you give me a light?"

"Sure thing." And he got out a packet of matches and struck a light for her. But he held the flame far from her, down between his slightly parted thighs, so that she had to lean in close against him, and over and down, to get at it. One of her freed breasts was squashed against him, just above his belt. She rested one hand high up on his closest thigh, breathing life into her cigarette. Then feeling for once in her life totally grown-up, she huskily whispered, "Oh God, I'm afraid I'm starting to spill ashes on you." And Alec, his voice sounding as if he had just caught an instant bad cold in the rain, answered, "Feel free. Go ahead, spill some more. Just don't set me on fire."

Kathryn sat up and nervously bore down on her cigarette. Alec dived for her left nipple, was starting to suck it through her dress. Remembering the Ambush, Kathryn whispered, "*Wait*," then laid her cigarette down in the aluminum drawer of the ashtray under the dashboard. She whispered, "Wait" again, then, like a mother struggling with fastenings in order to feed a ravenous child, unbuttoned her dress, let out a breast.

As they began the little settlings and hitchings of making themselves more comfortable, Kathryn experienced a moment of powerful doubt. But Alec was already starting to suck her exposed nipple and unbutton the rest of her dress. As he sucked and un-buttoned, she could feel her body changing its mind for her. She could feel it making a claim for itself, wanting what it wanted. She rubbed her nose back and forth under his jaw while he tried to work her shoulder free of her perfumed dress. "Let's get into the back," he urged her hoarsely. "We can lie down better there."

Kathryn gripped his hair in her fists and rhythmically massaged his skull with her thumbs while he dipped down to kiss her—her eyelids, her nose. Trying to decide, she stared up at the top of the gully through the fan of cleared glass being made and re-made by the windshield wipers. She could see how the wind was moving like a whip through the trees up there and how all the trees were nodding their heads as if in agreement.

¶

Jill Dalibard
from *The Lyrical Spine*, 1988

Then

It was always the meadow.
At morning it lay a knee's hitch
up to the tall sill
of my bedroom window;
then a gaze down.
It was crossed by a pale
curve of blue river,

where the cygnet with only one web
paddled beside
his two brothers,

and the tail of my dog
bounced dew
onto the red tiles
of the kitchen.

Then the hot summer
days when the river slept as we wandered
between brown cows which grazed
on green grass
among cakes of dung;
the sweet fumes of steam
rose from moist pudding.

So that now, when I visit
it is always the meadow.
I stride in the crisp
dusk, where balloons of breath
rise from the mouths of cows
cropping on yellow stubble.
And my leaping dog is gone.

Mother

Are tea-roses still warm in your garden?
Here it is only the white flakes
falling into the hole of the dusk.

At noon I imagined your body
tailored into the satin of Aunt Joan's sofa
for a chat after supper.
I phoned, felt your absence
cold as iced rain
pierce the eye of the day.

Summer retracts, the slow reel
of a film cranked back.
Are you in bed now, sleeping?
I picture your curly chestnut wig
on its post at the side of the vanity.
Your grey head floats
from the warm body of duvet
like smoke
from a snuffed candle.

❡

Richard Harrison
from *Recovering the Naked Man*, 1991

My Father's Body

I bathed with him as a child,
his enormous limbs,
the gentleness of a giant hand,
his huge cock at rest in the water. My father, naked,
and I was naked and small
in his silence.

All the things I knew too late:
how he slept with my mother,
how the scars came to his body.

Later, I saw him pale, almost white
stretched out on the couch,
his human body as long as furniture, as long as an animal,
the power to lift me, the world around me
gone, whitened with the death inside him
growing;
my father's body immense even in this quiet
like the home planet,
immense with all it had done.

My Mother's Breasts

My mother lamented
her large, pink breasts.

She envied the small women,
the straightness of their backs,

how their breasts did not swell or cyst
or tug with the earth, the need
for relief from the pressing bruise of milk.

In her bath, before
I felt what I felt as sex, she
would call me in to scrub her back
in the afternoon,

she could be taken care of,
she could fold into the pleasure
of warm water, unthreatening love
and forget the pain of her breasts;

she would close her arms
around them like a prize,
her head tilted in the steaming room.

Do not hate me, mother.
Long after they were denied
I would have touched them with my face,
the wet, warm saucer of my hungry mouth.

¶

Jennifer Price
from *Still Lives*, 1991

Entrenched in cement,
muted cannons protect
the perimeter of Westmount Park,
guard the memorial to the war dead —
boys robbed of sneakered Friday afternoons,
tossing the pigskin and watching
high-heeled secretaries
rush home from work.

Karate Man

Under perfect cover of shaded book
I watch him move.
Against rough comfort of nearby tree
I feign disinterest.

A shift of eyes propels me
from silent sterile paper world to green,
wet, pulsing screaming laughing,
the park and him, armless karate teacher.
Kicksteps in the park Thursdays at six.

Cartoon body, Thalidomide form.
No arms, just odd little hands gesturing.
Step Turn Kick Hai
Jab Jab Hai Hai.

I watch for moves that call for arms,
eyes flying from him to book to him.
His body flashes. A boy tumbles
over back, across armless shoulders.
Thuds mutely against wet grass.
Kick Step Turn Jab Hai:
triumphant, he lifts he face into the sun.

Jennifer Price

By dark the park is quiet,
trampled grass spotted with abandoned toys
dropped by children fleeing
darkness and the creatures
who own the park by night.

Watching

He is black-clad.
Eyes hidden by tinted glasses
reflecting the playground in miniature—
    tiny swings tracing perfect little arcs,
    mini-slide with Tom Thumb children
    clamouring and squealing and wearing
    the smallest pink dresses.

He slumps on a bench
on the edge
of the laughter and hopscotch,
the wide-open faces of childish glee.

He is long and sinewy,
out of place in this chubby universe
of pastel T-shirts, mud-caked knees
and mothers, drawing their wagons
in a circle of supervised sunlight.

He is watching,
lips curled into a wolf smile,
the parading of someone's little princess
wearing only blue underpants,
tiny crescent wedge of promise.
His pelvis tips slightly, straining.

§

Patricia Stone
from *Close Calls*, 1990

Close Calls

THE LAST AUGUST WENDY SPENT at her uncle's cottage in Haliburton she saw that the poster of Stephanie Baker was gone. She walked through the general store, past the shelves of cottage amusements, and stared at the bulletin board. The square of cork where Stephanie's picture had hung was a deeper brown than the faded corkboard framing it. Everything else on the board looked untouched from the summer before—packages of fishing lures, hooks, lethal-looking sparkling flies, traps, rubber worms.

Wendy glanced around the store; maybe the poster had been moved to another spot. Or a new one put up to replace the old one, which had looked more yellow and torn each year.

She went back to the cash register. Her mother was buying things to take to their uncle's cottage: eggs, bread, bacon, orange juice, bags of chips to eat while they played euchre. "You know that girl Stephanie Baker? Her poster's down," Wendy said. She looked at the store owner, ringing up the purchase. She wanted to come right out and accuse him of removing the poster. Of giving up, losing faith. She felt as if someone had stolen, or she herself had lost, something precious. She hadn't expected this. The week in Haliburton and the poster of Stephanie Baker's disappearance went together. She felt cheated, as if time were moving along too fast. She hadn't been given a chance.

She had been daydreaming about Stephanie Baker for years. By the poster's description, Wendy knew they were the same age, but Stephanie had long straight blond hair and a sweet, even-tempered, smiling face. She had not been frozen at ten years old. She had grown into her teens with Wendy, a perfect friend that Wendy met and rescued from Northern Ontario lake-pirates or kidnappers looking for ransom. A favourite fantasy involved white-slave traders. Stephanie had been stolen for her blond beauty, her virginity. She was drugged and being kept—where? Sometimes in a winterized, but isolated cottage; sometimes in a cave or in the back of a van. She was always unharmed whenever Wendy found her—except in one or two daydreams which got stretched too far and Stephanie's spirit was deadened by the time Wendy arrived. Her wish to live had dried up. Her beautiful hair and face were grey and withered like an old woman's. She might have been beaten or tortured. The horror of these things was not imaginable in a real way.

In every dream, Wendy risked her life to save Stephanie. Once, she even died rescuing Stephanie.

"Did they find that girl?" Mrs. Seldon asked, lifting her eyebrows doubtfully at the store owner.

He shook his head, which was over-sized and nearly bald, tufted by grey hair at the crown of his head. He punched the keys on the cash register. "Only leave a reward notice up for five years or so." He did not look at them. When Wendy's father came into the store each summer, this man had a joke to share, always a smile. Even with Bill, two years younger than Wendy, he'd have a few words and a wink. Women didn't quite measure up. Each summer, he pretended never to have seen Wendy or her mother before.

Wendy stared at the man and realized that he would, from here on in, figure in her daydreams as a culprit.

"She might still show up," Wendy said to her mother weakly.

"Whatever you do, don't be as stupid as that poor foolish little girl," Mrs. Seldon said as she reached out a ten-dollar bill.

Wendy tried to carry the memory of Stephanie Baker's photograph in front of her eyes, but after a few months it began to fade. She felt that she was betraying a trustworthy, constant friend, a central figure in her girlhood dreams. But she wasn't dreaming that kind of dream much any more. She couldn't look directly at Stephanie in her mind now.

By Christmas, Wendy's hair, which she had been growing out for a long time, was to her waist. She ironed it to make it gleam and hang even straighter. Her brother's was shoulder-length. The fights between him and their parents were becoming fierce. Wendy and her girlfriend Gloria wore short skirts, eye shadow by Yardley, and earrings shaped like hearts from Kresges. Each night before turning the light out, Wendy sat in her bedroom and raised the hems on her dresses and skirts. Every afternoon, when she returned home from high school, her mother had let the hems back down. Not a word was ever said.

She had started to go out on dates—and with older guys. It disappointed her to discover that they were not as smart, not as smooth or relaxed as she had expected. She met John, a law student in his early twenties, who drove a red convertible sports car. His parents were well-to-do and owned a large grocery store in town so the Seldons allowed Wendy to go out with him, despite the fact he was eight years older. He was in law school at Osgoode Hall, which impressed Wendy's parents.

One night near Christmas he drove Wendy up to Toronto to the house of another law student. It might have been where he stayed while going to classes. There was a Christmas tree decorated with lights and icicles in the living room.

"I'll leave you two alone," the other guy said. He winked at John. She felt sorry that he was leaving the room since he was handsome, more so than John, and in a way that resembled the man she had begun to fantasize marrying some day. But she felt he was a bit silly—he had underestimated her by winking like that.

John pretended to conduct an interview with her. They sat on the floor by the Christmas tree, drinking and smoking a joint. He leaned forward, holding an imaginary microphone, and asked her questions.

"And what do you think of sex?" he asked finally into his fisted hand before stretching it across to Wendy's mouth.

She had been stumped by that. The answer—that she was a virgin and terrified—wasn't something she had the nerve to reveal. What she knew was that the act he was putting on made him transparent. She felt above him suddenly, furious that he and the winking law-school friend dismissed her as small and unimportant. When he loomed over her and pressed her backward onto the shag carpet, pulling at her clothes and burying his face in her neck, she felt only the slightest fear. Although she was quite drunk and stoned, and his weight on her was suffocating, two facts remained clear in her head: he was in law school and there was another man in the house to hear her if she screamed. She announced it was time he took her home.

She had an image of herself as a whirling solitary figure, moving through dazzling events. She liked the belief that no one knew the real Wendy—and that she had dipped only a toe into the vastness of her life.

One night, when she came in from being downtown at the Globe restaurant with Gloria, eating shoestrings and gravy and drinking Coke, Wendy found a letter from her mother lying on her pillow. The blankets and sheets had been pulled back as if the bed had been prepared for a hotel guest.

In the letter, Mrs. Seldon said she had always loved Wendy and that she had always wanted a baby girl and how thrilled she had been when Wendy was born. She wondered what had gone wrong. Wendy could hear her mother's careful, deliberate, ferocious tone in the letter. It ended with an announcement: No socializing on weeknights, and a curfew of midnight on Fridays and Saturdays.

"But I have to go out on weeknights," she said to her mother the next morning at the breakfast table. "Everyone else goes out. Anyway, I'm the one who gets the high marks."

"If you stayed home, your marks would be even higher," her father said.

"Look at what happened to that girl in the poster, what was her name—" her mother began.

"Stephanie."

"Look at what happened to her."

But Wendy, who had carried Stephanie around like a favourite character in a book—perhaps Mary in *The Secret Garden* or one of the pony-riding girls in an English novel—could not see what had happened. There was nowhere to look. When she looked at all, she saw beautiful Stephanie Baker with her blond hair fanned out over a plot of deep rich grass in spring, her eyes closed as if asleep. Or her hair rising underwater like the petals of a sunflower, her eyes closed and her lips open, iridescent bubbles rising past sunken treasure to the surface.

Mrs. Seldon shook her head and set her mouth as if she were gritting her teeth to clamp down on a wave of nausea. She shook her head and looked away from Wendy at the kitchen wall. "Don't you ever...." She stopped short.

It was unusual, because generally Wendy could rely on her mother to provide a graphic portrait of any person's tragedy. When Wendy had first tried waterskiing at the Haliburton cottage and had not known to let go of the line as she neared the dock, Mrs. Seldon had been walking to the shore with her Instamatic. She happened to snap a picture just as Wendy was about to be sliced in half by the jutting diving board. The photograph turned out to be a blur of Wendy contorting sideways at the last minute, a red smear of blood where the diving board grazed her waist as she flew past.

Afterwards Mrs. Seldon relished showing the photograph to people, and shivering and rolling her eyes. She always related a story to go with the photograph—of a boy who had water-skiied at a high speed into a face of granite cliff bordering a lake. When he arrived dead at a nearby hospital, nothing but pulp and blood, the emergency nurse was his own sister.

In January, there was an ad in the paper for part-time sales clerks at Simpsons. Wendy applied and got a position in the young women's clothing department. In the mall, she met Gary, who worked as a sales clerk in a men's wear store. He was even older than John. Wendy felt that it was best to lie about his age to her parents. One night, he drove her to Toronto. They went to Yorkville first and walked up and down the streets looking at the hippies. They bought two marijuana cigarettes and drove out to the airport and smoked them in the car. They went inside the terminal to buy chips and pop and sat eating in silence, paralyzed by the drugs and the screaming chaos of a group of Italians who had just gotten off a plane. He told Wendy, in a sad, old man's voice, about his first love—a girl he had finally given up on when she told him at the top of a ski hill in Collingwood, "I've still got you wrapped around my little finger." The next day, Wendy couldn't remember driving home from the airport.

"You mean he doesn't go to school! I thought you knew him from school," Mrs. Seldon said after pressing for information one night at dinner and discovering that he worked full time in the men's wear store.

"How old is this fellow?" Wendy's father said, his face compressing and creasing as if she had just announced she was fatally ill.

Revised guidelines were imposed: Wendy was to date boys, not men. Nineteen was the cut-off age.

Wendy's parents had not gone to school long, and they wanted their children to do well. They were self-taught. Each weekend they lugged home books from the library in order to keep abreast of changes. All anyone talked about was the rate at which the world was expanding. Every morning, Wendy and her family listened to the radio's litany of murder, political dishonour, and human cruelty. Most of the events were staged in small, unheard-of towns in the States that became landmarks overnight, because of mass murders or appalling tornadoes—something Wendy thought she would like to experience just as Dorothy had in Kansas with Toto. She'd like to see that twister crossing the Kansas farm fields—a black, soul-shaking funnel of dust and terror.

Mrs. Seldon often sighed after putting down a newspaper. "It'll be the last straw when we have to lock our doors before going to bed at night."

Things were happening in broad daylight—assassinations, muggings, armed bank hold-ups. It seemed impossible for journalists to get clear photographs of the people who committed the most horrible crimes—as if the criminals were missing some parts. Their pictures in the paper and on television were blurred and indistinct like the ones of Lee Harvey Oswald, Albert de Salvo. As if there were less than a full human life for the camera to capture.

In February, everyone was amused when one of the neighbours—a woman notorious for looking through her curtains and observing everyone's activities during the day—peered out her window in the middle of the night and saw a dark figure stalking through an adjoining yard. The woman called the police, who were quickly on the scene, shining their flashlights into the snow-covered backyards, finally revealing the culprit—a snowman that some children had made during the day.

"Never you mind," Mrs. Seldon said after she had told Wendy and Bill the story and they sat around the dinner table snickering at the neighbour's foolishness. "Doesn't it make you feel good to know she had the gumption to call the police?"

Mr. Seldon agreed. "In this case she was wrong, but what if it had been a prowler? We're lucky to have good neighbours."

Bill scoffed. "Who's going to prowl in February?"

The conversation switched to a girl at school who had gotten pregnant. At one time, she had come to the house to take piano lessons from Mrs. Seldon.

"Poor, foolish girl," Mr. Seldon said soberly, shaking his head and staring at his coffee cup.

This comment was directed at Wendy. She knew it and so did her brother. She glanced at him and caught the smug expression on his face.

"I've got to get going," Wendy said, looking at the clock on the wall.

"The meeting starts at seven."

"I'll drive you," Mr. Seldon announced.

"I can take the bus."

After Christmas—and after getting the letter from her mother that restricted the number of nights she could be out—Wendy had joined the Leo Club. It was the junior chapter of the Lions Club and the man who was a manager at Simpsons had encouraged Wendy and the other young girls at the store to join. She was appointed secretary. A girl Wendy's age with an advanced, sophisticated manner was appointed president.

"Why won't you let me drive you?" Mr. Seldon said. Wendy shrugged. She pulled on her mittens and wrapped a long purple scarf around her neck. "Maybe I'll call you to come and get me."

Her father looked offended.

It was a sharp winter night. At a dip in the road, the woods and the houses of a more distant neighbourhood were silhouetted against the twilight sky. It was only six and already the street was quiet. It was the season when people made excuses to stay in.

Shifting from one foot to the other, Wendy played with the snow about the bus stop, scooping it into a small mound and running her boot heel down the sides so that the melting snow would re-freeze into ice. Balancing on the slippery, gleaming sides, she could look down and make out the layers of water freezing as each surface turned to ice. Across the street, the light from a kitchen lit up the snow of a backyard and its now famous lopsided snowman, a dark scarf draped about its peculiar, neckless torso. A hockey rink in the next yard was strung with yellow lights.

The cold passed through Wendy's ski jacket and chilled her unbearably. She pressed her mittens to her face and felt her pinched white skin. She tightened the scarf about her neck and hugged her coat to her body, hands thrust into her pockets. She was tempted to walk home, give up the idea of going to the Leo Club meeting. But they were going to the Globe restaurant afterwards for shoestrings and gravy. At home, her father's pipe smoke and the roar of the hockey game would filter through the walls to Wendy's bedroom. And her parents would seize the opportunity to continue their harangue about homework, Wendy's choice of friends, the length of her skirts.

The cold was freezing the air that she breathed and making her gulp. In the winter, the bus was often late, held up by traffic toward the town line where the network of factories began or by a snowplow, or a block in the road. Sometimes, the driver stopped at the city limits for a coffee in the bowling alley behind the gas station—and a ten-minute talk with the fat, made-up waitress who served donuts and coffee in Styrofoam cups. The bowling alley was a seedy place with Coke-and-hamburger ads thumbtacked against a dull green wall. Sometimes, fights broke out in the parking lot.

"I don't want to hear that you've been hanging around that place," Mrs. Seldon told Wendy more than once, darkly. "It'll be all anyone can talk about. Once people decide something, it's hard to change their minds."

Wendy and Bill were somehow diplomatic representatives to the world, the guardians of their parents' reputation.

Each time the bowling-alley conversation ensued, Wendy turned her face away so that her mother wouldn't guess she had already, out of curiosity, ventured into the place. Her daydreams about Stephanie Baker had given her a sense of what it was to disappear and be a poster on a fading bulletin board. She wanted to make her life chock-full of things-happened, just in case. She wanted to have more experiences than she could remember. It would be no good to disappear like Stephanie—be imprisoned somewhere and have a lot of wide open space in her heart and head where memory and sensation could have vibrated instead.

She continued to massage the pyramid of ice, feeling in the darkness that each side was as smooth as the next. Over the roofs of the houses, Orion was clearly a Greek god ready to hunt. The beam of headlights illuminated the sky over the crest of the hill and headed toward her.

Just in time, Wendy thought. She had been on the verge of turning back. She fumbled in her pocket for the fare and groaned as she realized that the lights weren't those of the bus.

A station wagon slowed down for the corner, its tires slipping on patches of snow missed by the grader. The driver looked in both directions and began to pull away. Then, he hesitated and glanced out of the car at Wendy. He waved as if he recognized her. Leaning forward, she peered through the darkness. A muffled tune from the radio trembled against the windows of the car, which was jerking as if the motor were about to stall.

It was too dark to see. The door swung open and the heat of the car's interior flowed into the night air. The driver withdrew his hand. "Heading downtown. Want a lift?"

Wendy pictured the bus driver with his hand in his pocket, leaning comfortably on the counter, the waitress with sugar donuts on tea-cup saucers, resting her elbows on the counter near him.

He'll notice that I'm hesitating, Wendy realized. She felt embarrassed. If she had to wait much longer for the bus, she would be late for the meeting. "That would be great!"

"Hop in then."

She slid onto the seat and leaned back awkwardly when the driver reached in front of her to pull the door shut. They started away and Wendy turned and smiled at him. She wondered whether she should tell him something about herself—what school she attended or why she was going downtown. He was bound to think she was ungrateful or rude if she sat without talking. She thought these things drowsily. The warm air rushing from the vents was affecting her like warm milk or flannelette sheets.

"Thank you for stopping," she said. Her teeth clicked like hard sharp pieces of marble. "I'm going downtown to a Leo Club meeting." This fact tended to impress adults. Maybe she went to school with one of this man's kids.

"Fine." He nodded and continued to drive in silence.

She had never come across anyone who didn't ask what the Leo Club was.

He's not interested in talking, she thought. Relieved to be out of the winter night and on her way, she settled back and let the familiarity of passing homes mark the route. In the gully between the church and Conlin's store she saw some girls from school—Gloria among them—with skates across their shoulders. She waved and then realized they wouldn't recognize the car.

"Friends of mine," Wendy said.

She tried to look over her shoulder at her girlfriends but the window was fogged over. Gloria was having the same problems at home that Wendy was having. The two of them left school each day at lunch with

Ted, a boy in their class who had his own car, a silver-grey Camaro. They drove to Dines restaurant at the mall and ordered hamburgers, onion rings, and milkshakes. They always smoked a joint on the way over and ended up stuffing the food into their mouths like wadding.

Wendy had been in trouble over this. She had been selected to act as a prefect in the cafeteria at lunch during certain days of the week. The vice-principal had made a production of giving her a school sweater with the school's colours—gold, brown and white—on the arms. But it had been reported that she kept missing her prefect duty, and he had called her in.

She had never been called into a principal's office before. This man had a savage reputation.

"What's the matter with you?" he asked her.

He was a man with a permanently exasperated face. He asked her this in a fatherly way and she felt taken aback. She had expected him to be harsh. Her eyes filled with tears because she thought maybe he was right and something was wrong with her. She shook her head and shrugged her shoulders, trembling. Suddenly, she recognized his strategy. He was manipulating her, figuring out the best way, the quickest and cleanest, to get at her.

She had handed in her prefect sweater and only felt badly once or twice when she and Gloria went to Dine's in Ted's Camaro.

She took her mittens off and resisted the urge to rub the window clear of fog. People didn't like that because it streaked the glass. Wendy had not gotten over her childhood enjoyment of writing her initials with great style and flourish on steamy windows. The radio was playing country and western music but it was distorted by interference, too much treble. The lights of downtown began to brighten the sky ahead and Wendy thought lethargically how reluctant she was to have to step outside again.

Snapping out of a daze, she saw they had taken a turn onto a street which headed north for some ways and eventually led out of town. She looked around to orient herself: a different neighbourhood, but a familiar one. Her grandmother lived three blocks from here.

The driver's expression had not changed. With one hand on the wheel, he continued at the same speed. It seemed more polite not to point out that this was an unusual route to town. He could be taking a different way. Who am I to know all the roads? Wendy thought. But she felt uncertain. He had created a barrier, an odd feeling in the car, by refusing to speak.

The houses were getting shabbier as they neared the edge of town. Driveways were cluttered with snowy bed springs, old motors, broken chairs, tires, and cords of wood. Wendy recognized a house where she had attended a birthday party years earlier—a girl from her grade three class, from a poor, ill-fated family, who nevertheless had had a wonderful birthday party. The mother had led a noisy, foot-kicking bunny hop around the living room.

They continued northwards in tight, constrained silence. Wider spaces between houses. No one was walking along the road.

Wendy realized she had to speak. She tried to think of something courteous to say. She forced the words past her lips. "Are you going downtown?"

"I'm going up ahead a ways," the man said, lifting his hand from the steering wheel to gesture.

She stared at his hand which was enormous, a fleshy baseball mitt.

"I have to pick up a friend who works with me on the night shift," he added, without looking at Wendy.

He was forty, she thought, maybe fifty. When he had pulled up at the bus stop, she had assumed he was somebody's father, a neighbour, someone whose house she had visited on Halloween nights. Not many people drove down her street at six o'clock unless they lived in the neighbourhood.

As the landscape slipped by, Wendy pretended to be watching it. What he had said could easily be true. The factories in town did have night shifts. She looked sideways and saw that his lips were pursed to whistle but nothing was coming out. With a jolt, she knew that something was wrong. She looked ahead again and began to pull at bits of fluff—tiny balls of wool on the mittens that her mother had knit. Wendy cleared her throat.

"Where is it that you work?"

The Leo Club meeting would already be started. She could walk in late—but what if one of them was trying to call her at home right now? "Mrs. Seldon, we're wondering why Wendy is late." Her parents would be helpless, beside themselves.

A knot tightened in her stomach.

The stranger named a factory in the city which produced sheet metal. His voice rose naturally.

He'll turn around and go back before long, Wendy assured herself. But where will the other man sit?

The prospect of a second silent and menacing stranger in the car made her dizzy.

From the corner of her eye, Wendy looked at the driver. Above the fur collar of his dark green parka rose his featureless face, double-chinned and shadowy. Wendy's face twitched. Her left eye fluttered for the first time in years. She touched it with her finger. A feeling of panic, painful and trembling, gripped her heart. She tried to calm herself: Tell him to stop if he isn't going to drive straight downtown, she rehearsed. Tell him to let me out, thank you, and I can walk from here.

The words kept dying in her mouth.

Trusting, waiting things out, felt safer, easier. He would turn back. Or he would meet his friend and then drive back to town.

They passed another patch of houses. The scratchy radio music was being drowned out as the road became rougher, making the paint-spattered ladders and tools clang in the rear. Wendy turned in her seat to look at them and, lifting her eyes, saw through the back window that the city's lights were disappearing into the distance. She faced ahead again.

"Where does this friend of yours live? I don't want to be late and I probably already am." Wendy bit her lip. Was that too anxious? Too rude? She didn't want him to know how frightened she was. Somehow, her safety lay in concealing that.

"He lives close to here."

She waited as they rushed into the darkness. Every mile or so, a farmhouse appeared, set back in a field, aglow with lights. Wendy was struck by an image of her parents relaxing in the overly warm living room at home, reading, watching TV. Her father would still be feeling annoyed that she had insisted on going out on a weeknight, even if it was for a Leo Club meeting. Through a farmhouse window, Wendy saw people moving through their evening rituals, unaware of what was racing past them. A sensation passed through her chest—she had been lifted outside of normal life, she was on the other side of a screen, apart from what was safe, knowable.

She sat stiffly on the seat, waiting for this strange, unbelievable moment to end. After another space of silence had passed, she said loudly, "Where are you going?" She felt her heart racing, partly from the belief that she was insulting this man, a good Samaritan who had stopped to give her a lift on a freezing winter night. This had to be awkward for him. She had the odd feeling that it might be her job to protect him from feeling awkward—or from picking up on her own tension.

She stared hard at the driver's face, then at the road, and back again at his face, trying to will him to look at her, to stop the car from heading into the depths of the countryside, taking her with it. The night was suddenly a place she hadn't known existed.

This time, the man remained silent.

She decided to throw herself from the car as soon as he began to slow down.

Even if he doesn't slow down, she thought, I'll throw myself out. It would be better to land in a ditch of snow—better even to be hurt in the fall. In a quick succession of blurred images, she imagined being run over by the car, dying from exposure once she began to search her way back to town, being pursued in a field, tackled.

She reached down in the darkness of the station wagon to touch the handle. A sick feeling vibrated through her body. She stared down through the green pallor cast by the dashboard and saw that the handles had been broken off the knobs.

She put her mittens back on, took them off, plucked at the wool. Her heart bolted inside her chest.

He would turn to face her. What would he say? What would she do? This can't be happening, she said to herself. This can't happen. Her life was something that was too real for this to happen. What did he want? She had never had to fight with a man. He'll rape me, Wendy thought. She could not visualize it further than that: just the word itself dangling in the blackness inside her head. But rape was often followed by murder. He wouldn't want her to be able to identify him....None of this would happen. None of it could happen. Not to me, Wendy thought.

They were now miles from the neighbourhood where she had waited for the bus. She thought suddenly of Stephanie Baker. The pressure and chill of nausea swelled in her throat. Maybe the girl had just run away. But not for six years. She might have gone through the thoughts Wendy was thinking now. Maybe she had been knocked unconscious first and then killed. Wendy had never considered her own death before. Not as something this close. Death was an old woman in a narrow bed, gaunt and leather-faced, hands folded, yellow lace, ready to pass on.

She looked out the car window. There were no street lights now, no fences. It was scarcely a road that they were on. She had no idea where they were. She knew only that they were heading north, away from town. The stars were behind them.

The car came slowly to a stop and the engine shuddered. A fallen fence lay across the path—or maybe he had driven down a dead-end country lane. He turned on the seat to face her.

Unable to stop herself, she said, "What?"

He stared, unblinking, at her. "Is it worth a kiss to get back home?"

Wendy stared back at him. "No, I can't." Her voice no longer belonged to her. "No!" she cried as he moved his hand along the back of the seat toward her head.

He leaned against his door. "Isn't it worth a kiss to get back?"

Somewhere, Wendy heard the sound of doubt. He was unsure. He had never done something like this before. She would do it. She would lean across the seat and kiss him—quickly, the completion of an agreement, an arrangement. She would kiss him and then back away and he would keep the promise he had made. But what if he didn't. The voices in her body were drowning each other out, but the deepest one, the judging one, was a bass humming noise, the strongest voice there, something close and essential speaking to her, calling.

If I kiss him, I'm dead, Wendy heard herself thinking.

He would take the kiss as a sign of weakness, of encouragement. She remained frozen, the round door knobs pressing into her jacket. She let the voice deep in her throat that was desperate and shrewd have its way—she began to plead with him. She twisted the mittens in her hands.

"Take me home—I promise I'll never tell anyone a word of this. I'll never describe you. Just take me home."

She explored his face with her eyes and pleaded.

In the darkness of the car, his face changed expression. He smirked.

"How old are you?"

"Sixteen." Should have said fourteen, thirteen, the voice in the back of her head said.

"You're awfully foolish to have taken a ride with me."

"Yes," Wendy said, barely audible. She felt a quick fury at his fatherly, reprimanding tone of voice.

His arm shot out. Wendy screamed and realized that he had tried to scare her back into muteness, passivity.

"Let me go, I'll find my own way home. Leave me here," she begged him. Maybe she was going to be all right. He wasn't going to carry out some dimly formed plan in his head after all.

"Get out of here, then," he said. He reached in front of her and she shrank against the car seat. He grasped the knob and wrenched it around.

The car door flew open, and the winter night cut its way into the car. As he leaned forward and grabbed her purple scarf, Wendy rolled past the open door onto the snow. She felt the scarf tightening around her neck. Twisting, she released a faint scream and whirled dizzily so that the scarf unwrapped and the stranger was left tightening it in his grip.

In great awkward leaps, she floundered through snow drifts. A fence post rose ahead of her, a foot above the snow. She pinned her eyes to the wood that someone's safe, methodical hand had lowered into the ground.

He's after me, Wendy thought wildly. He would catch her. She tasted something strong in her mouth. Any minute, he would bury her in the snow beneath his weight. She listened past her heaving breath to catch him behind her and, in mid-motion, shot a look back. The tail lights of the car were moving up the laneway, already a half-mile into the deep darkness of the countryside.

She kept fighting her way through the snow, falling and gasping from the exertion. She scanned the eerie blue-black night. She would call Ted. She would give directions. He would drive to get her in his Camaro. He would drive her home and she would never tell her parents what had happened.

A light flashed in the distance and Wendy saw a farm's yellow windows through a stand of trees. She stopped to rest her heart and catch her breath and wonder at still being alive. She felt the sudden, strange triumph of having escaped something inescapable—of knowing what others had known, but never lived to tell. She thought of Stephanie's poster and tried to see beyond it to a vast twisted darkness until the image evaporated in her mind.

¶

Su Croll
from *More Great Dinners from Life*, 1988

Banjo Poem

You got a dance hall for parading
with a bar for drinking
and a floor for dancing
You got women   wanting to feed you
and clothe you
and put you up in their hope chests

Bet you never went hungry
with a banjo like that

Things are different up here
Come on in   and close the door

Now you got to earn your keep   Get up and chop me
some wood   you got to fill up   my big Franklin stove
fore we get any heat in here

And here it is   baking day   My kitchen's sweet
and ready   pewter's all polished   cupboard's full
with plenty

It's cold outside
but we're under this tent
You   me   and your banjo
And you can play that music
'til bread dough rises
Then we'll punch it down
and set to square dancing again

Beginning With the Dog Paddle

Her father kept paddling and humming to himself
old songs that we didn't know   about bonnie
prince charlie   we were embarrassed and spoke
too loudly—*he's not deaf   you know*—only moving
slower   like a snail   or clams coming to slow
salt water boils   that year
we went to norway bay   had hot dogs
by the beach   fire taking
too long   pebbles hurting our feet   we walked
with tiny steps   and made squealing sounds
'til we could get to the car
for our flip flops

her dad was covered   silvery hair
over his chest and legs   I'd never seen
that before   and so skinny
like an athlete   he dives right away   makes
an arrow in water that is too cold
for us   he swims into the middle of the lake
like an olympian   I want
to ask jenny about her dad   but I can't
form the question with my lips   can't move
it out of my mouth

canoeing the islands up in norway bay
and naming them   jennifer gave them names   mythical
animals   or characters from c s lewis   I see her dad
in the grocery store   he comes in
every morning at nine for a loaf of whole
wheat bread   unsliced   and walks
with a cane   I can't ask
if he remembers me   and I know he's not
deaf   but count back his change
very loudly

¶

Robert Majzels
from *Prodigal Son*, 1988

from Act One

DAVID: Listen to me, Benny.

BENNY: I'm not taking any lessons from you. You were the one supposed to come home covered in glory. Look at you. You came home with your goddamn tail between your legs.

DAVID: At least I didn't make it by climbing over someone else's back.

BENNY: You didn't make it at all.

DAVID: Making it. Is that your religion? Is that what it's all about, Benny?

BENNY: You wouldn't know what it's all about. You wouldn't know enough to come in out of the rain.

DAVID: Right, and you: you'd be out there selling paper umbrellas.

BENNY: You're a loser. A dud.

DAVID: You're a pig.

> BENNY *starts toward him.*

Don't, Benny. We're not kids any more.

> *They stand in a stalemate for a moment. The ghost of*
> HELLMAN *appears on the steps to the bunkroom. He is old as he*
> *would have been before he died, but he is dressed in the uniform*
> *of a Camp prisoner and his head is shaven. His shoes are worn*
> *out and one of them is wrapped in cloth.* BENNY *does*
> *not see him.*

BENNY: I'm going to wash up.

> BENNY *exits U.C.* DAVID *stares at* HELLMAN.

DAVID: Papa?

HELLMAN: So much noise.

DAVID: Don't be angry, Papa. Benny means well. It's not that I'm ungrateful...

HELLMAN: It's cold in here. At night it gets colder. Sometimes you can't get to sleep from the cold: the shivering keeps you awake.

DAVID: I know, you're disappointed. I let you down. I didn't want to. I didn't think it would end up like this. I thought...but I can't change all that now. Still, try and understand. I was trying. I was trying to do something important. I thought I could change things.

HELLMAN *moves D.C. and begins rewrapping the cloth around his shoe.*

Papa, are you there? Listen to me, Papa. All right, I know: the arrogance. I, David Hellman, will change the world. But I was just a kid. You don't get marks for trying. The road to hell is paved...Everything is measured by results. Intentions don't count for anything. But what if we'd won, what if we'd built a strong grassroots movement, penetrated the factories.... No, I know. The arrogance—there was too much arrogance. But, Papa. Papa, can you hear me? I let you down, Papa.

HELLMAN: *(working on his shoe)* This shoe is finished. Like a sieve. Everything passes through: the cold, the water.

DAVID: Papa, I want to talk to you. I want to explain.

HELLMAN: *(shrugs)* Explain. Sure, explain. Explanations help to pass the time. We look for causes. We argue how we got here. Why. Everybody is interested in the why. Should I have gone to temple more often? Observed the Sabbath? Should I have left in '39, when there was still time? Explain: it passes the time.

DAVID: I need your help, Papa. Tell me what to do.

HELLMAN: *(working on his shoe)* The most important thing is the feet. You want to survive, you have to protect your feet. *(points to* DAVID's *sneakers)* Those shoes are no good. They look fine now, but they won't last a week. I always told you: never scrimp on shoes. The worst part of it is I had a good pair. At home. You walk out the door one morning, and that very same night you're in here. You never know. They don't let you go by the house to pick up your good shoes. You have a good pair of shoes? Wear them, David. That's my advice to you. Feet are the most important thing.

DAVID: Papa, listen. I know, you're disappointed in me. You didn't think I would end up like this.

HELLMAN: When I first came here, at night sometimes, lying in my bunk, I let my mind wander. I tried to imagine the promised

land. When you come to this place, you have to have something to dream. You have to have an idea of paradise. It keeps
you alive. Oh, not the paradise they told us about when we
were children: not that picture like a postcard: land of milk
and honey, golden rivers in golden sand, palm trees heavy
with fruit. No. Here, every man makes his own promised
land. Sometimes, it's a going back. Sometimes it's nothing
more than a going back to my father's old medical office in
Warsaw: the clean white jacket, the sterile instruments all
lined up neatly on the table, his patients, so polite and full of
awe. Sometimes that was my promised land. Sometimes I
remembered the lessons in Shul. Then it became something
vague, something very abstract: a concept you have to dig out
somewhere in the clauses of the Torah. *(whispers)* For some
here, it's Israel: Jewish armies driving their enemies into the
sea. *(shakes his head)* So much blood. But most often, for me,
when I first came, it was America. Not your America. What
did I know about your America? My America was as distant
as the rabbi's paradise. But simpler. Very simple. Like a child's
building block. You know, a six-sided cube with the word
America stencilled on every side. The same word, in thick
square letters on every side. But in different colors: America
in blue. Turn it over: America is green. America red. I could
turn the cube over, around and around in my mind, and no
matter how I turned it, the dream was always there, always
the same. Just America.

DAVID: Papa, you're not listening. I have to talk to you.

HELLMAN: Yes, I know, I know. It was all straightforward for me, too.
At first. At first it was very simple. After the Kapo, it was
different. After the Kapo, things were more complicated.

DAVID: *(he has heard something about the Kapo before)* The Kapo,
Papa?

The ghost of HELLMAN *vanishes.*

Papa, wait.

BENNY *comes in through the living room, carrying a towel. He
picks up a dish of cake and a fork from the floor, and comes down
into the bunkroom eating.*

DAVID: Benny, what did he say about me?

BENNY: What did who say?

DAVID: Papa. At the end, he must have said something.

BENNY: Oh, for Christ's sake, David, will you forget about that?

DAVID: I'm just curious. Come on, what did he say?

BENNY: What difference does it make? He was old, sick. He didn't know what the hell he was talking about.

DAVID: Did he talk about the Camps?

BENNY: He never talked about that stuff. You know that.

DAVID: He talked to me about it. That's what he talked about, on those long walks, when we were kids.

BENNY: Come off it, David. Everybody knows the survivors never talk about it. On account of it's too painful to talk about. I saw a thing about it on TV.

DAVID: What the hell does TV know about the Camps?

BENNY: They know a hell of a lot more than we do. They had some actual survivors.

DAVID: Talking about how they never talk about it?

BENNY: They've got experts: doctors, historians, guys who didn't drop out of college.

DAVID: That's just like you, Benny. If the TV told you Jews had two heads, you'd run out and buy an extra pair of earmuffs.

BENNY: If I had two heads, I'd have given you one a long time ago.

DAVID: I know what he told me. Maybe he never saw that program on TV: he didn't know he wasn't supposed to talk about it.

BENNY: Why do you want to start in on the Old Man again?

DAVID: Because he would have understood. Because that's why I had to leave home. That's why I did what I did. That's why I can't take that job. I think Papa would have understood. Because they put him in prison, too.

BENNY: It wasn't a prison; it was a concentration camp.

DAVID: What's the difference?

BENNY: He didn't do anything to deserve it.

DAVID: That makes no difference. It's still political.

BENNY: It's not the same if you didn't do anything.

DAVID: You think he never did anything?

BENNY: They just picked him up. Like all the others.

DAVID: What about the Warsaw Ghetto?

BENNY: What about it?

DAVID: He fought in the uprising.

BENNY: Did he tell you that?

DAVID: He was in the resistance.

BENNY: Oh, come on. He was a poor schmuck, like all the others.

DAVID: That's how they caught him. His family left, but he stayed behind to fight.

BENNY: They picked him up on some country road.

DAVID: He was on a mission for the resistance.

BENNY: He was out riding his bike.

DAVID: He was delivering supplies.

BENNY: He was going for a picnic. He had a basket of food.

DAVID: Supplies for the Ghetto.

BENNY: Oh, for Christ's sake…

DAVID: They took him because he was part of the resistance.

BENNY: They took him because he was a Jew.

DAVID: You don't know.

BENNY: And you do? Why do you have to make such a big deal out of it? Listen to me, David: they went through the Camps; not you. If you're looking for some fancy psychological justification…

DAVID: Maybe what happened to them makes us different from most people, makes us more sensitive to injustice.

BENNY: That's a load of crap. What about me? I'm the son of a Holocaust victim, too. There's nothing wrong with me. I don't have some weird sensitive thing.

DAVID: Well, maybe I turned out more like him than you did.

BENNY: He never killed anyone.

DAVID: *(pause)* He killed a man in the Camp.

BENNY: That's a lie. My Old Man never killed anyone.

DAVID: The Kapo.

BENNY: You're nuts.

DAVID: He told me.

BENNY: That's a load of crap.

DAVID: In the Camp.

BENNY: Shut up, David. You're sick.

DAVID: He had to do it, for all the prisoners. He had no choice.
BENNY: Sure. Our Papa killed some big armed guard in the Camp and got away with it. Make a movie.
DAVID: A prisoner. A Kapo. A kind of trustee.
BENNY: Go to hell.
DAVID: The man was a collaborator, a Kapo.
BENNY: Papa never killed another Jew. You want to try and tell me he killed some Nazi, that's one thing. I still don't believe it. But he never killed another Jew.
DAVID: The guards put this Kapo in charge of the toilets. The toilets were in the cellar of the barracks: an open row of bowls along the wall. They'd march the prisoners down there in a line and sit them down, in groups of twelve, to take their turn on the toilets. The prisoner sits there in the open with his pants down around his ankles. And everybody standing there, waiting and watching while you try to take a crap. Nobody ever thinks about that part of it. We try and imagine the pain, the hunger, the fear; but we forget about the humiliation.
BENNY: I don't want to hear this stuff.
DAVID: When the Kapo blew his whistle you had to get up and move off, and the next group sat down. The Kapo was a Pole: a huge man, about seven feet tall. And he had absolutely no hair anywhere on his body. All blubber and muscle: a giant hairless walrus. The guards kept him around for entertainment: a sideshow. In the toilets, he had this stool on the end of the row. And a whip: a short leather whip with a knot in the end. He'd sit there on that stool, with his whip, and from time to time, when the spirit moved him, the Kapo would start whipping some prisoners while the poor guy was sitting on the pot. Maybe the guy was too slow moving off after the whistle, maybe the Kapo just felt like it.
BENNY: You're making this up.
DAVID: He'd whip until the prisoner fell off the toilet, and he'd keep on whipping. The guy would by lying there on the cement floor, in the water and piss, with his pants still down around his ankles. And bleeding. But the Kapo kept on whipping, swinging that whip down, over and over, and grunting like a

pig. Whipping, whipping, whipping. And all the time the guards are standing around, watching until they figure the guy's dead. Then they have to wait a while until the Kapo gets tired. All that's left is a mess of blood and skin and bone and shit. When he stops, a few prisoners carry out the body, and the next group takes their turn on the toilet. The next group is lucky, because he's too tired to do it again for a while.

BENNY: Papa killed him.

DAVID: The Kapo terrorized them. He took whatever he wanted. They were scared to death of him. He took their food. He kept getting stronger while they got weaker.

BENNY: Papa couldn't have killed him; not alone.

DAVID: Papa had a fork. *(picks up* BENNY's *fork)* Just a mangled piece of old iron with two prongs on the end. But it was metal, and sharp. He knew he couldn't tell anyone what he was going to do. It was late at night. He waited until everyone was asleep.

BENNY: Why would he take the chance?

DAVID: Someone had to.

BENNY: Not him. He didn't have to take the chance.

DAVID: That's just it. Don't you see? He didn't have to, but he did. The lines were drawn; he had to choose. He decided to do something about it. He chose to act.

BENNY: You're trying to make it political.

DAVID: It was political.

BENNY: What's the point of this fairy tale? I'm a Kapo? Is that it? I'm some kind of a pervert with a whip?

DAVID: I'm not talking about you; I'm talking about Papa.

BENNY: You don't know what you're talking about.

DAVID: He told me.

BENNY: You were a kid and he told you this story? You don't remember. You had a dream.

DAVID: I remember. It's not something you forget.

BENNY: Is that right? The Old Man went down and killed this giant, single-handed, like Jack and the Beanstalk, David and Goliath?

DAVID: The Kapo was asleep.

BENNY: He killed him with this, this fork thing?

DAVID: That's right.

BENNY: Bullshit. That's not what happened and I can prove it.

DAVID: How?

BENNY: You say he had this fork thing?

DAVID: He found it, in the Camp some place.

BENNY: He had it before he went down to kill the Kapo?

DAVID: I told you that's how he killed him.

BENNY: Impossible.

DAVID: What do you mean, impossible? He told me the whole thing.

BENNY: He didn't have the fork.

DAVID: He used it to ...

BENNY: He didn't have the fork until after the Kapo was killed.

DAVID: He never told you any of this.

BENNY: The fork belonged to the Kapo. Papa took it from his bunk after he was killed. *(grabs fork from* DAVID*)*

DAVID: What are you trying to prove?

BENNY: *(hops up on top bunk)* Anyone can make up a horror story. You got it all mixed up. So, there's this freak: he's seven feet tall, a big vicious maniac. And the Nazis get a kick out of watching him tear Jews apart.

DAVID: You don't know any of this. Papa never talked to you about it.

BENNY: You say. What if he did? What if he told me all of it?

DAVID: You said he never talked about it.

BENNY: Maybe I don't brag about it. Maybe he told me everything after you left. You think he just clammed up for seven years? Seven years without anyone to talk to? Maybe he started to talk to his other son, his first son. I mean, his wife's been dead for a long time; his favorite son's fucked off on him: vanished. So what's left? Good old Benny, that's what. The guy who stuck around to do the shit work, the guy who took care of the house, the guy who busted his butt to earn a living when the Old Man got too sick to work. The guy who sat by his bed and wiped his chin when he couldn't swallow his soup. Maybe the Old Man told that guy a few things, too, before he died.

DAVID: About me? Did he say anything about me?

BENNY: We're not talking about you. We're talking about the thing with the Kapo.

DAVID: Papa killed that Kapo. I don't care what you say, he killed him.

BENNY: You really want to know what happened? I mean, really? All right, so there's this crazy Kapo down in the toilets. And he goes around killing the prisoners. But there's more, there's something else. This Kapo likes little boys, you understand? He picks out some young kid in the Camp, and he makes him his boy. Which wouldn't be so bad: I mean it happens, in prisons, right? And a guy like that, usually, takes care of his boy. Except that this Kapo is too big, and too rough. So the boys don't last long. That's the Kapo. So what does our Old Man do? What does he do about this crazy bastard? Nothing. Same as everybody else. All of them: they all shut up and mind their own business; and, most important, most important, they stay the fuck away from this Kapo. Why? Because they're smart. So one morning they find the Kapo down in the toilets, and he's dead, stabbed to death. And nobody knows who did it. Nobody's sorry, but nobody knows who did it. Maybe it was one of his little boys, couldn't take it any more. The guards don't know. The Jews don't know. Our Papa doesn't know. So, Papa sees the Kapo's dead. So, he goes up to the bunk, and he finds the fork there. He figures, the Kapo's dead: he won't need it, right? What should he do? Should he leave it for the guards to pick up? Should he leave it so someone else can get it? He takes the fork. That's how you survived in the Camps. That's how he got the fork. That's all.

DAVID: You just made all that up. He never told you about the Kapo.

BENNY: *(tosses the fork down on the bunk and comes down)* Sure. He only told you. Nobody else; just you.

HELLMAN *appears and walks over to the bunk. He picks up the fork and examines it.* BENNY *does not see him.*

¶

Roma Gelblum Bross
from *To Samarkand and Back*, 1986

The Stepmother

A WEEK AFTER SAVO DJON'S FUNERAL, my mother announced that we must pay a visit of condolence to the girl's stepmother, Fatima. But I did not want to go. I ground my heels into the carpet, refused to talk to her and avoided looking into her eyes. The memory was still fresh in my mind, nightmarish and painful: the small coffin being carried away from the square, and Fatima standing there, in the midst of women dressed in blue mourning capes, as if none of it was her fault, crying and wailing as if she really cared.

Then, I had not even been allowed to go down and join the mourners. "We are not Uzbecks," Mother said. "We were not invited." Now she wanted me to go down and face Fatima, stand there not knowing what I should say or do, and listen to my mother saying things she did not mean.

"I'm not going!" I announced.

But my mother was adamant. "It's the custom," she said. "We must go and console the bereaved. Fatima is our landlady. She was kind to us. We owe her that much."

I stepped out with her into the open veranda that connected our house to that of Fatima. I had more than one reason to be unhappy with Mother. That morning I heard her talking with our neighbour, Masha Kronenberg, like us, a refugee from Poland. They agreed that after what had happened we could not possibly go on living there. I had lost my friend; now I was going to lose my beautiful bright room with the arched window looking towards the city and the little sunlit square.

I looked down. The sun was setting and the square was carpeted with long shadows. Hundreds of birds chirped loudly, settling down for the night in the mulberry trees. The street beneath was, as always, teeming with people: herdsmen driving their cattle, old turbaned men on donkeys, women in capes and veils gossiping noisily and street vendors shouting out praises of their goods. My friend Samenchuk was there, playing on the steps of the wooden mosque. In the distance the beautiful dome of Tamerlane's tomb sparkled and shone, its turquoise tiles reflected a myriad little suns. Mother took my hand. "Let's go now!"

A minute later we were standing in front of the carved wooden door that opened into Fatima's inner yard. Mother pulled on a wire loop and a bell clanged. I still hoped that I could run away or convince Mother to go in without me. Scenes from that terrible night held on to me. It seemed that they were going to stay with me forever: Savo Djon's screams, and me lying shivering next to Mother in the dark, dogs barking, then the tumult downstairs, police questioning Fatima, her pale face illuminated by the flickering light from an old lantern, then her voice saying, "She is dead, Commandant, dead." I wished it were a dream. But it was not. I tried to wriggle my arm out of Mother's grasp, but she held me tightly by my wrist, as if she knew where my thoughts were going. She raised her other hand to ring again, but at that moment the door opened and a woman in a blue mourning cape let us in.

The inner yard of Fatima's house was suffused with the warm glow of the setting sun and smelled of herbs and roses. She sat in the middle of a raised wooden platform on a low stool. Her shoulders were hunched and her face hidden in a mass of falling gray hair. We stopped in the entrance and stood there for a while quietly. When Fatima raised her head, I gasped. She looked so many years older than a week ago. Her face was pale and wrinkled and her eyes were swollen.

"Fatima!" Mother cried, stepping nearer. "Fatima, I am so sorry. It took us some time to come, I know, but here we are..."

She tried to pull me with her, but I preferred to remain where I was.

But there was a time a few years back, when I greeted Fatima with friendliness and smiled at her. It was after Mother and I first arrived in Samarkand after months on crowded refugee trains, and saw Fatima waiting in the entrance to the house to greet us. She was one of the few Uzbecks who had agreed to rent rooms to refugees. We had received her name and address scribbled on a piece of paper, at the train station.

It was winter. We were cold and frightened and did not know what was awaiting us at the end of the trek through yellow puddles on dark windy alleys. When she brought us up to the long dark room and left us there, I thought we would spend the night huddled together on the mattress in the corner. But she reappeared after a while. She carried a basket of coal in one hand, a teapot in the other, and on her head she balanced a brass tray. It was loaded with fragrant pittas, raisins and nuts. We had been living on dry bread and thin soups for months. This looked like a miracle. She lit a fire in a small square pit in the middle of the room.

"Eat, drink, please!" She spoke Russian.

"Thank you." Mother pulled me to the fire and, her hand shivering, poured the tea into the small round cups.

"Handsome woman," she said to me in Polish. "God bless her."

I did not think her wrinkled brown face was handsome, but I liked the smile in her dark, slightly slanted eyes and the huge silver amulet that hung from her neck on a heavy chain. I was also intrigued with the silver earrings made of small coins that dangled from her ears, and the embroidered hat on top of her head, two thick braids coiled around it. With her face reddish in the glow coming from the coals in the pit she looked to me as if she had emerged from a fairy tale—a gypsy or a mysterious queen.

She still looked like a mysterious queen to me a few days later, when she took me to her house to show me how she baked her pittas. I watched her mix the dough, form it into flat pancakes, then squat in front of the fire like an ancient priestess. She threw the pancakes on the smoke-blackened wall of the oven and then sat and waited. With my legs drawn up beneath me I stared at her, at the fire, at the pancakes rising, then falling off the wall. She grabbed them and brushed the tops with a yellow mixture made of yolks. She made small pittas for me from the remnants she scraped off the walls of the container and engraved my name in the dough with her long, dark fingernail.

She had also once showed me her silver amulet. It had hinges and a minute door that opened to reveal a tiny scroll densely covered with letters. She said it guarded her from bad luck and diseases and also from the evil eye. It was supposed to ensure her a long life, prosperity and happiness in marriage.

A few weeks later I met her daughters, Savo Djon and Alua.

The first thought that occurred to me when I saw the two was how very little they resembled each other. Savo Djon was skinny and dark, her face long and nut-brown. Her almond-shaped eyes, set deeply in their sockets, stared at the world sadly and thoughtfully. Alua, the younger, was chubby and light-skinned and her cheeks were red. Her hair was black and shiny, like a well-polished turtle shell and she tied to the ends of her braids small bells that tinkled as she walked.

When we were all older, when I was ten, Savo Djon fifteen, and Alua fourteen, I heard women in the street say that there were young men after Alua from the time she was twelve. "She is like a red apple," they said, "pink outside, inside sweet and white. No wonder the young men want to take a bite." But it looked as if no young men wanted to take a bite off Savo Djon, they said, unless they liked dry almonds, and there were not many such men around. And they laughed at their own smartness. But I felt offended, for I liked Savo Djon. She had taught me my first words in Russian and in Uzbeck and played with me often, though I was younger than she.

Savo Djon told me many legends of Samarkand. The one I liked best was about the beautiful princess who brought from her native land a small gray worm as a betrothal present. Though the worm lay in a golden box studded with precious stones, the people of Samarkand were offended, for they considered it an insult. Many merchants in the old bazaars wore their beards dishevelled, to demonstrate their sadness and confusion. But they combed their beards very soon after, for the princess placed the worm on a mulberry leaf and the worm spun the most beautiful white cocoon. She then taught them how to make the finest silk in the world, and the merchants had many reasons to rejoice, for the world came to their bazaars on camels, horses and donkeys and they became wealthy and famous. The women of Samarkand were the best dressed in the world, for even the poorest wore silks.

But Savo Djon's dress was not made of silk. It was made of dark cotton, its sleeves were too long and they partially covered her hands. It was Alua who had the silk dresses and velvet vests to go with them. When I asked her, she said she did not like silk dresses. It was hard for me to believe. She also said that Alua was going out more and needed them, while she preferred to stay home.

This was true. I never saw Savo Djon go with Alua and Fatima when the two went visiting or into town. They were a sight to behold then, for their dresses were long and colourful and their vests were embroidered with sequins. They wore square tibeteyka hats artfully embroidered with roses and leaves and had dainty slippers on their feet. Unlike other older women Fatima never wore a cape or a veil, and many years of balancing various things on her head made her carriage erect and proud. Savo Djon said she did not mind at all, that she liked being alone, and yet I thought that once I noticed some sadness in her eyes when she said goodbye to them at the door.

In my second or third year in Samarkand Savo Djon revealed to me that Fatima was not her real mother. I was taken aback. She was the first person I knew who had a stepmother. All my knowledge about stepmothers came from the few fairy tales I knew —"Cinderella," "Snow White" and "Hansel and Gretel." I looked at Savo Djon with pity.

"Don't you miss your real mother?" I asked.

"I never knew my real mother," she said placidly, "so why should I miss her?"

"But what about Fatima?" I asked. "Is she the same to both of you?"

There was a slight tremor to her voice when she said: "Fatima is a good mother to me."

But I knew she lied and I started regarding Fatima the way one regards a strange and ferocious animal in the zoo. I thought about the differences between Alua and Savo Djon, I thought about the dresses. I remembered Savo Djon's sad eyes when the two were leaving her alone at home and I knew she was trying to conceal things from me. Soon I was to notice even more.

In my third year in Samarkand I started going to a school for refugees' children, where I had Polish and Jewish friends. Repeating what they heard from their parents they said the Uzbecks were "uncivilized" and "backward" and that we all lived in "wild Asia." When I asked my mother for the meaning of the words, she hesitated before answering. Then she said that it meant that people here had different customs and understood things differently from us. I was not satisfied with Mother's answer, for it did not explain the malicious expression that appeared on my friends' faces when they said these words. I questioned Mother about it, but she would not respond.

In spite of what my school friends said, I liked Savo Djon and I liked Samenchuk. I continued playing with them when, in the summer, my other friends scattered away to other parts of the city where they lived.

In the beginning of the fourth summer, when I was nine years old, I noticed that I grew up almost as tall as Savo Djon though she was fourteen. But then everyone said I was tall for my age. I also noticed that her skin became yellowish and all of a sudden she looked as if she had shrivelled. She told me she was sick with malaria in the winter. That was the year when Savo Djon quit school and started selling pittas in the square. I was surprised to see her there, but she said she had to, that Fatima needed help and money. And yet I knew well that Fatima was no poorer than her neighbours, that the women in the street treated her with deference not only on account of her age, and that Alua went to school. Savo Djon said Alua was the smarter one. I knew this too was untrue. Alua could not tell stories. Alua could not speak Russian. Savo Djon could.

I often watched her out in the square, where the pitta sellers competed for the street trade with vendors of grapes, figs and pumpkin seeds. They formed a group of their own beneath the largest mulberry tree and converged noisily on passersby, many of whom came on camels, donkeys and makeshift carts. But Savo Djon never mingled with the others. She stood apart from them and waited till a customer approached her.

It was also the summer when I first saw Savo Djon's room. I went to get some pittas from Fatima's bakery, in the rear of the house. The door to Savo Djon's room stood ajar. I peeked in. The room was small and dark and contained only a narrow bed and a wooden shelf on top of which was a kerosene burner and two bowls. It looked as if Savo Djon did her cooking there, for a strong smell of food and spices came out of the room. When I mentioned it to her, she was startled.

"How do you know I don't eat with the others?" she asked. I told her I saw the kerosene burner and the bowls.

"I eat different food than they... that's all," she retorted. But I saw she was uneasy about it and I knew that Fatima was to blame for it all.

One windy evening, Savo Djon's tibeteyka was blown away. During the short space of time when her head was uncovered I had noticed something very strange. Savo Djon had gray hair. Patches of gray hair covered her scalp. She put the tibeteyka on and ran away as if she were frightened. I knew that gray hair came from age or from worry, and Savo Djon was not old.

Then, one day she fainted and lay flat on the pavement. The pitta vendors scattered. Alua sprinkled Savo Djon's face with cold water from Suleiman's jug and she recovered. I was in the entrance to the house in the evening, when Old Suleiman came to ask for his payment. He brought the water from the springs up in the hills and sold it by the glass. Fatima became angry when he demanded payment for four glasses. She quarreled with him noisily and called him a thief. He called her old witch. They settled for two pittas and Suleiman went away, cursing. I overheard the women in the street say that Savo Djon did not eat enough; they also said Fatima used to behave towards her differently when Savo Djon's father was around, before he went to the front, like my father.

It was then that I made up my mind to help Savo Djon. I thought I could write to her father. But where was he? Did he speak Russian? Then I decided to read to her the story of Cinderella. Perhaps she would understand. Perhaps she would write and complain to her father. I had an old Polish book with colourful pictures and I brought it down to the square. She regarded the pictures with interest, then handed the book to me.

"Read, little one," she said gently.

I read slowly and distinctly, to make sure she understood. From time to time I lifted my eyes to examine her reactions, but she just stared at me out of her dark sad eyes. The sadness was still there when Cinderella put on the slipper and turned into a princess.

"Why are you sad, Savo Djon?" I asked. "The story ended well for Cinderella."

Savo Djon pondered my question for a while, then said, "I am sad for the stepmother and the stepsisters."

"What?!" I almost screamed. "Perhaps I should read it again?! Perhaps you did not understand?!"

"I understood well, little one. You read well and clearly."

I was proud but not happy. I felt I was shrinking a little under Savo Djon's gaze. "How can you, Savo Djon? They were bad and ugly and cruel to Cinderella!"

"This is why I am sorry for them, little one. Their hearts were full of hate and envy. Cinderella worked hard, but she was kind and healthy. And she married a prince. So why should I feel sorry for her?"

I knew I was failing somewhere. I did not know what to answer. The ground was slipping beneath my soles. I made a last, desperate effort.

"That means that you are also sorry for your stepmother and stepsister. They treat you like a servant. You are like Cinderella, Savo Djon! They wear nice dresses! They send you out to sell pittas in the street! You live in a dark room! You don't even eat with them!"

She did not answer. She just looked at me thoughtfully for a long time and I thought that I noticed tears in her eyes. She then said, "It's getting late, little one. I must go home."

I remained all by myself on the steps of the mosque. The neighs of camels settling for the night in some remote caravan-serai came from a distance; a woman sang lullabies to her baby on a balcony across the street.

I put the book under my arm and walked upstairs to our room, which was dim and cool like a mystery. I sat by the window. The clouds were now crimson. The nippled minarets and towers of Registan glistened in the distance. I opened the book and looked again at the picture of the stepsisters and the stepmother, trying to gather sympathy for them. But I could not. This is what they meant by the word "backward," I thought. They just cannot understand the simplest thing. Then I threw the book into the corner, the way one throws an item that has outlived its usefulness. Summer ended soon after and I went back to my winter friends from school.

The following summer—my fifth summer in Samarkand, Savo Djon and I grew closer. That was perhaps because I needed a friend more than ever. As Father's absence lengthened, Mother became more nervous and had less and less patience with me. She slapped me frequently and spent more time away from home. So I spent longer periods of time out in the square playing with Samenchuk, who was a liar, but fun to be with, watching Savo Djon sell her pittas and talking to her on the steps of the wooden mosque. It was nice to be spending those long free hours on the square. I liked the smells of spicy foods that wafted from the stalls, the colours and the sounds that surrounded us. When Mother's voice summoned me, I dragged my feet unwillingly up the stairs, then waited impatiently for the next day.

That fifth summer was unbearably hot. By the time the last days of August came, everyone wished an end to it. The cotton fields were in bloom earlier than usual. The tufts that floated in the air irritated children's eyes and they walked around looking as if they were crying. The last of the mulberries were ripening on the trees, sweet and mushy, perfect food for the thousands of silkworms that spun white cocoons on their leaves. The women in the street talked about heavy winter coming and about some strange disease of the silkworm that was spreading, that might affect the cocoons and cause the butterflies to emerge deformed and die. Otherwise, things were the same.

On one of those days I came down to the square wearing new white shorts with a red butterfly sewn below my belly. Mother cut it out of an old pillow and stitched it on clumsily. Samenchuk gave a long whistle at the sight of me.

We were going to harvest the last of the mulberries and Samenchuk was ready with his white sheet, which he spread under the tree. Savo Djon was already there with her pittas and she smiled at me. She squatted in the shadow of the tree taking her midday rest. The pitta vendors in their colourful dresses and hats looked like a bunch of flowers laid on the yellow ground. Summer insects danced in the air and a group of butterflies whirled towards the women. Samenchuk climbed up the tree. He shook the branches and it started raining mulberries. The women picked them from between the folds of their dresses, laughing merrily and jokingly scolding the boy. He came down, tied the corners of the sheet together and carried the load to the other side of the street, where there was a wooden awning above a store entrance. We divided the loot between us, then squatted under the awning. The ripe mulberries melted as we ate them, their sweet nectar spilling from the corners of our mouths. Then we sat there silent and tired, watching the pitta vendors and chasing some lethargic flies from our legs.

Around noon time the street became very empty and quiet. People must have gone to find shelter from the heat in the cool interiors of their homes. Only the vendors remained, but even they were not as noisy as always. Old Suleiman sat in a shady corner and drank the spring water from his jug, a very unusual thing for him to do.

I noticed the woman in the dark cape right away. At first she looked like a long dark shadow. She came from the alley that led to the cemetery and approached the group of women in slow limping steps. They did not converge upon her the way they always did. They just sat there and stared.

Savo Djon was closest to the alley and the woman addressed her first. The girl rose to her feet; it was customary for a younger woman not to remain seated in the presence of an older one. The woman asked her to uncover the pittas, then pinched them one by one. She told Savo Djon to bring up the bottom one. She then lifted her veil.

Her face was wrinkled and her eyes were very small. She unbuttoned her dress and brought out a dirty leather pouch. She took some coins out and counted them into Savo Djon's hand one by one. When she stopped I saw Savo Djon shaking her head. She was protesting something. The woman seemed angry. Suddenly her small eyes rested on Savo Djon's hand. She then lifted her head and examined the girl's face. Shrieking shrilly she took a step backwards. Savo Djon's eyes widened in fright. She retreated, the pittas falling to the ground and rolling away in the dust. The pitta vendors yelled, rising to their feet. In a minute they were gone. Savo Djon too disappeared into the entrance of the house.

It all happened very fast. Only Samenchuk, I and the old woman remained in the sunlit square. She stood there a while longer, then looking stealthily around gathered into her cape the pittas that rolled from Savo Djon's hands. She shouted something in Uzbeck and waved a clasped fist in the direction of the house, then scurried back to where she had come from. Only then did I ask Samenchuk for the meaning of it all. But he seemed angry and restless, then hurried away too. I remained all alone. I ran home, hoping to find out what had happened. But all was very quiet there too. Mother was away, at work. The carved door to the inner yard stared mutely at me. I climbed up on the veranda and pushed the wooden shutters that opened out into Fatima's garden. The garden was empty. Only some birds chirped faintly in the pomegranate trees and the open entrances to the house gaped at me dark and mysterious. I went to our room then, closed the shutters and curled up on top of my mattress. Overcome by heat, I fell asleep.

I awoke to the sound of screams. It was dark outside. Mother let me sleep through supper. I was hungry. At first I thought I was waking from a nightmare. It's Savo Djon. I sat on my bed and listened. The screams were coming from that direction. She has lost the pittas and Fatima was punishing her. I hated Fatima! I slid off the mattress and went to the other side of the room, where my mother was lying immobile on a low bed. In the light of the moon I could see that her eyes were wide open.

"Mother, what is it?" I whispered. "Has it been going on for a long time?"

"No, no, calm down."

She made me lie next to her and covered my ears with her hands. But I could hear.

"It's Savo Djon, Mother. I know. She lost her pittas today. Did you know Fatima was not her real mother? Yes, she is her stepmother and she will kill her…. Call police, mother. I'm afraid."

"The police station is far away. Besides we are strangers here. We do not know their customs." Mother was afraid too. I could hear the shots of the falling whip. I wanted to scream too, but could not. It went on like this for a terrible while. Then the screams ceased as if cut by a knife. Terrible silence followed. Then there were loud knocks on the front gate. Mother and I rushed out and we saw a dishevelled Fatima running towards the gate with a lantern. Two policemen came in. They demanded to be admitted to the inner yard. And then her awful words: "She is dead, Comrade Commandant, there is nothing to search for. She is dead."

¶

I stood leaning against the whitewashed wall of the yard. The woman in the blue cape brought in a tray with grapes and yellow figs which were artfully arranged on top of fresh green leaves. She then put some coals in the cavity of the small samovar. She laid it out on top of a low table with nacreous inlay and brought it to where Mother and Fatima were seated. Mother motioned to me to come nearer. Fatima looked at me, smiled and handed me a cup of tea. If she only knew what thoughts I harbored in my heart. We drank in silence. Fatima fingered the silver amulet on her chest, all the while looking to the ground. When we had finished drinking she lifted her head and cast a hazy glance around her.

"It's a heavy loss for us all," she said.

Mother nodded and I looked at Fatima hatefully.

"I loved her like my own daughter," she said.

Mother bowed her head low and I had a sudden urge to run away and never set my eyes on Fatima again. She must have noticed our silence and reticence, for she sat staring sadly ahead, her fingers clasped around the amulet. Then, stuttering slightly, as if trying to overcome a strong hesitation she began talking again.

"Madame Solomonovna," she said turning her eyes upon Mother, "when I married her father, Savo Djon was only a tiny baby. Alua was born very soon after, so I could still nurse Savo Djon for a while. So you see," she said with a tiny smile, as if the memory was a pleasant one for her, "sometimes they both sucked at the same time, each at one breast."

Mother just sat there silently, her hands clasped in her lap, the fringes of her black shawl touching the ground. She turned towards me as if she looked in my face for answers, but I had none. What Fatima was saying made everything for me so much less comprehensible. Fatima must have understood, for she said, half sadly, half angrily: "You must have harsh thoughts about me, Madame Solomonovna."

Mother started pulling nervously on the corners of the shawl. "Well," she said finally, "you know...we heard Savo Djon's screams that night, then we saw the police...and also people talk...."

"Yes, yes, I understand." Fatima nodded sadly.

I looked at her and all of a sudden she was only a sad old woman, so different from a mysterious queen in a tale. As if sensing the change in me she took my hand and pulled me towards her. She held my head in her lap and I hid my face in the folds of her robe. She smelled of balsam and of soft warm silk. When she started talking again I got up. She told Mother then how lucky she was to have such a smart and healthy girl. Mother answered that she was indeed. Fatima then said that she too was lucky in having at least one healthy girl.

"We did not know Savo Djon was sick," Mother said after a pause. "She never missed a day out in the square."

Fatima lifted her head. Quietly, as if afraid to be overheard she said, "Madame Solomonovna, do you know what leprosy is?"

Mother nodded.

"Savo Djon was a leper."

"What?!" Mother's eyes widened and she just sat there rigid like a sculpture. "Little Savo Djon... a... leper?"

We talked about it at school once. The teacher said there were some sicknesses here, in the Orient, that were extinct where we came from. She mentioned cholera and leprosy and said cholera was not the worst, for one died fast. About leprosy she said some things that were too frightening to think about.

"I knew about it for five years," Fatima went on. "I have prayed to Allah for enlightenment. I also visited a few of our old healers and wise men. They told me it was not as contagious as people believed if one kept clean and took in certain spices and herbs. But the Russian authorities think differently. So I decided to hide her. You know, Madame Solomonovna what would have been the alternative?!"

I watched Mother. She knew.

"Yes," she said with an expression of horror on her face "Yes, I know…a leper colony."

"A leper colony in the desert!" cried Fatima. "Where they live like animals, worse than animals, their limbs falling one by one, their faces a rotting wound, till they die, their bones scattered on the rocks. Could you do it to your child, Madame Solomonovna?! Could you?"

A shiver ran through Mother as she looked at me. Her lips curved down unhappily and there were tears in her eyes. I started crying. The woman in the blue cape brought white cloth and rose water to wash our faces. Fatima dropped her hands into her lap in a gesture of helplessness and fatigue.

"For five long years I managed to keep it a secret. Believe me, Madame Solomonovna, it was not easy. We lived in constant fear. I had to engage her in the selling of pittas to keep her out of school and protect her from being forced to work in cotton fields. Otherwise there was no need for her to work."

I squatted on the edge of the wooden platform. So it was all different from what I thought. Fatima motioned to the woman in blue and she refilled our cups.

"Satan himself," Fatima cried clasping her amulet, "Satan in person must have sent the accursed woman to our street that day. She used to work with lepers. She saw what others did not. She threatened to notify the authorities. May she hang by her tongue! There are severe penalties imposed for hiding a leper."

My mother raised her eyebrows questioningly.

"There were not many choices left, Madame Solomonovna," Fatima sighed. "We knew the police would be here before dawn. So we agreed, she and I, that I should beat her till she bled.…That way they were not going to touch her. That's what I told her…that they won't touch a bleeding leper… Savo Djon tried not to scream…." Fatima started sobbing uncontrollably. I was scared. The woman in blue rushed to her side, but she waved her away.

"Savo Djon tried not to scream," she sobbed. "But it was too painful. Believe me, Madame Solomonovna… my heart bled with every shot of the whip." She buried her head in her hands. My mother looked bewildered. I just squatted there, numb, not knowing what to do. I looked beyond Fatima's head. The pomegranates on the tree were ripe and red and deep shadows lay in the small arbour of vines. The sky was very clear and the woman in blue stood in the entrance to the house watching us all respectfully.

Then I saw Mother leaning towards Fatima and I heard her whispering, "But Fatima, dear Fatima, did it not occur to you that she might die of the beating?"

Fatima straightened her back and looked into Mother's eyes, her head held up proudly.

"Madame Solomonovna!" she said. There was a note of disappointment in her tone. "Madame Solomonovna, I know you are a learned and intelligent woman…and yet, yet you do not seem to understand…" She paused and looked at me. I knew she would have preferred I was not there. Then, leaning very close to Mother, her face tense and almost cruel she whispered hoarsely, "Do you really think a leper colony in the desert would have been better?!"

Crickets started chattering somewhere in the grass. My mother lifted her hand to her lips.

Fatima got up, like a queen at the end of an audience. My mother rose to her feet too. The woman in blue stood erect, then bowed deeply.

I knew then it was time for us to leave.

ש

Grant Loewen
from *Brick*, 1989

ECAUSE HIS DAY IS GOING TO BE TOO BUSY TO PLAN, Brick concentrates on the car. It's a straight two-mile shot along the highway into town, the snow thick and predictable under the wheels of the '64 sedan. If he can get to Wire's tonight with the beer he doesn't much care what happens today anyway. *The Sabre Truth* would be typeset by now and although Moore will go by the printers to look over the proofs and likely withhold his go-ahead over several spelling mistakes in order to make himself look stupid, the bi-weekly student paper is likely to be at the exits at the end of the school day as usual. "Useful to stuff boots with tonight," Brick thinks. Then he concentrates on the road.

I imagine Brick's highway feels a little like the road I took to Wire's camp on a warm day in March: a thick winter road. That was the first out-of-town trip I made with the '64 Comet. Travel had compacted successive snowfalls into bony tracks and bonded them to the roadbed. Mine was the first vehicle to come along after the last cover and I had my hands full to maintain forty miles-per-hour. Through my grip on the wheel I negotiated the contract between summer tread and the twin backbones below the morning's snowfall. The tires slid off, searched, wrestled back up. Whenever I dared risk a glance at the speedometer the needle showed the same.

Even at forty a white luminescence quickly rose and fell in my peripheral vision. It was the doeskin moccasins of dancing giants whose feet flew through the regions of black sticks on either side of the car; one of those mythologies on the outside of car windows. When rolled down the vision disappears but the magic is breathable for one breath.

Wire lived with Shirley and the kids north of our home town on the same geographic edge that runs like a fault line between bush and prairie in our province. A hundred enterprises kept him busy in one part of the southeast or another. In summer he raised bees, joined framing crews, custom combined, fought forest fires. But winters he cut wood: lumber, ties for CNR, pulp for the chipboard plant. From January to March he'd move into the bush, further east each year, wherever the cutting permits took him. He'd have set up his landing there in the fall: mill, trailer, supply shed. Once set up he'd find enough reasons to stay out there for days at a time even before cutting started. Weekends he made a point to be home.

I approached Wire's turnoff, turned, and, as if it sensed my own intimidation, the car immediately fell off the skewed tracks. I was barely off the road and stuck good, but knew right away there was no point in going on with a noisy, rubber-smoking attempt to get back onto the disjointed trail to the trailer. My brother's skidder could make short work of it in any case.

"So, Sod, what have you come for this time?" Wire said after I'd pushed myself and the Old Stock into the trailer.

"You're not so terribly frightening," I said.

"Says who?" He indulged his first impulse to mock me, to piss around the boundaries of our love. "Me and the chainsaw've got the pines whispering, the aspens trembling and the birches shivering. Did you hear? Pop'lar 'pinion says I'm the number one fright throughout the riding."

"I guess not." For Wire, people and politics were a metaphor for the region's population of trees and their opinions. People lived beside roads, too, for instance. They had similar life expectancies to the sticks in this part of the world. They died in large fires, from old age, and at the hands of armed and licensed predators like himself. The metaphors were a way to deal with his isolation, I think.

Later we were overheating the trailer, working through the beer, and complaining about the wicked world; about how, here we were, thriving in local economies of thrift and industry for his part, of sprouting social and professional status for my part, and both of us unable to convince the other of a reason why, therefore, the world was damned: something we both knew, or felt, not knowing why. It was a rare topic between us. I think we adopted a feuding stance, politically, in order to avoid the subject after that.

I defended the political process that night. I said the process was democratic, responsible. Wire said it was a democratic joke, that the government was elected for the one thing it knew how to do: carry a mace. The walls and ceiling of his trailer enclosed three pieces of furniture which defined a kitchen, a bedroom and a shop. The floor was a piece of worn white linoleum splotched with our rapidly drying boot marks. Wire set out a meal for us and while I ate and drank he moved back and forth between the kitchen end, where he produced graham crackers, cheese and tomato soup, and the shop end where the snowmobile's carburetor was being cleaned in a bath of gasoline. The fumes made it difficult to taste the cheese. The sheet metal stove glowed red around the base of its exhaust flue from the furious, nearly visible immolation of a stick of pine Wire had added to my initial overdose of poplar sticks in order to boil the soup faster. An erratic heat spilled against my back and I started to sweat.

"I drank a lot of wine last winter but the freezer/oven cycle of temperatures in the trailer doesn't help it. It was better when I left the bottles outside and just threw them frozen into a pot of water on the stove until the ice disappeared. Sorry I don't have any left. Shil's batch from the fall was a small one this year—we finished it up at Christmas. The poor crop of chokes must've discouraged her. You were there at the Wiebe's fiftieth, eh? That was Shil's wine—the red. Chokecherry and white raisin—nice colour."

As bottles increased on the table my democratic arguments emptied. I conceded that the political process in our part of the world did not work as a democracy might, yet it depended on the democratic ideal to effect social control. Wire said the government's social contract with the people, beneath all the rhetoric, was a death warrant. I said no to this. I said that justice, however modest, was distributed to some who were otherwise oppressed and harassed, that improvements were effected by the influence of individuals on cabinet members directly.

"OK. Let's go. Let's go see a minister right away and effect one of those improvements." Just one of his brainy ideas we never acted on.

If Wire didn't like an opinion he immediately challenged it with a chainsaw, it felt like. I didn't like to see my ideas mocked, but I had the presence of mind to change the subject. I had to hit him quickly and hard so I said, "What should I do next, Wire?"

"You? What you are doing, probably."

I chewed a wood chip. "Help me," I countered. "I want to figure things out, do something, get somewhere."

"Let's go to the lake. How much fuel's left in the car?"

"None. I could go for some. The car's stuck." I was confused. Needing what I thought Wire knew about stuff, I fell easily into his agenda.

"What's that? How much is in the car?"

"Enough to get back on. Not enough to get to Falcon Lake. But we can stop along the way. What's the problem?" I said, trying to recover from his manipulations. Yet I wanted to encourage his plan; to understand him. This time more than ever. I wanted to know why he'd quit teaching for this hands-on life. No, I wanted to know what to do.

"What's my problem? What's yours?"

More confused, I blurted out: "Everything! Graduation for sure. Going away. Getting somewhere!" I was such an inarticulate asshole around Wire. Everything tugged in the wrong direction.

"Let's go to the lake," he announced. "I've got this guy's motoneige in payment for dock timber. You don't have to be back tonight, do you?"

"No. Of course not. But why don't we take my car?"

"Where we're going a snowmobile's faster. The machine needs gas is all. A minute before it ran out of gas I realized that every other piece of equipment around here runs on diesel. Good thing I was in the yard. Oil I've got in the shed there."

I got a length of hose and two fuel cans from a shed next to the mill and filled them from my car's tank according to his instructions.

"Will two cans get us there?" I asked politely.

"One will get us there, the other gets us back. You go as far as you get, one way or the other," Wire assured me.

I knew I hadn't left myself enough gas to get back to town on, but I already felt too stupid to question him. I must have been desperate for some shred of guidance to put up with this pain-in-the-ass brotherhood. It wasn't Falcon as I'd assumed, but Whitemouth Lake to which we were going. With the fuel from my car and several yanks on the starter cord, Wire got noise from the snowmobile. I climbed on behind him and together we headed up one of the skidder tracks which ended a half mile from the landing in a maze of fallen trees and piles of brush: Wire's harvest of usable timber waiting for him to drag it out to the landing. I was struck by Wire's industry; the force in his hand, once applied, to make a living in this peripheral place. A problem developed.

"Can't get the power," Wire screeched over successive revving and dying sounds from the engine.

"What?" I shrieked in response, knowing full well the meaning of all the noises. Several surges of power got us around and back to the trailer.

"Have to look at that. Feels like a fuel-supply problem." I followed Wire into the trailer and threw several sticks into the stove while he gathered handfuls of tools into a small tool box and went out. "Make some coffee: whatever you can find—help yourself," he said, pulling the door shut.

I filled the kettle from a five-gallon Reliant, placed it on the stove lid and listened to the contradictory sounds of small motor repair: whistling, coughing, blowing, spitting; never a word. I needed a play by play of what was happening to our transportation so out I went. Wire revealed nothing. "Can I get my flashlight?" I offered. Then I followed him in again where Wire placed a wet lump of carburetor on the bench and beside it several nuts and washers that dropped out of his mouth into a greasy and, now I noticed, bloody hand. "Sorry. Is that bad?" I said.

"Just a knuckle. Let's have some coffee while I fix this: in the coffee tin there. It's easier to take the entire carb inside, clean the jets and I think the float was sticking. The thing's filthy anyway."

We took the same route, skirted the cut clockwise through some unpacked snow where the machine rolled slowly back and forth dodging trees, testing our balance. We came across an obvious trail that took us away from the scene of Wire's work and towards Whitemouth Lake.

On the trail the going was good: bumpy, but softened by the warmth. Without stopping Wire pulled his feet from under the engine cowl and kneeled diagonally against the seat.

The echoed roar of the machine receded to the back of my consciousness and a sense of solitude, before and behind, replaced it. Wire reached for a switch and extinguished the bobbing beam of light ahead of us. Silver light from a rising, bulging half-moon flickered through the passing sticks. The giants danced again without their slippers: muscular black wind-sculpted shapes. Now I had the leisure to seek them across the moving moon-mottled floor.

We veered off the track and struck a tree. I think the crack of the machine against the tree and the sudden silence spooked me less than the sight of Wire lying beside me in the snow. I found myself thinking about the night we'd spent in the same bed when I was a kid. I forget where, but I remember feeling abandoned in a foreign house where Wire had two friends who filled rooms with model airplanes, montgolfiers, electric devices, and where the air was crammed with adventure. This was the first time I'd listened to him breathe.

He didn't move and I, too, lay in bewildered comfort. I lifted my head to have a look at him. He was ghostly white but not visibly damaged. I waited for a grey-black spot on his forehead to lump up and explain his look of sleep. I stood up in deep snow and examined Wire's body in the moonlight. My shadow fell across him and I moved around, kneeling to examine his face.

Then an awareness of some sort confused me and I decided to rescue Wire, to call in a helicopter and fly him out within minutes to emergency, to brush the hair out of his eyes along the way, to hear him speak. I could not remember touching him before. But the helicopter wasn't coming, there was no phone, I could not even run the machine, or rather, it was wrecked. I carried the body draped across my back for about five hundred yards until I heard Wire's voice.

"How about cancelling the trip to the lake, kid, and turning us around?"

I put Wire on his feet and as he stood shaking and hanging on to me I felt the clean slicing shame of my mistakes: attempting to carry Wire, thinking I was taking him home when I'd continued towards the lake, not thinking to make a camp and keep us both dry and warm. His concussion was serious and he suffered some delirious minutes on and off, but he could manage enough lucid moments to take over the tasks of his own survival and mine.

Wire walked back to the wreck clutching my shoulder for stability on the undulating trail, now pocked with the marks of my footsteps where I'd staggered off the hard track. Once under way, the rhythm of our exhaustion, our bobbing shadows, and the warmth of the work took over the task of moving us along. I felt the heat of my muscles against the shivers running along my damp skin. I was too warm or too cold, thinking I should know which.

I wanted to walk all the way back, to just keep going, but Wire had a look at the snowmobile and decided it could be run with a few makeshift repairs. He thought it was fifteen miles out; that we'd do better to try for ten miles-per-hour on the machine than walk for fifteen hours, if we could even do it in that.

My job was to build a fire, get myself dried off and to stay out of the way of business beyond my competence. While I was about this, Wire righted the machine, which had bounced back several yards from the tree, tore off the shattered cowling and windshield, kicking at the hinge that held a large piece. The gas tank had split, but with a cord from a sleeping bag which I hadn't realized was in the pack, Wire tried to bind it tight enough to hold fuel for the duration of our return.

The repairs failed. Wire became incoherent and lost most of the fuel. I used the rest of it to create a blaze, which at first was too large to be useful and then was quickly swallowed up by the snow beneath it. Bad mistakes. Wire came to his senses long enough to instruct me to stuff one sleeping bag inside the other, to set them on our clothes in a grave-shaped hole in the snow scraped clean to the ground, and to lay both of us down together in that bed, naked, our parkas thrown over our heads and upper bodies.

I did it. For a stupid minute I hoped I would die of embarrassment before he did of hypothermia. The full-length feel of Wire's clammy skin, his grasp, and the inhalation of his expired breath: all turned magically to comfort. It was mid-morning and we were both warm and wide awake when we heard our rescuers' snowmobiles along the trail. On early morning patrol a warden had stopped at Wire's landing because my car had partially blocked the road and the plough operator had stopped, gone and knocked on the trailer door, and radioed in. The warden arranged a search. So here they were, two wardens and two police officers, in time to get us home for lunch. Wire and I stood in our steaming hole, nude as winter birch ready for whipping.

¶

Bryan Sentes
from *In the Way of Knowledge*, 1989

The Lost Psalms of Anselm of Canterbury (1033–1109 A.D.)

I

At dawn, I came from the green hills
　　Pale and moist with spring mist;
Left the yew in its morning stance,
　　Let the rowan kneel still;
Left the stream's quiet chuckling
　　To the minnows and toads;
Left the larks to twist their songs,
　　Sparrows to their quick flight;
Passed the freshly furrowed fields,
　　The ox's trudge and groan;
Passed through the village and its smells
　　Of peasant life at dawn;
Mounted the slow rise surrounding
　　The monastery's wall;
Traced their careful and smooth stonework,
　　The curved arch of the door;
Turned and filled my sight with the sky,
　　The far and massing clouds;
Stood and prayed in thanks for this day,
　　Turned again and entered.

II

At ease in my high cell, I rest
    My legs from the climb's strain.
I consider the day's duties,
    And allow them to pass
Clear from my mind, for these define
    My life in earthly days.
I carefully list all duties
    Of one of my Order
That border my vocation,
    And, listed, let them pass
From my mind's attention also.
    Family I recall,
Ponder my own small place
    In the ranks of human
Souls that walk the face of the earth
    Under the loving face
Of God the Almighty Father;
    And on that focus
Body and all the faculties
    Of the created soul.

III

Once, I listened to two dispute
    The proposition that
All Creation is a codex
    Revealing the Design
Of God, the way that words reveal
    (By making visible)
The private thoughts of their author.
    If this is true, what of
All those who are illiterate?
    And what created man
Can claim he has interpreted,
    Not some treatise composed
By some mundane mind, but the thoughts
    Of God that sing like choirs
Of wise angels in harmonies
    And sublime chords no man
Can hope to transcribe in truth?
    The learned may dispute
And climb on Reason's wings along,
    But not for all such flight.

IV

But if God is everywhere, why
    Cannot all men see Him?
Can it be true that one must learn
    To see His great Presence?
But if one were to stare into
    His Face, one would surely
Die. Therefore, it is human pride
    That dares to measure God
By the scales of the fleshly eye;
    A deadly sin again
Trips humble and sincere desire
    For Him into the Pit.
So, we must not seek to prove Him
    By our human senses.
And all the pagans and the heathen
    Had faith in gods of stone.
Some even worshipped trees, and wound
    Around their trunks for praise
The entrails of living men.
    Pure faith answers nothing.

V

No man is Reason and senses
    And faith held together
In a wrap of clay. Man is one
    Undivided being,
A unity broken only
    In thought and abstraction.
And being made by a loving
    Father, must have access
To that love so he may return
    Love. In quiet, passive
Meditation, then, I ponder
    What passes are open
Through this high range of questions.
    And that I see my pride.
No one comes to the Father but
    Through our loving Saviour,
And one need only approach His
    Portal and knock humbly.
So now I call on memory
    Of all the things He said.

VI

"Unless a man be born again
    "Of water and spirit
"He shall not enter the Kingdom
    "Of God." But what water?
What we sprinkle on infants' brows
    Is purely symbolic.
Surely the water that God breathed
    Over is meant: chaos
And darkness that threaten to drown
    The helpless human soul.
"And what is spirit?" one asked.
    "No man knows," He said,
"Where the wind comes from or where
    "It goes, but everyone
"Heard the wind. We of the spirit
    "Are like that." Thus, I will
Rest like a leaf, blown and carried
    By the wind where He wills.
Already my spirit lightens
    And rises to God.

VII

Withered and frail through vice,
    Yet rising higher through
The blinding clouds of sin, I come
    To light at last before
What I conceive You, Lord, to be.
    I knew You incarnate
In my idea of You, wrought
    Of dross metals, hardly
Gold, that constitute the substance
    Of even my finest
Thoughts. You still reside beyond
    The lofty heights you've brought
Me to; I knew my conception
    Is true as it can be:
I do not seek to understand
    So that I may believe,
But I believe to understand.

VIII

Give my faith some understanding
        That You exist as I
Believe You to exist. I know
        There is no thing above
My thought of You; no greater thing
        Can I conceive at all.
And can it be that such a thing
        As I think you to be
Does not exist? Only the Fool
        Says in his heart "There is
"No God." For it is more perfect
        To exist than not to,
And what can I imagine
        More perfect than You, Lord?
I understand that You must be,
        For Your perfections pass
Far beyond what I can conceive.
        Now, knowing, I believe
As one whole man: intellect,
        Faith, passions, together,
A small created trinity.

IX

But now, the great grey seas of doubt
    Begin to boil and churn,
And though I had danced over them
    With the faith of a saint,
They trip, and toss, and buffet me
    Till I near drown in fear.
My heart thuds, thundering blood
    In my ears, and the storm
Passes away, leaving only
    A quiet stiller than
A heinous soul before the Seat
    Of Judgment. And then, there
Rises a shadow, an island
    That navigates the seas
Anchorless, at random, a ship
    Of imagination
Alone. No more perfect island
    Could be: rich forests,
Choirs of paradisal birds,
    A temperate halo.

X

That much I could see from this far
        Off. I swam to its shores
And crawled onto its beach. The sands
        Were white, and soft, and warm,
Lightly fragrant with salt and airs
        Breathed gently on breezes
From the pale throats of flowers,
        Still, on the fresh foliage.
Birds fashioned songs of audible
        Quicksilver, suddenly
Gone, then sung again. And streams
        Splashed from the forested
Cloak mantling the island's peak.
        Around its slopes I saw
Animals, perfected by some
        Husbandry of genius:
Golden flanked deer with opaline
        Eyes; ghostly grey squirrels
Quicker than shadows; and angel
        Feathered birds in vast flocks.

XI

Sodden, trembling, and cold, I
    Watched, muted, a woman
Approach with the ease of a Summer's
    Dusk. Her eyes and hair were
Jet, her flesh a living ivory,
    And her voice, music
As vibrant and soft as the blue
    That gives way before night.
She was the angel the pagan
    Parmenides mistook
For a goddess; the consoling
    Woman Boethius
Loved as Sophia; the angel
    Who called my mind from earth
To the contemplation of God,
    Who showed me now in ways
My earthly soul could comprehend
    Faint reflections of His
Infinite Perfections. I knelt
    And sang a prayer of thanks.

XII

With dusk, the sun ignites the clouds
    And burns them red as blood;
My soul is calmer than the dawn
    Our Blessed Lord was raised.
My being sings the praises of God
    Who gives to all who search
Some understanding of His Love
    For every man with faith
Enough to rise on Reason's wings
    In rapture and in hope.

translated from the Latin by Frank Lambdin

¶

April Bulmer
from *A Salve for Every Sore*, 1990

Eddy Goss

He buys a blue salt block and a big bag of
oyster shells for his chickens. Tells me:

Jesus Loving Christ, she makes a
man feel lowly, with her beauty
and never takin a lover. I was
drinkin a bottle a Orange Kik
when I seen her cross the field
in her summer work dress, her
boots round her neck so's she
wouldn't wear them out. I heard
her singin Little Betty Blue
lost her holiday shoe, as
she got close. She had a apple
box a rags and dirty clothes. I
watched her dark head bend over
the water like she was a whisperin
her sins to the rocks.

Sure would like to take tea and
porridge cakes with Miss Graham.
To rub the soreness from her body
at the end of the day with
a bit a fish oil.

I'm saving my treasures so her
Pa'll let me have her. I got a

sack a onions, two jars a pickled
eggs, a piece a lace curtain, a
ostrich-feathered hat, two skinny
cows, and a sorry-lookin scrub
horse. Give all I got to spoon
with Miss Laura Graham. To share
with her my daily bread, a
glimpse of the moon.

Angels

I measure George Sidney's shoulders
for a belladonna back plaster. *The pain feels
like broken wings,* he says.

He tells me the angels came again last night
as he was brewing tea.
Appeared as steam on the kitchen window,
rustled in the gingham curtains.
Five of them stretched
from the oven to the ice box,
clean and white as nighties drying on the line.
Then they fluttered like moths
around the light bulb.
George flaps his arms and gives an arthritic wince.
And sang, sang hymns as the kettle whistled.
George makes a soprano squawk.

They beat their feathered arms, rose
like prayers through the stained ceiling.

¶

Ken Decker
from *Backyard Gene Pool*, 1982

Molecularclockevaluation

The nightwatchmen know that they may quit their jobs at any time.

"If these next three minutes go all right," they tell themselves, "then we'll stay for another three."

In this way they work through a long string of triadic clusters of minutes which have gone well.

¶

Sharon Sparling
from *The Glass Mountain*, 1984

Chapter 1

CHLOE PRESSED THE DOOR SHUT. It was early. The nurse had roused her for breakfast at six, but she wasn't hungry. Dr. Homsy would undoubtedly have something to say about that. She never did eat breakfast, and disliked it that her personal habits were now the subject of scrutiny.

The solarium was empty. Stuffed vinyl chairs were still poised in animate clusters from the previous evening: cream chairs and blue chairs. She noticed a tear on the arm of one, where anxious fingers had compulsively plucked at the stuffing. The housekeeping staff had mopped the black and white checked linoleum, and sunlight rolled in the southwest windows with golden heaviness. Screened windows. Thick protective screens, she noted with a tightening of her lips. They were, after all, on the third floor. Chloe couldn't imagine any of the patients, drugged, dazed on diazipam or piportil, taking the big step.

A shaft of sun touched her bold red dress, casting a diffusion of the colour, staining the floor and walls about her. An unapproved colour, red. Those endorsed as soothing were most shades of blue, one shade of insipid pink, a British manor-house dining-room green, and off-white ranging in tone from clotted cream to café au lait. A pale coat of enamel on the old upright piano was from that vapid spectrum. The day of her admittance, she had been told there was a piano, and after three weeks of ploughing through a bizarre collection of nineteen-forties novels from the nurses' lounge, musty and spine-crumbly, she felt ready to play.

Chloe crossed the shining tiles and sat on the bench. The lid pushed open with a clatter; the strings hummed. Many of the keys had been stripped of their ivory, and the exposed wood beneath was scratched and marked. She touched one. The wood was smoothed and darkened with absorbed body oil. Anonymous initials were carved on the surface, and a date. E.M. 1947. The year she was born. The marks stretched across thirty-eight years. I was here. I was. Sad, sad initials, Chloe dismissed them from her mind and ran a quick arpeggio. The instrument, if jangly, was in tune. Dust motes jumped in the vibration, sound waves expanding outwards, rebounding off the cream walls. She flexed her fingers and began playing, carefully and deliberately as a child might; a child's piece. What was it called? Her hands moved automatically. She recalled the cover of the sheet music, a picture of the boy Mozart seated at his spinet. The print inside was enlarged and the fingering, simplified. "The Music Box." The process of playing felt alien, like returning home after a long absence and finding it smaller than you had imagined, remembered. She ran through the piece again, staccato, an octave higher, *quasi senza pedale*. It really did sound like a music box. Delight was there, intact and shining, as when her pudgy dimpled five-year-old fingers first mastered the repeated scales, running up and down the keys.

The air pressure in the room altered slightly as the door opened and closed. Her illness (she chided herself that even in the stillness of her thoughts, she used the soft, protective euphemism)—her breakdown, her crack-up. Good term, crack-up. I am everything I am cracked up to be. Her crack-up had "sensitized her to subtle environmental changes." Mental environ. She glanced over her shoulder. A woman in a flowered johnny shirt stared back. Jane, Jane, plain Jane, insane plain Jane who wandered the halls in search of, what? Perhaps an attractive nightgown. The hem of the hospital one didn't quite reach her knees. Her heavy white legs were mottled by bruises, spider and varicose veins. Another of Chloe's sensitivities—an acute sense of smell. From across the room, she knew the coffee in the cup was black. Turning back to the piano, she decided to try something different. Another golden oldie. "Für Elise." Da da, da da, da, da da, da da... Oversized slippers slapped the linoleum. A hand flashed past her left eye, depositing the coffee on the piano top. The liquid slopped over, dripping a streak of brown on the pale enamel. The woman sat beside her on the bench as she continued to play, trying to concentrate, keenly aware of the sweet, acrid odour issuing from Jane's white flesh. The woman's knees brushed hers. For all the attention she was giving to the playing, it could have been someone else pounding out the Beethoven. It could have been a piano roll. Her arms, stiff and tense, moved by habit, not feeling. All that she knew, was the moist warmth of the body beside her. Why didn't crazy Jane go away and drink her coffee elsewhere? Why didn't she jump out the window?

"Pretty," the woman croaked. "I never took piano lessons. My sister did. I always wanted to, but they didn't let me. Did they let your sister take lessons too?"

Chloe smiled again. The old nuisance probably spilled yolk on her johnny shirt. Maybe that's why it had little flowers: stains wouldn't show. Save on laundry bills. But this was an exclusive loony-bin—sanitarium. Sebastian had seen to that, had looked after her interests when she had been in her little state of catatonia. It sounded like a vacation, an island off the coast of California.

She shifted to the right. So did crazy Jane.

"Teach me to play." Jane's heavy arm descended with a crash on the bass keys. Then the left. She was a lifer. Paranoid schizophrenia. A walking testament to thirty years of psychiatric experiments: electroshock therapy, LSD, and a small lobotomy. Not a whole lot of dura mater left, thought Chloe. Sebastian had left specific instructions that she was not to be fed so much as a valium.

Jane's hands, with their clenched fingers, bashed the piano. Smash, crash. The cup rattled, shook, and spilled more coffee down the front panel. Chloe blocked Jane out and continued the piece, but she couldn't hear. It was impossible. Her long fingers formed the correct patterns, pressing inaudibly into the keys as the pesky woman banged away at the bass.

"Come on. Give me a little lesson." Jane reached between Chloe's arms, her bloated hands smashing the notes, pushing her sticky warmth heavily over.

"Stop," Chloe screamed. "Stop." She froze with her hands raised over the keyboard. "For the love of God, stop." She squeezed her eyes shut and tried to will the woman away. Why was she permitted to wander around and bother people? Why wasn't she confined to her room? Chloe wished she had some chocolates. Maybe she could be bribed away. Bribed out of sight, out of hearing.

"I'm a good listener, but they never let me take lessons. I wanted to take lessons. I asked them. But they only gave my sister lessons." Jane yelled to be heard over the noise.

"Stop that! Stop what you're doing! Stop. Stop." The coffee cup was doing a little dance along the edge of the lid. Jane now banged all the black notes, hand over hand. Chloe's head was bursting, spinning, cracking.

"You can teach me all those pretty songs. I can play for my sister. Then she'll take me home. They were all wrong."

"For Christ's sake, stop that noise! I can't stand it!" Chloe stood abruptly, jerking up one end of the bench and dumping the fat woman on the floor. Jane stared uncomprehendingly from her prone position, the pathetic blotchy limbs splayed across the checked tiles.

"You offensive old cow!" Chloe kicked the side of the piano and the coffee cup finally tipped over the edge of the lid bounced off the keys. Brown liquid splattered everywhere. Jane shrieked and tried to roll away, tried to jam herself under a chair. An unreality descended on Chloe. Jane, floundering on the floor reminded her of an amoeba, struggling, threatening to change shape, to divide and become two Janes, four Janes, eight Janes; all emitting sharp piercing cries. She turned and drifted out of the room, down the corridor. Jane's screams grew fainter and Chloe ignored the nurses who brushed past her in their race to investigate the commotion. "What do I care?" she thought. "This has nothing to do with me."

§

Sandy Wing
from *Casualties*, 1984

Casualties

THE BIRD FLOPPED AT HER FEET, beating dust onto her shoes. The iron trap had bitten the bird almost completely in two but somehow its front end was still alive. Wings flapping, beak sawing noiselessly open and shut. Melanie knew what she was supposed to do. Lindon would do it without thinking. In fact, he came down to the garden every hour or so to make sure none of the crows were suffering, to make sure they were all dead. And when he found a bird like this one he'd lift his foot and let his steel-toed boot come crashing down on its head. Put it out of its misery. Well, she'd be damned if she'd do anything so barbaric. Damned if she'd walk around all day with crow guts on the bottom of her shoe. She'd have to soak her feet for hours before she felt the filth of it, the stink of it, was gone.

She moved to the other end of the garden, skirting the rest of the traps. Eight of them altogether between the rows of corn. All of these birds dead, thank God. Lindon had told her that if they wanted any corn this year—and they needed it because the poorer quality stuff went for cow fodder—he'd have to use the traps. He'd tried scarecrows, aluminum pie plates bobbing and flashing in the wind, even sending the kids down in shifts to yell and stomp whenever a crow landed. The birds couldn't have cared less. So he raised a fence around the corn patch to keep out dogs and cats and kids and hauled the traps out of the barn. Big clinking iron affairs looking like shark jaws. Meant for badger or fox, not crows. He dragged the traps down onto the lawn next to the house, spread out a tarp and painted them. A brilliant, almost luminous red so that if anybody did stumble into the garden they couldn't miss them. Melanie watched from the kitchen window but after a while she had to turn away, appalled by Lindon's calm face, his whistling as he sloshed the paint over the traps. He could have been painting the picnic table, whitewashing the fence for all the difference it made to him.

She picked corn, stuffing it into the pillowcase she'd brought. Lately she found that she was still doing things for five people instead of only four. Picking too many tomatoes, making too large portions at meal-time. Still doing things for herself and Lindon, for Joey and Shelley, and for the hired boy Calvin. Even though Calvin had been gone for a month now. Back at his mother's sitting all day in a rocker on the front porch, his head bandaged and lolling. The stump of his left leg jutting out over the edge of the chair seat. A vegetable now after the accident.

And maybe she was going to have to start doing things for five all over again. No, there was no maybe about it. She recognized the symptoms—the headaches and backaches, the cramps and nausea. But five would be reduced simply enough to two, to just her and the baby, when she left Lindon. *When she left Lindon.* The words came easily to her, naturally. She'd been saying them for years now, waiting. Waiting for just the right moment, the right reason. She'd almost left the day of the accident. No one could expect her to put up with this any more, living in this torture chamber, this slaughterhouse. But people had said after the accident that Lindon wasn't entirely to blame, wasn't really to blame at all. Calvin had been careless for an instant and it had cost him a normal life. Nothing Lindon could have done about it. Certainly forgivable. But it was a beginning. A point of reference. All she needed now was some final push.

A crow landed on the fence beside her, close enough that if it had wanted to it could have leaned down and pecked her on the top of the head. Or if she'd been fast enough she could have reached up and grabbed it around the neck. It watched her, tipping its head and focusing one black, non-reflecting eye on her. Then it flew down into the garden and sauntered between the traps, inspecting the corn scattered around them. It stopped beside the trapped crow, cocking its head, beady eyes watching its fitful flopping. Then it reached down and gave the other bird a vicious peck on the neck. Melanie flinched, looked away. Saw a flurry of black out of the corner of her eye as the crow flew up and lit on a stalk of corn. Lindon said crows were probably the worst kind of birds around here. Real scavengers. Opportunists.

The accident. It always came to her early in the day after Lindon had gone to the barn and the kids had left for the neighbours. Like now. Flashes of it creeping into her head. A blaze of light—the sun had been white hot that afternoon—a square of brilliant blue sky. That would be what she'd seen out the kitchen window. She was standing at the sink washing tomatoes. Tomatoes so ripe they were almost rotten. She had to handle them carefully while she rinsed them under the tap, dried them. She thought then (or had she only added this later?) that they were like breasts. Smooth and tight on the surface but with a warmth, a ripeness just underneath. And then that terrible noise. The groan and screech of the hay bailer. Then the scream. The tomato had split open when she dropped it into the sink.

Lindon raced into the house then, his face ashen, sweat pouring down his cheeks. He dialed the hospital number and waited but when he opened his mouth no noise came out. He coughed, almost whispered into the receiver. Then he was gone again, not seeming to hear her cries of "What happened? What's wrong?"

The ambulance careened into the driveway, its siren suddenly choked off, followed by a procession of neighbours in cars, on bicycles, on foot. Vultures, she'd thought, they won't be happy unless Calvin's dead. They moved in a stream behind Dr. Hill and the stretcher bearers, out to the west field. She sat waiting a long time, wondering why she seemed to feel nothing. As if some connection inside her head had been abruptly snapped off.

They brought Calvin down wrapped in a tattered grey blanket. It was sodden with blood in several places, big black patches of it. His head was bandaged out to two times its normal size. She learned later, even though Lindon had warned everybody not to leak any details to his wife, who couldn't handle this sort of thing, that part of Calvin's skull had been ripped off, leaving the coiled grey mass of his brain exposed. Some people said the sight of it made them feel pretty damn sick. Lindon stumbled along behind the stretcher, something in a thick plastic bag held tight to his chest. She learned (also later) that this was Calvin's severed leg. Lindon shook his head from side to side and she saw that his face was still slick with sweat. No, tears. She was sure then, seeing Lindon crying, that she loved Calvin. Looking at Calvin's bloodless face below the bandages, convinced that he was dead, she thought that she had probably been in love with him for quite a long time.

She'd done it again. Picked too much corn. Not only picked for five but for about twice that many. She pulled a few ears out of the pillow-case and tossed them over the fence. Maybe the crows would eat those instead of the corn that wasn't even ripe yet. She made her way back through the traps. They frightened her; she kept imagining her own foot caught in one of them, severed at the ankle. The bird at the end had stopped flopping, its beak gaping open.

She locked the gate to the garden behind her and walked up the narrow dirt path towards the barn, letting the pillowcase bang against her leg. She went in through the side door to the barn, walking along the plank laid there. Squish of shit and urine with every step she took, residue from the manure pile only a few feet away. Lindon always smelled like this, like a manure pile. Even after he'd soaked in a tub for an hour and put on fresh clothes he still smelled of cow shit and hay. Or maybe it was the house that smelled that way or just the air. Very possibly it was just the air. But somehow she figured the smell had gotten into Lindon's blood, into his sweat glands.

It was dark inside the barn, the windows so covered with dust and cobwebs that next to no sun came through. The bare bulbs between the two rows of stanchions were on, shedding a gloomy half-light onto the cows that were in for milking. The steady chugging, sucking sound of the milking machine filled the barn. Lindon was down at the far end of the barn, hunched over beside a cow, milking her by hand.

"Why isn't she on the machine?"

Lindon turned and smiled at her. Didn't even jump. Somehow he always seemed to sense when she was going to show up.

"She's got a sore tit here." He poked at the cow's udder, sending a red swollen teat swaying. "The machine hurts her too much. "

She stood watching Lindon's hands for a while, his grip lightening every time the cow mooed, turned her head. Big liquid eyes somehow registering pain. When he was finished he swivelled on the stool and faced Melanie, using the cow's broad belly as a backrest.

"Got a problem, Missy?"

"Yes." She said it seriously, her face more drawn, more sour-mouthed than it had to be. Lindon leaned forward, touched her arm.

"What is it, Mel?"

"I'm going into town tomorrow morning to see Dr. Hill. I thought you might like to know."

"What's wrong?" Lindon still leaning so close. She fought back the urge to reach out and shove him away.

"I have stomachaches all the time and I want to find out what's wrong. Maybe it's ulcers." She heard a touch of pride in her voice.

"You can't have ulcers, Melanie. Not at your age. Why don't you go see that Dr. Williams in Montreal?"

She felt her heart race. "He's a gynecologist. I don't need anything like that." Maybe Lindon had seen her slip the specimen into her purse. Maybe he'd connected it with her trip into town to do "groceries." His knowing, even suspecting, would ruin everything. The element of surprise would be gone.

Lindon reached down, picked up the bucket of milk at his feet. "Do you want me to come with you? I could drive you in."

"No." She turned away, angry. She wished Lindon would have made more of a protest. Asked her who'd get the kids up and going in the morning, who'd make the breakfast, feed the chickens. Tell her the pain was all in her head. She'd have enjoyed going into town more then.

Lindon called after her. "Will you be back by lunchtime?"

Here it came. "Yes."

"Good. The new boy's coming over tomorrow afternoon. I'd like you to meet him."

She took a few steps back toward Lindon, letting the sack drag along the floor. "Boy?"

"Yeah, well I guess so. He's twenty or around there."

"Does he know what he's in for, Lindon?"

He stood up then, slowly, as if even the air was heavy on his shoulders. The milk sloshed in the bucket.

"What are you talking about?"

"I mean, does this new boy know that this isn't exactly the safest farm to work on?"

She watched Lindon's face go hard, felt a surge of pleasure as a flush spread up from his neck, darkened his cheeks. His knuckles turned white where he gripped the handle of the milk pail. He took a step toward her and though she kept her feet rooted to the floor she felt herself leaning forward, holding herself only an arm's length away, a fist away. She felt a rush of relief, disappointment, when he picked up the milk stool and pushed past her.

At breakfast the next morning she drank only a glass of juice. She'd been sick during the night, woken up all dry-mouthed and trembly from a dream, run for the bathroom. The whole thing had been clear as a photograph, not hazed-over like a dream at all. She even remembered the colours. The fleshy pink of the butcher's paper the package was wrapped in. The package Lindon brought to her. It had been tied with string and there'd been a price marked on it. How much she couldn't remember now. She opened it and Calvin's leg sat there in the middle of the paper, somehow miniaturized, shrunk to the size of a ham, a leg of lamb maybe. Still wearing the red-toed rubber boot, the faded blue jeans. Dried brown blood at the knee. She stood the dream until then, half-awake and marvelling that she could imagine anything so ridiculous. But then she saw herself turn to Lindon, the package in her arms. She'd smiled and thanked him. My God she had thanked him.

Lindon sat across the table from her now, sipping tea while he read from some farm journal put out by the co-op. Joey and Shelley sat at the other end of the table, going along with the silence. Joey had dripped strawberry jam all over the oilcloth.

Lindon laid down the paper. "Interesting article in here on bloat, Joey. I'll leave it for you to read later."

Melanie shifted in her chair, cleared her throat. Saw herself mirrored as Shelley made a face, placed her piece of toast ceremoniously on her plate.

"They've got some kind of serum that the calves take orally, on a tongue depressor I guess, that brings down the swelling. It says here," he picked up the journal again, "that it 'dissipates the water buildup and in two years the use of syringes, with their high risk of infection, will be obsolete.'"

Joey nodded. "It's hard getting those syringes in sometimes, too. Calf hide is pretty tough."

Melanie put down her glass, glared across at Lindon. "You let Joey do that? Stick needles in cows?"

"Yeah, why not?"

"Because it's a terrible procedure, that's why not. You can hear the calves screaming all the way down here when you do it."

"Use your head, Melanie. You're going to hear them screaming all the way down here if we *don't* do it. Screaming till they bust open or drown in their own water."

"Yeah, Ma, you should see." Joey leaned across the table. "They swell up like balloons and then—"

"I've seen it before Joey, thank you." She kept staring at Lindon. "I don't see why Joey has to do that sort of thing."

"He has to learn sometime."

"Why? Who says he's going to be a farmer?" She spit the last word out.

"No one. But while he's living on a farm it's a good thing to know." He let his eyes move away from hers. "Besides, we're shorthanded right now."

She got up, rinsed her glass out at the sink. Lindon. He would probably strap Joey in a harness and hitch him to the plow if the tractor broke down. She picked her purse up off the counter. "I'm going now."

Thank God she had her car. A gift from Lindon for their fifteenth wedding anniversary last year. She pulled out onto the highway and passed into the glen. There were no houses here, only tree-covered mountains looming up on both sides of the road and the river winding along to the right, widening into a pond every once in a while. Some of the trees, the sumacs and sift maple, the early trees, were already changing colour. This was what she loved about the country. The beauty of it. If she didn't look at the gaps in the trees where house foundations would be laid soon, the glen looked like it had when she and Lindon used to go walking after school. The quiet of it then. No whining chain saws, no people shouting. Only the sound of the river, the birds. The crackling of leaves underneath them as they made love. Their laughing as they picked bits of moss, pieces of leaf out of each other's hair, off each other's clothes. Shelley had probably been conceived out here in the glen. Well, there was no maybe about it. She had been. It had been too beautiful, too romantic out here and Lindon had been too gentle. Maybe if she'd grown up in the city with only movie houses and parked cars to find refuge in, she would never have had to get married.

The road took a sharp twist just before it entered Laurel and if you didn't keep the wheel turned just right, you'd end up sitting in front of Jerry Petrie's gas pumps. Jerry said he got half his business that way—by accident, ha, ha, ha. After the service station came the school, the library, the grocery store. Then the neat little clapboard houses. All of them nearly identical but trying hard not to be. A walkway lined with blue painted stones. A brilliant pink flamingo sprouting up between someone's tiger lilies. But all the houses still the same except maybe one. Calvin's. She stared straight ahead as she passed it but still she saw the front porch, the rocking chair out of the corner of her eye. Empty. She would have to ask Dr. Hill what that meant.

Calvin. Arm muscles twitching as he pulled the rabbit, Joey's rabbit, out of its hutch. The animal quiet in his hands, not struggling, kicking the way it usually did. Big back feet spotted with red. Calvin had looked at her then. Frowned, shook his head.

"Its feet got caught in the wire on the bottom of the cage."

"Will it be all right?"

"Oh yeah. I'll just put a board down so it don't happen again."

He handed her the rabbit then as if it were made of china. Startled her with his gentleness.

Calvin. Following her down into the back pasture. She was sure he'd followed her. It couldn't have been just an accident. He'd crouched beside her in the bramble as she dropped raspberries into a grey tin pot. His hands resting on his knees, then darting out to pick a berry, toss it in with the others. Fingers stained red. Black hair on the backs of his hands. She'd wanted to touch them, stroke them. Had she?

Calvin, shirt off, skin slick with sweat as he dug the marigold bed below the kitchen window. Grunting with each shovelful. A good head taller than Lindon, so much broader in the chest. No fat at the waist for her to pinch between her fingers. She tapped him on the shoulder, felt a tingling go up her arm. Handed him the glass of water, ice tinkling. Their fingers touched longer than necessary. She was sure of that. Calvin kissing her thank you the way he'd kiss his mother. On the cheek. Or maybe the mouth. Taste of salt. Smell of sweat.

And the weekend Lindon went away to an auction she'd prayed Calvin would come into her bedroom. And like a dream he had. Just a sound in the darkness and then the weight of him on the bed. So dark she could hardly tell if her eyes were open or not. Just the same she had seen every inch of his body, felt it with her hands. Felt the colour of his skin, his hair, with her fingers. Felt the sharpness of bone, the tensing of muscle. Heat of blood. A throbbing that seemed to fill both of them. For a moment not thinking at all, losing track altogether. Layer after layer of blackness peeled back.

No, it was all too clear, too vivid to be imagined.

Dr. Hill's office was in one of the little clapboard houses. The one with the gilt-edged swinging sign planted on the front lawn. Dr. Joseph S. Hill, M.D. M.D. for the past forty years as near as she could figure it. He probably hadn't been to a conference or a seminar or read a medical journal in forty years either. But people in Laurel wouldn't go to anyone else. Dr. Hill, they said, knew them all so well, knew their family history so well, that all he ever had to do was look at them and he knew exactly what was wrong, what to prescribe. No need for any messy, embarrassing examinations.

She was glad to see that there were no other cars parked in front of the doctor's house. She would have the waiting room to herself. She got out of the car and walked along the path to the side entrance. Down a few steps to the basement door. Ring the bell first then go right in.

It was always clammy down here and smelled of must and Mrs. Hill's laundry soap. It was always dark, too, half-light even with all the lamps turned on. She sat down on one of the vinyl sofas. She swore this must be the same furniture that Dr. Hill had had fifteen years ago. The same stuff she'd stuck to when she came in sweaty and terrified, pregnant with Shelley. Dr. Hill had ushered her into his office then and he did know, just by looking, what was wrong with her. Patted her on the knee, told her not to worry because she was one of the lucky ones. She had a good reliable boyfriend who wouldn't hesitate to do the right thing. Then he handed her a booklet on diet for the expectant mother and wished her good luck.

She'd been grateful to him then for taking control of things but she hadn't come back when she was pregnant with Joey. She'd branded him an incompetent by then, had seen too many people with chronic bronchitis die of lung cancer, too many people eat their way to a heart attack because Dr. Hill couldn't embarrass them with their obesity. And so on. People would be better off with the local veterinarian, who at least had some guts, some professional integrity. But Dr. Hill would do for what she needed. Even he could do a simple pregnancy test, refer her to a specialist in the city.

She dug her book out of her purse, read a few pages then closed it. She hadn't been able to get through a book in almost a month. Couldn't seem to concentrate. She'd have to get back to the library, take out her three books a week and read them all the way through or she'd end up like everyone else out here. With the intelligence of a scarecrow and half the personality.

She studied the pictures on the waiting room wall. A Norman Rockwell print, the one where the jolly-faced, bespectacled doctor (not unlike Dr. Hill actually) pressed a stethoscope to the chest of a little girl's doll. A calendar from Joe Petrie's Garage & Auto Parts turned to the month of February. A poster showing a stomach wearing boxing gloves and silk shorts, its inane grinning face spouting some garbage about "feed me right and I won't fight." And then the diagram that she guessed must come from Grey's Anatomy. Her kids particularly liked this one. Whenever an emergency forced her to bring them here they always wanted to look at the "skinless man." All the skin peeled away, replaced now by slightly yellowing layers of plastic. Lift all the sheets up, calendar fashion and the body was filled with blood vessels, little spidery capillaries, a heart etched in blue and a ghastly purplish red. Used and unused blood. Drop a sheet and vital organs appeared. Stomach, lungs, liver, kidneys, pancreas, internal sex organs, intestines. Everything you could possibly need. Then came the muscles, tendons, ligaments, cartilage. Raw red meat. And finally bones, fitting neatly between all the other parts. All so static, as if only a good shave would get the machine started. And then there was no promise that the parts would co-ordinate, work in unison, no promise that something wouldn't break its moorings. A heart plummeting into the coil of the large intestine.

She marvelled at the diagram's incompleteness. The blood vessels, nerve lines, sheathes of muscles were all severed at the neck, a large black arrow with the words "To the Brain" replacing the head. The head must have been covered on another page, a whole section of the book that maybe Dr. Hill never got to.

Dr. Hill peered around the door of his office, motioned for her to come inside. They sat down facing each other, he behind his desk, fingers touching on his blotter.

"Well, I haven't seen you in a long time, Melanie."

"Not since the accident."

He lowered his eyes. "Yes."

"I drove by Calvin's this morning. He wasn't out on the front porch."

The doctor looked at her, blank-faced.

"What does that mean?"

"Well, I guess it means his mother just hasn't got him up yet. It's still pretty early you know."

"Then he's still all right?"

The doctor nodded. "My guess is he'll be all right for quite a few years yet. He's got a good sound body—except for that left leg of his. His brain's looking after that part of him pretty well. It's the thought processes, the reasoning that I'm worried about. He can't think for himself. Worse, he can't do for himself."

She hadn't expected this. Maybe he'd read the section on the brain after all. At least enough to sound ethical, convincing. "Do you have the test results?"

"Yes." He flipped through some papers on his desk, pulled out a pink one. Glanced over it, then smiled up at her.

"Good news. The tests were negative."

"What?"

"You're not pregnant."

The doctor's face dropped. There must be more showing on her own face than she meant there to be. He coughed, stuck the pink sheet back into the pile of papers.

"I'm sorry, Melanie. You didn't seem too happy the other day when you came in for the test. I figured with Joey and Shelley practically grown up you wouldn't want to start all over again. I thought you'd be pleased."

"Well, I'm not." Or was she? She stood up and walked over to look out the narrow slit of the basement window. She'd counted on this. Counted on giving Lindon the news. Watching his face light up, then telling him she couldn't possibly have it, not here anyway. She couldn't be expected to bring up another child in such a monstrous environment. She'd have to move away, to the city maybe. She had to think of the child. Or something like that. She gripped her purse until her fingers hurt.

She turned to face the doctor again. "How can I not be pregnant? I have all the symptoms. The nausea, the tiredness—"

"Well, that's the other thing I wanted to talk to you about, Melanie. It looks like you might have a mild ulcer. Nothing to worry about. Nothing a good bland diet won't cure. A bland diet and maybe your trying to relax a bit."

She set her mouth in a hard, incredulous line.

"I know, Melanie, I know. You're under a lot of strain. Some things that happen are hard to stomach." He smiled. A sympathetic smile? Maybe sometimes all this got to be too much for him too.

"I think you should try talking to someone. A social worker maybe. Or I have a colleague in Montreal, a psychiatrist—" He paused and she watched as he studied her face. He must be waiting for some sign of outrage, some denial on her part. Well, he wouldn't get that sort of thing from her. She was surprised though. She figured he wouldn't recommend a psychiatrist to anyone short of a raving, foaming-at-the-mouth lunatic.

"I don't think you're crazy, Melanie. And I know, especially with haying going on, you've got better things to do with your time. But I really think a few visits with this fellow would help. This business with Calvin would make anyone sick."

"I beg your pardon?"

"I think a few sessions with a psychiatrist and this business with Calvin will be cleared right up. You'll be surprised how quickly things get back to normal."

Normal? There was no normal. Not here. Just clear things up. Clear it up the way she'd scoop up an offending heap of dog shit in the middle of her kitchen floor. Toss it out the door and forget about it. Out of sight, out of mind. But the stink of it still there. The stink of it everywhere.

"I think that's really where your trouble is Melanie. Upstairs." The doctor tapped his temple. "Too much thinking. Too much dwelling on things."

She stared at him, fought back the urge to fling her purse at him. Send it ricocheting off his bald skull, his bald empty skull.

"I can give you my friend's number if—"

"No thank you." She strode past him. Closed the office door behind her and leaned against it for a moment. She would need the drive home to think things through, figure something out.

She stood at the edge of the garden and watched Lindon sprinkle bug powder around the potato plants. He was almost finished so she waited. She could afford to wait now. At this stage a few minutes didn't matter.

Lindon sealed the can of bug killer and looked up. He walked over to where she leaned against the garden fence, stepping around a crow trap that gaped unsprung on the edge of the corn patch.

"So what'd the doctor say?"

"He said I'm pregnant."

And there it was. Just like she'd expected. All the tiredness suddenly gone from his face and replaced with something that looked like relief.

"When? When's it due?"

"Sometime in March."

He reached out to touch her, maybe to pull her to him, but she stepped away. Picked at some corn silk hanging on the fence. Watched Lindon out of the corner of her eye.

"I thought maybe we could call the baby Calvin." She saw Lindon flinch.

"Considering Calvin's the baby's father."

She faced Lindon full then, watching as a quivering set through him. He stared at the ground between his feet, hands thrust into his pockets, shoulders trembling. His head slowly, slowly swaying from side to side.

"You can't ..."

"Can't what?"

Lindon's mouth opened and closed, no noise coming out.

"Can't have it?" she asked.

"Yes. I mean no."

"Just snuff it out. That would be the right thing to do I guess, eh, Lindon?"

"Shut up." Said almost below his breath but perfectly clear, carrying its warning. A few more carefully aimed words and the brutal, the inexcusable would happen.

"Calvin and I did it every chance we got. Every time you weren't around—"

He came for her then. Rocked forward on his left leg and sent his arm arcing through the air. His hand hard against her face. She could almost feel the red print of his fingers emerging on her cheek. He grabbed her by the shoulders then, his face only inches from hers. Eyes red at the corners. He slammed her against the fence two, three, four times. Then he seemed to lose strength, let his hands slide down her arms. Head slumping forward. She stared past him, studying the neat rows in the garden, waiting.

"Get out of here. Get the hell out of here. I've got work to do."

She turned, walked up the path towards the house. It would only take her a few minutes to pack her suitcase.

¶

Stacey Larin
from *Signs and Wonders*, 1991

Tense

JUNE 21—Time was when it was pretty much an opened and closed book. Time was when you'd have a man and a woman and start at the beginning to go through the middle to reach the end and even though at first the possibilities seemed endless, when you got to the end, there you were.

That's why it's called *the* end.

So Janet thinks.

And has been thinking for some time: days, weeks, months? At least the last few minutes since she came home to kick off her shoes into the pile at the door, crumple her jacket onto a chair, poise her pen as that line about timeless love unraveled into the nothingness of the paper's blank labyrinth. Too many possibilities. Or is it probabilities? That her first class this summer, tonight, should have to be cancelled, leaving her displaced like her students, an illegal alien in her own home. Still, what choice did she have? Janet leans back from the study desk, pushes her notebook away, brings her hands up to her shoulders and neck to knead the muscles. Tense. Time. Where is Iain? Beyond the pooled light on the desk, the house is suddenly dark, very still. Even Schrödinger is nowhere in sight. Janet sits at the desk, listening. Unbreathing. Very still. Where is Iain?

She'd turned a last corner in the corridor and there he was. He glanced up to see her and waved her in, his tie dipping into a half-unpacked box of books, his hair as usual beginning to stab the air in the stubborn black shocks which had captured Janet's attention the first time she ever saw him. He still plastered them down with water every morning, driving off to work sleek as a Fitzgerald hero and rattling home later as hopelessly rumpled as a youthful Einstein. She stopped in the doorway. Inside the room, naked metallic shelves striped the walls; an uncurtained window diffused light towards the broad-backed steel desk. Iain placed a few books on a shelf and turned: the books staggered like dominoes. His tie dipped into the box again as she watched his long fingers with their bitten-down nails pry up another text.

Janet touched her own fingertips to the fresh white paint of the walls: the air still wafted pungent. She felt a twitch of an itch high in her nose: allergy? She glanced about, then back at Iain.

"Looks just like my office."

"Really? Was it hard to find?"

"It's on the opposite side of the building. I'll never find my way around this maze."

"I meant mine," said Iain.

"It takes time," said a voice from the doorway.

Janet and Iain turned and Iain scraped his fingers through his hair. The doorway held a woman who held a ball of black and white fuzz.

"I don't suppose you'd like a kitten," said the woman. Janet sneezed.

She'd turned: a young woman in the doorway held a small mottled kitten against the vivid chevron pattern of her knit dress. Her ash-blond hair was drawn back from her face into a severe spinsterly knot, but her pale eyes were framed by pointed black-rimmed glasses so unflattering that Janet saw instantly that she was beautiful and saw Iain turn and smooth his hair.

In the car on the way home, Janet held on her lap the kitten given to them by Iain's new colleague in the physics department, Vivian Wedgwood. She had found it by the road that morning on the way to the college and had been hoping to find it a home when she saw Janet and Iain.

"Poor little thing. It was pure chance," Vivian had said, stroking its white stomach as it purred on Iain's desk. "And what do you do, Janet?"

She opened her mouth to say I write, as she would, could have said even a year ago, and felt blood warm her cheeks as Vivian waited, as Iain waited too. What did she do? "Actually, I'll be teaching here also." She heard her voice after all. "English. As a foreign language."

"Really?" said Vivian.

"Yes," said Janet.

"I see," smiled Vivian, and stroked the kitten's stomach with a clear-lacquered nail. "Poor little thing."

Schrödinger pads by the study doorway towards the kitchen and Janet pushes her chair away from the desk to rise. She breathes again. Silly: no one will break into the house. It's not even dark out yet; but leafy shadows, palmate and pinnate, have already inked the windows. Janet snaps on the kitchen light and, in the incandescent flood, sees her own taut-jawed face peering in the window over the sink, the twin panes casting a ghost to the original ghost. Her doubled hand pushes her colourless hair back from her blackened eyes. Schrödinger weaves around her legs, paradox of rough pattern and mink patina, and she stoops to stroke him. Her watchcat: he keeps time for Janet, requesting his meals on a finely tuned schedule. Tonight, though, is the first night of the course Janet is teaching (supposed to be teaching) this summer, the same night she taught last term and the term before, Iain's night to feed the cat. Iain would always be home for dinner after she'd leave and, when she'd get back from class, he'd already be up in bed, reading *Omni*. Tonight he should be feeding the cat. Where is he?

She'd turned a last corner in the corridor and there they were: her new summer students clustered outside the classroom, silently watching her approach, as, inside, another group parroted the unintelligible words of their instructor. Janet smiled at the students, cleared her throat, tapped lightly on the windowpane of the door; and the teacher, short and stocky with coarse grey hairs trained across his skull and a frothy ring around it like a laurel crown, edged the door open.

"I'm sorry," Janet said, "but there must be some mistake. I'm supposed to be teaching English here tonight."

The man glared up at her. "This," he hissed in heavily accented English, "is Bothno-Ugaric," and closed the door in her face.

The students were still waiting quietly, clutching looseleaf notebooks and plastic pencil cases. Janet swallowed. This isn't really happening. The sharp dark eyes of the students pinned her against the door. Why do these things always happen to me? Still, she managed to squeeze through the knot of bodies. But although she checked the length of the corridor and the floor below, she could find no empty classrooms; each contained an instructor scrawling on the board, students hunched over their note-books, all pausing to stare at her as she glanced through the window, then scribbling again furiously, as if writing her into their accounts of Asian empires, differential equations, the schizophrenic psyche. Her own clicking footsteps echoing down the corridors made it sound as though she were being followed. She didn't check the other floors in the building. She returned to the students, who milled midget-like about her for a moment before closing in like a puddle.

"I'm sorry." Janet spoke slowly, knowing most of them were recent arrivals from the Orient, the Middle East, come to study Western technology. "We cannot have class tonight. I will check on room arrangements. If there is a change in room number, I will post it on the door here. Otherwise we will meet here next time."

She looked around at them and they looked back wordlessly, miniature adults, young men and women, no bigger than she'd been as a child. What had happened? What in the world had arrested their growth so while she'd sprouted like Alice dizzy on mushrooms?

"No class tonight," she repeated, hearing her voice desperately simplify syntax, acquire an accent. "Next time. Next time."

"Nesstime," they echoed en masse, and beamed at her.

Janet opens the fridge to get the cat food and Schrödinger backs off sideways with his tail curled over his back like a question mark. Almost a year has passed since they brought him home, since they moved here from the last place, since they both began to teach at the local college, but Janet is no closer to writing her novel, Iain is no closer to completing his doctoral dissertation, which will allow him to seek what he calls a real position at a real university. To these ends he consumes *Scientific American* at the dinner table, plunges into *Physics Today* in the bath, attacks *Nature* passionately up in bed while Janet brushes her teeth and scrubs her face. When she comes out of the bathroom, he switches off the lamp that always flares into darkness and she stumbles forward in the shocking blackness, her hands outstretched, until she blunders into the bed and stretches out carefully along its edge. Before moving again, she waits for the pounding of her heart to lessen, for the visual purple to wash like a balm across her retinas and rescue her from blindness. Silly, silly…but she knows that this cold war will continue night after night, that she will keep lying there, knowing this, unable to stop the same thoughts from crystallizing, the possibilities, probabilities, petrifying. She can't sleep but she can't watch the late-night news, can't make sense of another *Harper's* index. What in the world is happening? Then she feels a gentle vibration at the foot of the bed and Schrödinger settles for the night. After night. After night.

Janet closes the fridge and dumps congealed cat food into a dish. Schrödinger's spine undulates beneath her hand.

"Silly cat," she says. "You came out of it alive, didn't you?"

Iain told Vivian Wedgwood what had happened when she stopped by the next day to see if she could help them settle into their new home. Preparing tea, Janet left the kitchen door open to listen to their voices in the living room. Wasn't it nice to hear Iain sounding so animated again?

"…and then, after we'd checked all the kitchen cupboards, we looked at each other and realized there was only one more possibility."

"You don't mean—" Vivian breathed.

"Yes!" Iain exclaimed. "He bolted out of that fridge like a bat out of hell—frozen over, of course."

They both chuckled and then swivelled their heads towards Janet as she entered with the tray. Their eyes, similar shades of grey, were bright.

"So you found him there alive," said Vivian.

"The last possibility," Iain nodded.

"When all others collapsed?" Vivian murmured.

Iain grinned. "Schrödinger's cat lives."

"Whose cat?" Janet settled the tray on the coffee table and sat down on the side chair. "Did you find out who owns him?"

Iain said nothing for a moment, but when Vivian smiled and slid forward on the couch towards the tray, he said, "No, Janet, you re-member—Schrödinger, the physicist who designed that famous thought experiment to illustrate the probability wave function. I'm sure I must have rambled on about it sometime." He coughed.

"Oh," said Janet, feeling her cheeks tingle as she bent to pour the tea. "Yes, of course." The name suddenly connected with memory, snapped into place in Iain's own voice reading aloud from the latest journals and magazines stuffed into his worn knapsack, strewn amid his kitchenette dishes, scattered over the dimpled hotel-room bedcover. He'd had them forwarded during their honeymoon.

"According to Schrödinger," said Vivian, plumping a sofa pillow and settling back, "the observer was necessary to collapse the probability wave function of any experiment. He suggested the example of a cat sealed in a box in which a lethal gas would either be released or not, according to a random event, such as the radioactive decay of an atom. When the experiment is activated, the gas either is or is not released, but without looking we can't know."

"Yes, I see," said Janet, setting the teapot down carefully. She had heard Iain say all this often enough and could probably recite it herself. She looked over at him but he was looking at the sugar bowl. It was the one shaped like a miniature globe which she'd bought him years ago but only she used. He still shoveled sugar out of the box.

"According to classical physics, of course, the cat is either dead or not dead and we simply have to look and see. But according to a certain interpretation of quantum mechanics, the Copenhagen Inter-pretation"—she stretched the short a—"the wave function of the experiment contains the possibility of the cat being alive or the cat being dead. Its fate is determined only when we look inside the box and the wave function then collapses as one of the possibilities, or probabilities, actualizes, while the other vanishes." Vivian paused. "Do you see, Janet?"

Janet smiled. "Cream, Vivian?"

Vivian smiled back. "Not a drop."

Iain scooped sugar into his mug, helped himself generously to the cream, and said, "But according to another interpretation, the Many Worlds Interpretation"—he paused to slurp as Janet stared at him— "the moment the atom does or doesn't decay, reality splits into two branches, each with its own version of our fatalistic feline, but the wave function doesn't collapse. The cat isn't in limbo, as in the other interpretation, but is both dead and alive, and only when we look into the box does our wave function split again to coincide with two realities, one in which the cat dies and one in which it lives, mutually exclusive, mutually unknowable."

His voice had acquired what Janet recognized as its thoughtful, scholarly tone, usually reserved for the lectern and his practice runs in front of the mirror. She sat immobilized in the chair. Copenhaaagen?

"The observer becomes the creator, in effect. All he has to do is look, and possibilities become probabilities become realities." He took a gulp of tea and gazed off pensively.

"In this case, one or the other," said Vivian, lifting her mug and tapping it gently with a long fingernail. She looked at Janet through her cat's-eyes glasses. "Which will it be?"

Sitting at the kitchen table, Janet watches Schrödinger, finished with his meal, saunter over to the doorway and then suddenly sink to a crouch, tail tip flickering, rump quivering, whole body ready for the spring, tensed. She tries to see what has caught his attention: by radar or sixth sense? But even as she scans the hallway he rises again, turns, leaps fluidly onto a kitchen chair, flops to his side and begins washing a paw. Janet tries to relax, watching the cat at his ease, but she finds her own body sitting stiffly, uneasily. Lately she feels besieged by signs and symbols, strange relations. Politics speaks religion on the east coast and fires flare insatiably out west; the cat rolls over to wash his ear and rain falls in unutterable salvation. Schrödinger looks at her with eyes half-lidded in bliss, faintly foreign, alien, ineffable—what was it? Bothno-Ugaric? Something Slavic; and while grown men budget for shuttles to and from the flag on the moon, children on peace missions crash into oblivion. What order of life is this? Men and women throughout the world at war with each other—what future can they promise? To themselves, to their children…. She can't say. She can't think. *How long?*

And Schrödinger blinks: he has become her constant companion, despite (because of?) her allergy; she can't fathom how she got through the first few years of her marriage without him. Sometimes she forgets he is (nominally) Iain's cat; sometimes, in fact, when she is home alone with him in the study, trying to write to the rhythm of his throaty rumbling, unable to write, language paralyzed at the pen-nib, she forgets she is even married to Iain. Sometimes, as if across a great divide, she sees herself pausing in mid-step in the doorway of her apartment bathroom the night of the day Iain began teaching, and Iain, sitting up in bed with a copy of *Omni* on his knees, saying that it looked like the time had come to tie the knot, and she then finding herself completing the step into the bedroom without objection.

It seemed sensible, the thing to do, at the time. What else had she ever wanted? A home, a sense of belonging, of order. Better to be safe than sorry, her mother had always said. Her father, when home, never said anything, vanishing behind the noisy façade of the newspaper. And she'd always been very sensible, even Iain said so; why make waves? No moods, no scenes: an exceptional woman, the strong, silent type, he used to joke with his friends. That's what he loved about her, he'd growl softly in her ear. And then nip it.

And sometimes, lately, how long? days, weeks, months? she finds herself musing: and if I hadn't said yes? and if I hadn't agreed? and if I hadn't then walked through the bedroom door?

She looks at Schrödinger curled upon the seat cushion. And if I had tensed and then simply—turned away?

Iain placed the "Do Not Disturb" sign on the hotel room door after asking the hotel operator to hold all calls. Janet looked at the suitcases standing where the bellboy had dumped them, then at Iain.

"But I'm waiting to find out about that job. That English as a second language course. For foreigners. They said if there was any news, they'd phone."

Iain closed the door behind himself with a click and smiled. "We already have a second language," he said. "The language of love." He took off his blazer and draped it over a chair.

Janet stared at him and managed to stop the tremulous wave that rippled her throat. She didn't trust herself to say anything for a moment. Instead she sat down on the bed. After a minute she took off her jacket too.

Iain placed the "Do Not Disturb" sign on the hotel room door after the bellboy brought up the science journals clogging their mailbox downstairs.

"Must you do that?" Janet asked. Was that really her voice? She tried to smile. "The maids are starting to give me knowing little smirks," she said, and twisted her face in imitation.

Iain stood by the door, holding the books. He had grey smudges under his eyes. "I don't see why they would," he said. "I told you, Janet, a long time ago, I don't like to be interrupted when I'm reading. It's research, after all. This stuff's important. I've got to keep up with it." He sat down by the window, crossed one leg at the ankle over the opposite knee, opened one of the journals flat. The spine snapped. He bit at the nail of an index finger and looked at her. "Don't be so uptight. Why are you always so tense? For God's sake, aren't we married, after all?"

"Yes," said Janet. "We are." Married. The cottage in the country. The kids.

"I'm sorry," he said. He breathed out heavily and managed a thin smile. "I shouldn't have said anything. It's just writing this damned thesis—well, that's nothing to do with you. Forgive me?"

Janet looked at the neatly patterned pages of the book flattened against the table, wordless in violation. She closed her eyes. "Forget it."

When they got back from the honeymoon, they had the argument about doors.

"Obviously, doors are meant for closing," Iain said. "Otherwise we'd simply have doorways, archways, entranceways. But as soon as we hinge a door onto an opening, we indicate closure. People don't leave their doors open when they go out; doors become the locus, the sign, of 'locking up,' of separation between point x and point y. We always kept the doors shut in my house. A door's purpose is to be closed."

"But if people just wanted to be closed off from other people, or wanted to keep areas closed off from other areas, logically they wouldn't need any doors at all," said Janet. "They would just have separate, distinct rooms with unbroken walls. Which is absurd. How would they get around? Doors are connections, links; they're interfaces, belonging to two places at once, relating them. They're meant for opening."

Iain stared at her, opened his mouth, then clamped it shut, strode to the front door, and slammed it shut behind himself. Of course, he opened it first.

She watches Schrödinger's eyes slant into the sleep of utter comfort. Could she try one more time? "Sequence of tenses. Remember that? Very simple. Putting things in order. Verb tenses working together to reflect meaning." To create meaning. Possibilities. Probabilities. Certainties. And Janet would see her chalk-covered hands gesturing, sending up small puffs of white; she would watch the faint clouds hover around her, unsettling. "Now, what do we need here? Simple present? Or past, or future? Or present perfect, past perfect, future perfect? Or present infinitive? Or perfect infinitive? Past participle? Present perfect participle?..." She would gaze out onto the rows of faces, indistinguishable, undecipherable, even after a whole term, dwarf adults, wizened children, offspring of modern warfare, her own. *I would like to have known* or *I would have liked to know?* Which will it be?

Standing at the lectern, her heart pounding: *I don't want to know!* And the students staring at her, speechless.

"And she's quite a smart cookie, you know," Iain called from where he was lathering his face at the bathroom mirror. "Family's name is highly respected in these circles. Was already teaching while finishing her undergrad studies—got her doctorate last year. Already published quite a bit here and there. Wherever. Said maybe she could introduce me to a few people. Could be useful, what with all these contract negotiation problems. You know."

"Well—" Janet knotted her robe about herself slowly, then drew the drapes open at the window. The yard below was a fragile litter of still sepia leaves. Hadn't she just raked them all up yesterday? "I don't know—Do you think she's for real? Her name—With all that, what reason does she have for being here?"

"What's the matter with you?" Iain came out of the bathroom. He was wearing a towel with a faded Holiday Inn logo wrapped around his waist. "I don't understand you any more, Janet, there's just no talking to you. What do you want? Can't you just take people as they are? Or things? Why must you always complicate things?"

Janet looked at the foamy white beard blurring his jaw line and trembling like a swirl of soft ice cream at the tip of his chin. There were two long furrows brackcting his mouth that she didn't remember, that must have formed before her eyes. What was happening to them? She felt a draft graze her cheek. "Of course, she is quite beautiful."

"Really? Is she? I hadn't noticed," Iain responded. "Well? Like you've always said, appearances aren't everything, are they?"

"No," said Janet, watching a large creamy dollop separate itself from his face and drop to the rug. "No, they're not."

At the science department's spring party, Janet realized too late that something had been added to her orange juice. By then, she found herself travelling around the room with Iain as he talked but never herself talking, moving in his orbit as he moved, drifting her gaze around the room as Vivian drifted in and out of her field of vision with her glinting smile out of Lewis Carroll, her name out of Harlequin Romance. Were those glasses for real? Was she for real? Of course; after all, she'd given Schrödinger to Janet. Iain, supposedly; but she'd handed the kitten to Janet as their fingers brushed: "Here, Janet...." Janet found herself thinking about herself, at the moment, in the third person: *she found herself thinking about herself*...as if from a distance in space and time, in spacetime, much in the way that she had recently begun to write in her journal, adrift from the words, their signs, their significance, unable to connect with this language she must use which spoke as if human while conceiving the inhuman. Below the hubbub of the crowd, she seemed suddenly to hear Iain's murmur a few feet away, turned to see him leaning close to the head of the barmaid whose face was hidden behind a smooth sheet of hair. Wasn't that one of his students? Iain looked up with a taut smile to meet Janet's gaze, walked back with a fresh gin and tonic delicately beaded with moisture he rubbed away with his thumb. She heard him laugh warmly at her side, saw him turn an anticipatory smile to one colleague's joke, bend a serious expression to another's comments. She gazed down into her glass, still chill, watched light slow and still within the ice. Frozen. What does this mean? What does *what does this mean* mean?

"...first strike," someone was saying. "I tell you, it's up to us."

"Stick to our guns," another rumbled, "and we'd win it. Absolutely."

"Got to. Or all we've fought for till now would be meaningless," added a third, as the second echoed, "Meaningless, utterly meaningless," and Janet felt the ice trembling to life again in her glass as the murmurous voices meshed and enmeshed her like the newspapers, the television, people in the street with placards: the end of the world tomorrow! And tomorrow, and tomorrow, to the last syllable of recorded time. Who said that? The war to end all wars, communiqués to end all communication, language pared down to the x and y, the x and how, not why. She looked at Iain, who swayed in her vision and he was introducing her to someone named Black or Blank involved in the contract negotiations, and she watched his untrimmed rusty mustache bristle itself around her name as she heard: *contract: negotiation: strike:*

She blinked: but instantly the vertigo passed to leave in its wake Blank's voice politely asking about work, home, family, children.

"Not yet," said Iain, flexing an arm around her shoulders so that she felt jarred from within her the only two words she believed could still mean something, anything.

"Not now," she said, staring at the red mustache. Meaning. Meaningless. What does this mean?

"But eventually," Iain smiled, gripping her shoulder with his fingers and squeezing lightly. "Plenty of time."

She felt herself slipping through his grasp, insubstantial, felt the words slipping from her control, *No. Not now. Not like this.*

But she hadn't opened her mouth; and around them, people were yawning and reaching for their coats.

"Why not simply make it a glass box?" Janet had asked. Vivian looked at her silently and then bowed her head to her raised cup, but Iain put his mug down on the table and a little tea sloshed over the rim to ring it.

"You don't understand, Janet," he said. "It's an experiment in perception."

"Precisely," she replied.

Iain stared at her, speechless.

It was chance, pure chance, that had designed Janet's cancellation tonight, for her sake, for their sake, she is sure of it, a design, an order masquerading as randomness, as she rises from the kitchen table and walks towards the front hallway. Schrödinger follows soundlessly behind her. She doesn't know what it is she is looking for, but she knows she'll know when she sees it. As she approaches the front door, she sees her sudden ghost again, her face at the diamond pane of the door, as if she stands outside again, fumbling her key in the lock, entering to sidestep Schrödinger, to glance at Iain's windbreaker hanging from the closet knob, kick off her shoes by his below, head into the study where she writes. Supposedly. Where Iain writes. Supposedly. Where neither of them, she knows, has written anything worth writing, worth meaning, since they've moved from one place and another to their current stopover on this suburban cul-de-sac where their dead-end stares them full in the face, unflinching, arrogant, absolute. She knows this, just as she knows she has found what she was looking for as she looks at Iain's windbreaker,

Iain's shoes. The same ones he wore going out today before she left. She stares at them. Or did he?

Janet stares at Iain's clothes and, beneath the drumming of her pulse, hears the words whirring and clicking into position, things falling into place. The clothes are macroscopic objects, like Schrödinger's hypothetical cat, and thereby subject to irreversible thermodynamic processes. Not to quantum mechanical wave functions, which apply to the level of subatomic particles which correlate not into independently existing structures but into a web of correlations whose meanings arise from their relationships to the whole where "correlation" is a concept dependent upon the conceiver so that finally Iain's windbreaker, Iain's shoes, stand not on their own but as tools for correlating experience.

Which is ultimately representable by an ur-wave function where all possibilities are mapped.

So that either Iain did not wear those clothes earlier and is still out, or he did wear them and has returned home. So that either he is home, upstairs, alone, or he is home, upstairs, not alone. With the door to the bedroom closed. *Aren't we married after all?*

Janet stares at the clothes.

For God's sake. Yes.

Which will it be?

Schrödinger turns and pads noiselessly to the stairway, sits, curls his tail around his front toes. He looks at Janet with eyes that are wide black disks rimmed with green-gold, he, the survivor of the fridge, the ice-box. Janet remembers how, when they'd first noticed him missing, she'd been relieved, grateful, almost hopeful he'd run away. And if they hadn't found him? He shimmers suddenly in her gaze, solidifies. *And if I hadn't taken what was offered? And if I hadn't opened the door?* To know, to take the chance and speak, to set things in order. What other possible probable futures were collapsed, vanished, splintered away, unreachable, unknowable, at the turning point?

Janet takes a step towards the cat and he floats up the stairs to the dim second-storey hall where she knows the future waits, waits for her to see Schrödinger sitting at the bedroom door, his tail licking the broadloom in slow, steady waves, where she will stand listening, tense, a soundless noise coming from within as of the sudden tensing of readied muscle. All it will take is a twist of her wrist and she will have made the decision to discover, to perceive, to activate the reality that lies beyond the closed door, the future that both of them will have to live. It could be any, it could be all. But she will know only one, after she places her hand on the doorknob, opens the door, looks into the twilit room.

¶

Teresa Jurkowski
from *Ethnic Television,* 1993

Bread

A N AUTUMN DAY, her father on the back gallery, standing on a kitchen chair. He nails a board to the underside of the porch above, where the comers meet. When the sparrows come to build their nest, he is there every morning to greet them, with bits of toast or suet he tosses into the snow. A mug of coffee in his hand, he watches them from inside the house, tiny birds leaving tracks smaller than his fingernails as they hop from scrap to scrap.

Veronica looks again at a picture of her father and a few mates on board. Everyone in duffel coats and toques and with cigarettes dangling from their hands, leaning on a gun that for security reasons is covered by a tarpaulin. Her father is so young that it appears he is affecting the toughness, the world-weariness that he does, that he is merely playing at grown-ups. But it is only the appearance of pretense, only the image; he has killed people, shattered bodies that flew up in pieces like a handful of bread cast over the waves.

There Are Other Homes

A SMALL FERRYBOAT MOVES SLOWLY through a mist so thick the navigator seems scarcely to know his bearings. His young face is unshaven and his hair shiny with damp, and in the manner of old films a narrow band of bright light is cast across his fearful eyes. The camera cuts to a heavy crucifix on the cabin wall behind him, swinging heavily with the roll of ponderous waves, then cuts back to the man, whose lips are trembling a whispered prayer. His eyes are shut tight.

He falls to his knees when the vessel runs aground on a sandy shore, falls to his knees and weeps. He leaps over the side of the boat, forgoing the gangplank, and staggers through the icy water, the dissipating mists.

On the beach a group of children await him. They are dressed in red and yellow tams, heavy woolen coats, laced boots. In their hands are wicker baskets filled with flowers and bread. They sing to him a song of greeting. *O, les enfants,* is all he gasps before falling once more, to hold fast in his hand the tiny foot of a green-eyed boy who bends over him and strokes his weary head.

Veronica switched the television off and pulled the comforter over her face. She had to beware of programming that included subtitles in languages she could understand; it exhausted her. It looked like now even the Hungarian show had become fraught with danger. If only they could broadcast the Tasaday eating grubs and living in harmony, she thought, but even they'd been exposed as an anthropological hoax, villagers who shed their wristwatches and pretended to be a people untouched by civilization, for hard cash. If only they could broadcast from alien planets, she thought. But the Martians would probably speak better English than she did, and what was worse they'd probably be better dancers. There was no use for it; the universe was small; infinitely small, and its inhabitants shared shockingly similar problems. Even her living room was being overrun by Hungarian sailors and nimble-footed extraterrestrials, all of them with a bone to pick.

"IT ALL CATCHES UP TO YOU," *Undercover Man sighed, "this line of work." He swayed slowly in the hammock and sipped a pinkish-looking beverage with obvious distaste. Overhead a tropical moon beamed down lustrously.*

"It's not too late for you to get out, you know." He spoke to his charge without turning his face. "You're still young and haven't been involved in anything that critical yet. The missions we've been on so far—well, they've been child's play."

So that's what it comes to, Veronica thought to herself. Fretfully she twisted at the knot in her scarlet sarong and straightened her perfectly tailored linen blouse. An angry flush spread up her neck and cheeks.

The words came slowly and painfully. "I'm not good enough, am I? That's what you're really saying." Her voice was controlled, grim.

There was no reply for a moment, just the hammock's gentle creak and the distant sound of waves.

With a masterful swing of his leg, Undercover Man sat up, his back to her.

Damn, she thought, he can even get out of a hammock gracefully. Fascination overtook anger as she admired the oval of damp on his shirt between his shoulder blades. Damn, she thought, even his sweat smells alluring. She breathed in its sea-blown tang and followed him with her gaze as he stood up and traversed the small patio. He drew up a white rattan chair, twin to hers, and regarded her seriously.

"You have no idea what you're letting yourself in for. No idea. You have to give up everything."

"What do you mean, everything? A happy family life? A home in the suburbs? Please, please don't make me laugh."

"That sneer is most unbecoming." He was in control once again.

"Who gives a damn," she spat.

Undercover Man leapt from the chair and began pacing the small square of earthen bricks, his jaw set and his eyes blazing icily.

"Don't you see that being a spy means you'll never be permitted to be a whole person? Yes, that's right, scoff. It'll be a lifetime of being stuck with your ear to the wall and your body in the shadows, watching, waiting, listening, forever listening. People get into this business because they believe it will give them power. Good God, woman, they don't know what power is. Heaven

forfend you should ever form an attachment to anyone. Friends, family, lovers—you'll never be able to fully confide in a single soul. Your distance has to be maintained at all times, at all costs. One imprudent word, one misspent phrase and you could jeopardize the Free World! For God's sakes, don't you realize what you'd be giving up? Do you know what I've given up?"

He flung open the slat doors and returned with his travel bag, retrieving from it a small cloth envelope. With care he pulled out a black and white photograph and handed it to her.

"There," he said, "look."

It was a blurry shot of a boy of perhaps seventeen years of age, standing in front of a stone wall and smiling shyly at the photographer. In one hand was a rough nosegay of daisies and in the other he held a small knife, used for cutting the rugged stems.

She strained to make out the boy's features. Yes, the resemblance was there, the fine bones, the broad forehead, the well-shaped mouth. But something about his expression was not Undercover Man's at all: there was a hesitant expectancy to it, a sweet openness that she had never seen on his face. It could have been his father. His brother. His son. And when she looked back up at him questioningly, he whispered hoarsely, "Don't, please, don't ask. It's classified information."

We Love a Good Ghost Story

DOUGLAS'S BEHAVIOR HAS BECOME SO UGLY that his wife leaves him and his mother banishes him to the country place. No one wants to see him, no one wants to hear of him anymore. Everyone has given up on saving him.

He heads up north with a backpack of food, a bottle of heavy tranquilizers, and the idea of going cold turkey. He has done it many times before, but has never managed to make the sainted state last. He is up there for a few days, until the tranquilizers and his resolve run out. When he isn't sleeping or throwing up, he spends his time carving the bark off an ash tree with Henry's butcher knife, crying and talking to himself. One evening when he can no longer bear it he hitchhikes to the nearest village and heads to the bar, where with his last few dollars he knocks back a few beers and heads out again. The next driver who stops to pick him up, Douglas persuades to give up his vehicle. He does this by brandishing his butcher knife. The driver, seeing a tall, gaunt creature with scabrous face and hands, throws the keys into Douglas's lap and jumps out of his Corvette, glad for his life.

Douglas is right to think his luck is quite unbelievable. As soon as he crosses the bridge to Montreal, he can sell the car to some unscrupulous mechanics he knows and buy some dope immediately. And he hasn't even hurt anyone to do it. He can get quite a lot of money for a Corvette. He can buy quite a lot of dope for that money. And he thinks that, for all he cares, everyone he knows can drop dead after that. His head is quite clear, he is making plans fast. The only catch is that he is driving the car into the oncoming lane.

Douglas sails through the air like Daedalus. When he comes to, he finds himself in a shallow pool, in black water. Behind him is the front end of the Corvette, with the windshield ripped open. The other half of the car is upside down on the other side of the highway. Curious people have started to gather in the dusk at the roadside, but Douglas doesn't notice them. He is thinking that his right foot is on backwards and that if he wants to get into town he will have to fix it. All he has to do is to turn it around, like he used to do with his G.I. Joe. Douglas forgets that even G.I. Joe's leg finally snapped off, that after all, even G.I. Joe was only human. He leans forward and wrenches the foot into place, but in the wrong direction.

The last thing he sees is a circle of people revolving around him, young faces made wise and old ones radiant in the approaching glow of the ambulance headlights. He is unknown to them, neither an evil man or good, but they gaze upon him with eyes full of unearned love; they have hopes for this harrowed creature floundering in mud.

There is nothing left to break anymore and Douglas passes out, falling slowly back into the dark stream. Strangers' arms surround his body like spokes in a wheel, lifting him up and up and up.

The House Her Father Built

ON A COOL AND SUNLESS DAY Veronica borrows Ferdy's car and drives alone to the country place. On her way up the front stairs she realizes she's brought along the wrong key and will be obliged to climb through the bedroom window. At the side of the house she lifts a ladder her father made, so old now it sprouts moss in the fissures of the flaking spruce. When she was little her parents used to forget the key, too, and her mother would start an argument, which her father would cut short by saying he would climb in through the window. From the back seat Douglas, Henry and Veronica would clap and laugh, convinced that their father put a great deal of showmanship into the way he wildly flailed his long legs around as he tried to gain entry. He looked like the tail end of a frog frozen live, mid-leap into an icy pond. The thrilling part was whether he would get in before the window arbitrarily slammed down, guillotine-fashion, on his innocent body. This was a man's job, because their mother was far too nervous to climb the ladder or hold the window securely for him, and they were too little to be entrusted with these tasks.

They were kids and it never occurred to them that there could be more to his kicking legs than a desire to make the silliest of a silly situation, that perhaps he was afraid to knock himself out cold on a bedpost or walk alone through the dark house to the door that would let them in.

She has elected herself to gauge the damage of Douglas's ill-fated stay in the country. Once in the house, she moved swiftly from room to room, professional as an insurance estimator. In the boys' bedroom, the bedclothes lie twisted on the floor. On the paneled walls is a large unidentified stain, that looks deliberately, spitefully splashed on. She decided that the grittiness of the stain means it was made with orange juice. The other bedrooms are untouched.

In the bathroom, the taps drip slowly. She shuts them tight. A dirty bar of soap lies on the sandy floor. Without even looking, she empties bleach into the toilet and lets it stand.

The kitchen table has a box of Cap'n Crunch turned over on its side, surrounded by an array of half-empty bowls. Around the souring milk in the bowls are garlands of apple blossoms; it is old, pretty china that her mother's mother had once religiously collected from Steinberg's. The tablecloth is worn linen embroidered with coloured yarns; Veronica thinks of how difficult it will be to get the Kool-Aid stains out of it.

All of it can be cleaned up later, she decides, not wanting to look at it any more. It is surprising to her now she has gotten out of the habit of doing anything that needs to be done, preferring to seek out hiding places, quiet rooms where no one and nothing can reach her, where she can dream in peace. The attic is a place like that; she climbs the stairs, which creak with gathering damp.

It is warm here despite the autumn coolness, warm and empty. On the dusty boards Veronica lays down, feeling strangely comfortable as she used to, a long time ago, before she knew better. Overhead are exposed beams, measured and cut and nailed together by her father, some of them bolstered against the weight of snow, and she lays there counting them as far as her eyes can reach.

In the cold and heat he had worked, balancing on narrow planks of wood high up in the sky, high up in the sky, it had seemed to his little children, building a home for his family. A magician he was then, in overalls as baggy as a clown's trousers, pockets full of wondrous objects, brass levels, plumb lines colored blue, blue chalk, thick red crayons for marking wood, penknives with bone handles.

From the top of the house, the top of the tallest pines in the world, he waves to them before resuming his work. Patiently he lifts his hammer, to bring it down on the perfumed wood again and again and again, until the skeleton of their home rises up from his warm and aching palms.

HANDCUFFED TO THE HOSPITAL BED, Douglas serenades the police guard. "Chains, my baby's got me locked up in chains," he croaks, glancing slyly at the young man in the chair to see what effect he's having. But the young man doesn't find his performance the least bit entertaining. Douglas's luck has finally changed. Of all the officers in the Sûreté du Québec, he gets the one whose hero is Mahatma Gandhi, and whose sense of humor doesn't extend to laughing at people in pain. The man regards him with a steady, compassionate eye, and before Douglas can think up the right routine to woo his audience, he shifts forward on the vinyl chair.

"You told me yesterday you have a little boy," he says.

"Did anybody call for me?" Douglas asks, fearful of the man's gentleness.

"No."

"Nobody?"

"No."

"Got a cigarette?"

"I don't smoke," the policeman tells him, then adds, "but in the meantime you can tell me how you got here."

DOUGLAS'S SON, Spencer, crouches in the sand at the beach by the lake. In one hand he holds a bucket and, in the other, a spoon burnt black at the bottom, one of his father's old heroin spoons. Each time he digs the stain fades a shadow more. He is building a city that he will people with small pine cones he has gathered. Around the little sand houses he constructs fences with smooth stones he's chosen from the lake bottom, more for decoration than defence. At the outskirts he makes careful gardens with fresh trillium, where the visiting ants are friendly dogs and cats. Those who will live here by the sea will be busy and happy and having nothing to fear. It doesn't matter that this place may only last for a day, there will always be time to build another one, out of sand or out of snow.

Spencer is a very serious little boy. He enjoys reciting the messages in greeting cards for his family. Happy Birthday, Four-Year-Old. We're wishing you the very best. When he reads, he leaves out the exclamation points.

Spencer is a very serious little boy. He will work and work and work to be loved.

The House of Stone

THE COVERS ARE RIPPED FROM HER SLEEPING FORM *and a voice penetrates her dream. An urgent whisper, a man's voice, in her ear: "It's time," he says, "wake up." Her protests are useless, she wants to go back, back into the dark, but the man stands over her, holding her clothes and telling her to make ready.*

"But what, Lyle, what is it?" she murmurs, and he answers, "You'll see."

"We can't go," she says, "there's a blizzard outside. We're grounded until further notice. This is Canada," she sobs, "we're at the mercy of Nature here. If we go out there we may never be seen again."

"I've prepared for those eventualities," he answers, and gives to her heavy leggings, an alpaca sweater and woolen trousers. "Don't dress me, I'm not a child," she wails.

"Aren't you," he says, maddeningly calm.

"I want some coffee," she says, as he throws a fur coat around her shoulders and pulls a balaclava over her head. "Room service will only take a minute."

"Not at this hour," he says, and pulls her by the hand.

She is still complaining on the elevator down.

"This is crazy," she shouts. He corrects her briskly. "This is duty," he declares, thrusting her into the triangle of the revolving door. She circles back into the lobby, but this time he squeezes in with her and carries her off into the storm.

Outside the streets are a desert of blinding white. The tracks they leave behind them are swiftly filled in with snow. Noiselessly they move into the heart of the city until at their feet is the bottom of a staircase, carved into the side of the mountain above them. "Climb," he commands her.

"But I'm so thirsty," she cries.

He brings a handful of snow to his lips and kisses cold water into her mouth.

The wind whips down as they ascend. As soon as his foot empties its print she fills it with her own, following to the top. Dark trees surround them now, there is no path but the one he makes for her, gliding through snow.

The forest ends and turns into smooth hills where outcroppings of shaped and colored stones dot the landscape, jewels in gossamer.

"Do I know this place?"

"Do you?"

"I don't want to go."

His icy fingers grasp her wrist and they run between row on row of polished rock until he finds the place he wants. A granite pillar, the names etched in on it rendered indecipherable by the powdery white.

Exhausted, she kneels on the mound before it, and reaches for the shrunken buds of a plant whose stems stand petrified in snow. One touch and she is assured; within the blasted pods, the seeds of new flowers cluster in frosty sleep.

Her guardian stands at her side and she looks up at him, scarcely recognizing the face beneath the shapka, ancient and foreign, grimacing with cold.

"Remember him," he says, pointing to the ground, where deep beneath them in a tiny box is a frail lacework of icicle bones.

"How can I? He only lived for three days."

"For some that is a lifetime. Now tell me, tell me who he was."

There is no escaping his question. The words of reply are expelled from her mouth in tender, ghostly clouds.

"My brother," she says. "Born and died, blameless and perfect, in the spring of 1946."

"His name?"

"They never told me."

He kneels with her, waiting, until she leans forward and reaches out her fingers to write something in the snow.

THE PHONE CALL he's been dreading finally comes.

"Veronica," Douglas says. "I've been here for weeks and no one's even called." His voice is small and contrite.

"You could have killed someone" is all she can think of saying. The words are like stones in her mouth.

"I can't speak any more," she tells her brother, and places the receiver in its cradle before he has a chance to answer.

"It's over," Henry whispers. "No more lying."

Later that night, when she has just fallen into a fitful sleep, a noise awakens her: the sound of ringing in her ears.

¶

James Smith
from *Circuits*, 1981

A Child's Story: The Answering Machine

1. This is Alex. I never answer the phone personally. I am in right now, just three feet from the phone, but value my privacy. I screen the tape twice a day. If you are not offended, please leave your name, number or message at the sound of the tone.

2. This is Alex. If you speak, you are part of the circuitry of the big machine. Your voice is the participant here. Why are you calling me anyway? If you wish, you know how to talk to the machine. Your intrusion will be taken note of, and possibly reciprocated in the future. I cannot predict when, as this machine has no concept of future.

3. Alex here. There is a good chance the machine will dysfunction and not record your name, number or message at all. It will be as if you never called. Your voice will go to the same place the sound of a tree falling in the forest goes, when I am not there to listen.

4. Alex. Please leave a beep at the end of this message. If you have personal knowledge that this machine has been counterfeiting my voice in order to fulfill some design of its own, write to me at the following bleep.

5. Please—this is Alex. I do not own a telephone answering machine. I have had my phone taken out. Whatever this is, it is not me. Do not listen to it. I am very afraid. Things are happening around me that I now begin to understand. My ears are ringing.

A Final Vision

WELL, I PICKED THE PHONE UP & instead of the hum that says OK go ahead and dial, there were barnyard noises. I'm a resourceful person, and it only took me a few minutes to disassemble the black box. Inside, instead of coils and wires, there was a tiny & perfect pastoral paradise, glint of sun on tanned thighs, the smell of animal flesh, and the slow grunting of vegetables up through the loam; even the woodsmoke fresh & pure. I marvelled at how this could be. Reverently, I reassembled the casing. Jealously, I guard my secret, knowing someday the right connection will be made, and I will meet you down in there.

For now, I feel a secret happiness at every incongruous noise over & under, behind and around your voice on the phone. When I am in love, I think you might already be there & only waiting for me to smarten up, drop my body like work clothes & let the real me, tiny & perfect & naked, crawl out my ear & down into the receiver, finally arriving in the garden, just as the sun rises.

¶

Mark Cochrane
from *Three Years from Long Beach*, 1991

Three Years from Long Beach
for W.J.M., 1964-1987

> *… Westward, till all are drowned, those lemmings go.*
> - John Masefield

I

For days together we were boys again. Now, when I confront your dying on a highway later that summer, I return to what is mine, that moment on the path, chips of cedar in a gentle National-Park curve, and I summon the ghost of a black bear, one city block ahead.

Always the jar of peanuts rattles to a stop in my hands. Our eyes meet his and he springs back, heavy and offended, as if we have witnessed some masturbatory touch.

Don't move, you whisper, but already I understand the ground rules: the sprint to the car is not between us and the bear, but just between us. For if the bear so chooses, the slower man will lose.

Like acrobats we balance a score of careful, backward steps along the spongy, ochre mulch, and so round the bend in his line of sight; but just as we leave his ken the bear minces off the path, each down-step of the great paws into the lush underbrush as delicate as a mime's hands.

On every side the ferns rustle with a commotion of wildlife. We jog to the gravel shoulder of the road, heads swivelling.

Our parked car: I juggle keys at the door. Then from safe inside, the driver's seat, I ogle you through the passenger window, and shrug, and hesitate—as ever—to let you in. You grin. You knock. You mock horror, smear your face into the glass—an agony of compressed features, stretched lips. You duck and vanish in the vapour of a kiss.

Another decade rises from the east and still I am dreaming of bears. In my sleep the devil of your imagination, cones of teeth and a greatcoat like an old Russian, lumbers behind us in the sunbright tunnel of rainforest.

An apparition like this could torment a man into traffic.

In the dream, I fumble with keys. From across the hardtop
you pray for speed of passage. You sweat, chant,
you play
the intoxicate shaman of fear:

I condemn thee, for I have seen a great evil,
and now all I desire is to die.

More hallucination: the key snaps off,
an arrowhead in the lock's heart.
The galloping bear overcomes you,
                                   Ford Bronco
mauls you on the Trans-Canada:
indents your forehead, crushes your chest;
unfolds a grizzly length, his head to assess me;
is swallowed by a forest recess.

2

We pass another day, the next, on the beach—lonely in May, rippled hard as a bodybuilder's tummy. Floating in litres of Riesling I read Wilde and bathe in a shallow tidal pool; probe the fingered sphincters of sticky green anemone.

The sun floats coins on my clean tub of sand. Empty bottle contains a message. So warm I am, helpless, I exhale into a pee. Burning I yelp and you smirk at my fervour, sucking your stone of hashish.

All this gay innuendo, an apology for never doing wrong. On Florencia Bay, backed by cliffs too steep for bear feet, you watch as I slide into sleep.

I waken alone, raw with salts: you have receded, a mirage in a black leather jacket, tracking yourself one mile down the tide. A squinting profile, stoned and alone, a sliver of wood perched on a jumble of rocks. Calvary.

But you return and we wade. The frigid Pacific squeezes an ache into the bones of our calves, then deeper we pogo to preserve every inch of dry flesh from the rhythmic onslaught of froth; chatter about scrotums shrunken to snakehide and cupped in our hands / as we hug
our own chests in our arms.

When I splash, your revenge makes my heart stutter.

When you dive, a perfect arc, you never crack the water:
you fall forever, meteoric.

Laughing, I feel the icy spike in our foreheads, submerged. But there are no trident-tough or musseled gods under here, barnacled or kelp-whipped, or phosphorescent as pissy-eyed cereal-box prizes.

(I could regret not drowning together.

I have wrecked myself three years, despising memory. Since my unsuccessful wisdom-tooth surgery and your death, I have lost the power to smile.)

The ache a numbness, numbness lead, I'm cold and unreactive, sinking with the ebb, my dead-fish arms, blood cold-dense, I fall from of all sure footing and my lips will not be said—

so I swallow salt
capsuled kelp

to see what vitamins it brings,
or dream I'm drowning in my pool
tanning under an angel's rings,
till tendrils trickle down my throat
to bleach the driftwood of my lungs,
a searing sting that sings and sings
but still I am

3

not dead. The sea spits me up and we crawl to Tofino.

Back at the cabin, I bathe again, cold marrow that warmth can never penetrate. Hours later I am still shivering in waves, Birdy on TV via satellite as you slip that polished tokestone into my mouth, urging tight pangs to my bronchi from your perch on the cornice of the tub.

Always you said: Once with a man before I die.

This loam we inhale, homey as oatmeal
cookies, chewy with tar
—but again, on the twin
mattress that is mine
the only ecstasy
I can attain
is sleep.

¶

This is my dream of September 14, 1987:

You are washed. Your bad skin porcelain-clear, my Perrault doll. Your pale blue eyes.

We meet naked in the ocean; we say goodbye without speaking. For the first time in a decade I wake up crying, the tang of blood on my tongue, a shooting star in the dawn-grey window.

The mists are huge on Long Beach. One errs to seek Japan in the distance. Just westward of what is actually seen, seals and orcas make pulp of themselves on the crags of an island, small and delectable, its eerie surf music a mythic amalgam.

A bright patch of turf near the maw of a whirlpool, blowhole of the planet: not even light can escape this place.

Fellow of infinite jest, the lemming king amuses a citizenry of sheep with an eternal prank.
    Leaping from a cliff's edge
                he lights safe on a high ledge.

His punishment: no gesture is definitive.

4

Next morning we drive cross-Island to Nanaimo. Sour gusts of Port Alberni, milltown on the fjord, waft and wince us back to a motel we sipped four nights ago, the bar where woodworkers in Dayton boots, Macs and black T-shirts rolled up their poor Player's and tattooed the floorboards while an imitation Boss stomped his nothing hours across the stage.

Glory days.

But today we pass on, past the ballsy goats of Coombs, and I hate you now for the songs you never stop singing, the corny homegrown social-ism, country ballads that soothe my hot paws on the wheel till the rattle of the ramp subsides and we bob silent in the sooty womb of the Queen of New Westminster.

The engine ticks as it cools.

Blame me for something, bastard.

5

But it is later, the ferry riffling the Strait between real Gulf Islands, the nebula of city lights no illusion, that I situate and fabulize your fair confession:

I must warn you. Today we are perched on the prow of a ship and the wind drags tears from your eyes. But nothing fills me. Fills me entirely. Understand it is impossible for me to say there is nothing you could have done. A few months from now
in an acid fantasy
I will embrace the high beams
of a prairie night:
my perfect trajectory
like a vaudevillian
from ditch to twin spotlight.

Understand I will not show the decency to involve or indict you. You will spend time, perhaps, hooking for my pant leg, only to prove that you were causal, that the cold observer changes what he observes, deserves a beast's share of shame.

But simply understand you will be absent.

Chameleon tongue, the landspit of the Tsawwassen dock withdraws us into the living continent;

and our lights cut a widening swath
through the darkness on the highway ahead.

¶

David McGimpsey
from *4 Poems,* 1990

The Trip

The trip was supposed to be simple enough:
drive Hank Williams from Knoxville TN to Canton OH,
give him time to dry out, straighten up
for a New Year's Eve concert the next night.
But I had to bring the car from Montgomery AL,
the first capital of that confederacy, 1861,
where Jim Crow ruled supreme as cotton, 1954,
& where blood was spilled not thirty years ago
for daring to cast a vote, sit anywhere on a bus.
I had to take the first cadillac cowboy's cadillac
all the way through the Smoky Mountains
& through a heavy wet snow
that grounded all the planes.

I was to take him wherever he wished.
& Ole Hank (he annoyingly referred to himself
in third person) wanted to go on
just another wild ride.
He needed some shots for the pain in his back
which was real at one time, but that day
he was riding the crest of a junkie's heat,
a hot spell that eats the user like a fever
from fix to fix until, someway, it dies down.
First business in Knoxville was to see
the doctor who would oblige Ole Hank.
Instead of starting north
we tooled around the south in the white caddy.
A dusty bottle of whisky from Fort Payne AL
was soon shattered, empty on the road. Then, then, then
we got to Chattanooga TN to see another doctor
another needle that I guess he couldn't

brave himself to spike.
Picked up some chloral hydrate tablets —
something to keep him from drinking
(you kept Hank from drinking by knocking him out).
The mountains were grey in the snow
but still missing the Christmas magic
Dolly Parton has associated w the region.
Travelling through you could never tell
throughout these fields, stench;
is left to fester on the battlefields;
gangrene, osteomyelitis, pyemia, peritonitis,
dysentery, typhoid, pneumonia, malaria
& of course just plain shot to death,
like Lincoln. Just passing through
you wouldn't know. God is silent that way.
Hank had a guitar back there
& now & then he'd manage a few stray strums,
or an out-of-tune chorus to "I saw the light."
The guitar was so big in his scrawny lap,
so sharp in its angles,
it looked like it might mangle him
like a big greasy machine.
I tended, even then, mostly to be disgusted
at the extent of his illness,
his Jack Daniels emaciation,
where you could see too clearly
the bony machinations of the lower jaw,
& his teeth always exposed,
brown w tobacco tartar, his lips
deprived of any healthy puff of fat.
But it was true:
he could sing your ass off,
sing you to the very brink of the country western
understanding of the world.

He wasn't the first to burn out his or her star,
& he won't be the last. He had spina bifida

& a talent for expressing loneliness,
maybe more than anybody before.
& for the longest time those songs,
so plaintive yet so sweet, nestled
in the deepest parts of my day-to-day.
Made me afraid to reach out,
seized up my knees like an ill-advised surgery
that replaced slippery cartilage
with rusty sheet metal & pins.
"Are you OK, Mr. Williams?" I asked
& he cussed & took a slug & said
"Ole Hank's alright" & we slid along,
the cadillac smooth as a skiff in the bayou,
silent, watching the grey winter forests of Tennessee,
way into the southern ridge of the Appalachian plateau
over the muddy tributaries, catfish thick,
of the Mississippi & Ohio rivers.
Jesus was on my mind, his mercy
wouldn't bring us through the snowfall, would it?
Jesus wouldn't bring us through —
through to that place like heaven
& by dawn we were in Chattanooga & Hank
saw his man & limped into the car
w another head-full of bootsauce.
He is coming.
To Chattanooga where the rebels pitched well
but disastrously lost the battle of Chickamauga,
Yankees storming their position on Missionary Ridge,
chanting, Chickamauga! Chickamauga!
& Grant's men forced General Bragg into Georgia
Nov. 25 1863, demoralizing the CSA,
the blood of the young in the creeks,
smell of gunpowder in the fog, a huge
American flag raised at the top of the hill.
Yessir that doctor fixed Hank up pretty good
& gave me some little white things
that would keep me wide awake well into northern OH.

By the time we got back to where we started,
behind schedule,
already intolerably weary of driving,
the car stank of malt
& Hank needed more than a day to straighten up.
More than a decade.
I saw Knoxville again,
the first time I left my wife in 1984,
& it was incredible, host of the World's Fair,
& I took in the humidity like a tonic
& lay around drunk just about anywhere.
Knoxville too was occupied by Union troops
in the autumn of 1863 & they resisted
any & every attempt to oust them.
I asked Hank if he wanted to stop here,
pretend all the night was a dream
& start again fresh,
maybe drive into a snowbank for fun.
But he said no & made gestures with his hand
as if to say: not now, Ole Hank
is busy making music history.
"I will you you (sic) still & always will
but that's the poison we have to pay"
is what the wreck coughed out in the back,
his last contribution to the lyric.
Snow, let it, powerful, drop heavy.
From then on, he said, I was the boss
& let loose & drove North East
& we were pulled over by this Tennessee cop.

Who snarled at the room-sized sedan
"Hey, 'bama boy," he said, looking at my plates
"that's one lawwng car. Who's in back?"
That's all he wanted to know.
He was only there because of the snow
to watch traffic through the Virginia/Tennessee border

where, by the way, Ulysses S. Grant,
a reported boozehound & certain military victor himself,
seized the Virginia & Tennessee rail-lines
in the first serious offensives of 1864,
more dead, of course, both sides. Afternoon.
"Hey, if that guy is Hank Williams
that guy looks dead," the cop said
& caught some thick flakes in his meaty palm
& licked them like a clumsy bear cub.
& we drove on into the thick Allegheny forest,
into those beautiful blue pines, & mudslick hollers.
Into Bluefield VA, an unremarkable town,
except Mr. Williams had a doctor there
whom he said he'd like to see,
but passing through, Hank was passed out,
the chloral nitrate, the whachamacallit I thought,
& stopped & had a sandwich by myself
dry roast beef, & a heart warming beer.

I had another & another until I was pestering
the waitress, saying, "didja know
Hank Williams is this big time Dodgers fan"
because the waitress admitted she liked Brooklyn too.
"& every year he gets choked when the NY Yankees
best them in the end, those Bums." Oh, O.
Hank never saw them play w Jackie Robinson
but he heard of him hustling out in AAA
for the Montreal Royals
at gentle Delormier fields not far from the
foot of the Jacques Cartier bridge.
In the end she wasn't impressed.
She turned off the grill.
Late night, had to travel slow through the snow,
Hank looked really bad.
We would never make the New Year's show.
I didn't want to find out.
I threw some take-out in the back seat,

a white paper bag that was never opened.
I thought I heard him stir when we started out
& if he had any life then
I'm sure he was thinking about the beer I bought,
the new life inside the long white cadillac.
I think it was full of song stuff.
I guess he didn't stir, passed through Princeton WV
& we were close to the limit of Confederate excursions.
WV was quickly incorporated into the Union.
I was thinking we were just nitwits travelling
but 40 miles north I realized,
it was obvious, Hank Williams was dead.
Tony Bennett's version of "Cold Cold Heart"
would no longer rouse him to violence.
I stopped in Oak Hill WV to tell somebody
there was a dead man, cold, in my car, his car,
whatever. & they came & said I was right
Hiram Williams was dead at the age of 30.
Police headquarters, telephone calls.
Excessive eulogies flowed from then on,
from people who wouldn't shake a hand before
& who looked on while the last stage of illness set in.
"The Hillbilly Shakespeare" they said,
which is only as accurate or inaccurate
as calling the Bard the Renaissance Hank.
Schubert, it seems, is the logical parallel,
but it too doesn't matter, I'm tired
& I don't know what to say any more.
Oak Hill WV, hundreds of miles south,
(too late, anyway) from the Canton OH promised land.
Canton OH, site of the Pro Football Hall of Fame,
Mike Ditka's jersey there in a football-shaped building.
Just north of Salinville, the Northernmost point
of any rebel excursion: Greycoat calvary raiders
under General Morgan surrendered there July 26 1863.
Although, once, St. Alban's VT was raided
by about 30 Confederates from their base in Canada.

Mansel Robinson
from *Colonial Tongues,* 1992

DEL *enters first. He sneaks a mickey out of his pocket and has a drink.*
EDNA *catches up with him.*

EDNA: There's something I want to talk to you about.

DEL: I need a cigarette. *(He rolls himself a smoke, slowly and fastidiously. He spikes his coffee)*

EDNA: *(At the window)* Come on, Del, you're not rolling for the queen, I'd like to talk today.

DEL: I can't wake up without a smoke. *(He finally finishes and sits contentedly with coffee, hair of the dog and cigarette)*

EDNA: By the time you wake up you won't have a pot to piss in—

DEL: Give me a minute, alright?

EDNA: Or a window to throw it out of.

DEL: Jesus, you're crude.

EDNA: Whatever it takes to get your attention. What? Is the house on fire? *(She takes the letter from her apron pocket and puts in front of him)* Yes. (DEL *looks at the burn, looks at her. He reads the letter. Twice. He pulls the mickey out and pours them each a shot in their mugs)* Del, it's eight o'clock in the morning.

DEL: Drink it.

EDNA: Is that your solution?

DEL: Drink it. *(They each drink)* When did you get this?

EDNA: A week. Two. I didn't say anything…. I didn't know what to do. I've been trying to come up with a plan.

DEL: Do? The bank has called in the mortgage. There's nothing to do except *(Pours more rye)* pack.

EDNA: This is my goddamn house. No one tells me to pack.

DEL: The bank's house. And you've been told.

EDNA: Are you still drunk, boy? We've been evicted? What are you saying? 'Screw it'? 'That's life'?

DEL: Have a drink.

EDNA: I don't want a drink! *(She swipes at the mickey.* DEL *snatches it to safety)*

DEL: Easy, old girl.

EDNA: *(Coldly)* If they were coming for that goddamn bottle you'd get up on hind legs. Two weeks I've been sitting on this. What do I get? A shot of rye and a 'go easy old girl.' Thanks for your advice.

DEL: How long were they supposed to wait?

EDNA: I sit in the same church with the son of a bitch and he wants my house.

DEL: His house.

EDNA: Whose side are you on?

DEL: Did you read that letter?

EDNA: This is your house, too!

DEL: I've been thinking about that.

EDNA: You think a lot, sitting on your arse in the beer parlour.

DEL: That's right. I got a lot of time to think. Unemployment does that for you. What I think is this: It isn't one house, it isn't just our house. Ten years from now, 15 maybe, Main Street will look like somebody kicked her front teeth in. Ma. My guess is that this town is dying. It might already be dead. Those goddamn diesels don't need firemen. They don't need the shops. The roundhouse either. It's over. We just got our notice a little early. That's what I think.

EDNA: You were a scrappy kid. Did what you wanted, not what you were told. If you were 12 and I said the bank was coming for our house they'd find a boulder through their front window tomorrow morning.

DEL: I'm not 12.

EDNA: The bullies never got away without a scrap when you were a kid.

DEL: I grew up.

EDNA: Any man who can't figure out the wringer on a washing machine is still a boy.

DEL: You can sometimes beat a bully. But the pros, that's a different story. You don't argue with them. The bank is a pro.

EDNA: Should have killed all the bankers in the Depression.

DEL: There's nice Christian talk.

EDNA: Christians, Jesus, I share a pew with Cyrus.

DEL: Maybe you should have married him instead.

EDNA: I'd rather kill him.

DEL: Marry him first, so you can collect the insurance.

EDNA: *(Diverted)* He's married to Martha Petrunka. Use your head.

DEL: Kill her, marry him, kill him, collect, keep the house. Problem solved.

EDNA: I like Martha!

DEL: You see? He married a woman you like too much to kill. That's a pro.

EDNA: Jesus, what nonsense have you got me talking?

DEL: Go see him.

EDNA: I did. What do you think, I've been sitting on my arse?

DEL: What did he say?

EDNA: He said I should take in boarders. Boarders.

DEL: Well?

EDNA: Well, what?

DEL: Why not?

EDNA: I'm not raising my kids in a hotel. It's bad enough they got a brother who uses this place like one. That's all we need, four or five goddamn boomers sniffing around Hazel, feeding their booze to Butch.

DEL: Maybe they'll be more interested in you.

EDNA: What's that supposed to mean?

DEL: Maybe you ought to get married again.

EDNA: *(Surprised laugh)* Married? Are you still drunk, pup?

DEL: I think it would be a good idea.

EDNA: Do you now?

DEL: What do you think about it?

EDNA: Did you have someone in mind or was I supposed to pick him out at gunpoint?

DEL: You aren't... old.

EDNA: You almost broke your face getting that one out.

DEL: Well, you aren't.

EDNA: Thanks, pup, but I've had it with boomers. *(Catches herself, gets back on track)* He talked in numbers. Not words. Numbers.

DEL: Cyrus is a banker.

EDNA: He's an adding machine.

DEL: It's his job.

EDNA: His job is to serve the community.

DEL: Isn't that in the Bible somewhere; Genesis, maybe?

EDNA: Keep your heathen tongue off the Bible.

DEL: No. Sounds more like the New Testament. Matthew, Mark, Larry, Moe and Curly Joe.

EDNA: Drunken pup. Should've drowned you at birth.

DEL: What kind of offer did you make him?

EDNA: What do you mean offer? I offered to stay in my house.

DEL: You gotta come up with a plan, ma.

EDNA: I work. I pay my bills and give him whatever's left over. That's my plan. It was good enough last year and the year before that. It should be good enough now.

DEL: But it's not good enough. *(He waits)* Is it?

EDNA: It's good enough for me.

DEL: It's not good enough for a bank.

EDNA: It's the best I can do.

DEL: 'A' for effort. But it don't pay.

EDNA: I didn't wake you up for your lip.

DEL *pulls some change from his pocket and spills it onto the table*

DEL: That help any?

EDNA: If you'd go to work—

DEL: One trip a month buys fuck all!

EDNA: You aren't too big to wash your mouth out with Sunlight soap.

DEL: Nothing. *Rien de tout.* Zip. Zero. Fuck all. The railroad, ma, it's finished for me. You wanna see an ancient artifact? *(He does a rough pirouette)* One fireman—but there's no firing left to do. The diesels took care of that. Stuff me with feathers, hang a sign on my neck and stick me in the goddamn railroad museum. I'm fuck all.

EDNA: You're a human being—

DEL: That's the nicest thing anybody's called me in a week.

EDNA: —but you roll over like a spayed dog.

DEL: So what kind of a plan can we cook up? Bootlegging? Government's got that racket sown up tight. Grow a little marijuana to sell in Toronto? Moss maybe, but pot don't grow on these rocks. Buy Butch a guitar and make him a rock'n'roll star? Skim a few bucks from the hockey pool? What's that? Fifty bucks a month? Better'n what I can depend on from the CPR. Maybe we can collect beer bottles. Yeah. As a family. Up and down the lanes, day and night. There's a growth industry for you. Collecting pop bottles. We can do that until the pensions come in. Or I could get a paper route.

EDNA: They can't do this!

DEL: You can't make the earth flat by wishing it.

EDNA: They can't do this.

DEL: Why not?

EDNA: Because…

DEL: Pretty good, Socrates.

EDNA: We fed them for a hundred years.

DEL: Don't give me that CCF-New Jerusalem hogwash! We'll get a thank you card on the way out the gate.

EDNA: It's not our fault the CPR took your job away. We made them rich.

DEL: Should've made ourselves necessary.

EDNA: They need people like us.

DEL: Hands are 10 cents a pair.

EDNA: We are not just hands. We are not just employees. We are people.

DEL: That's the problem. We're not quite robot and we're not quite slave. Too smart and not smart enough.

EDNA: I am not a slave.

DEL: Whatever you say. Don't fire until you see the red of their taillights.

EDNA: What are you, working for the bank? It's only money.

DEL: Spoken like someone with no cash.

EDNA: Right, Del, blame the victim.

DEL: It's too late. We didn't fight back soon enough.

EDNA: Fight? I raise a family. I pay my taxes. Why should I have to fight? I'm not the enemy. I'm a citizen.

DEL: You watch too many commercials. They only need you at election time.

EDNA: Del, don't fight me. Help me.

DEL: Boarders, ma. Your only hope. *(He mimics the cretins he describes)* Drunken young men prowling the halls at night—

EDNA: Not in this house.

DEL: Leering, lonely young boomers—

EDNA: Never.

DEL: Horny as goats—

EDNA: You're criminal.

DEL: Pockets jingling with coin, remember, and looking for the love mother used to give them.

EDNA: There's something evil about you. All we need is time.

DEL: Time's up.

 The roar of machinery off-stage. BUTCH *is flying in the first wall. It should be something of a triumph for him—his dream is taking shape.* EDNA *is helpful,* DEL *might even be disruptive of the process. When the wall is up,* EDNA *hangs a photograph.*

BUTCH: *(This speech should modulate between self-mockery and biblical prophecy. A little bit of ham would not be inappropriate)* Like everybody else, they've put it in the criminal code—memory has been outlawed, it's treasonous to keep a past, history is a crime—like bestiality or sex with an imbecile. Now. Three lousy letters to sum up our lives. Remember that other three letter word, Hazel? Remember it, Del? That's right. God. *(Smiles. The smile vanishes)* There's a sign up in God's window. 'Under New Management.' If God's still around he's playing for a farm team, he's with a D-class circus, a sideshow freak, God's on workman's comp, retired without a pension, panhandling in the subway, bumming smokes in the tavern. God isn't dead. He just wishes the rumours were true. Kicked into the street by sons and daughters, granny- bashed. We toss him out of his home, we raid the fridge and crap on the carpets. And all we've allowed him to keep is a Polaroid snap from better days—God at the beach with a beer in his hand, a sunburned nose and a child on his knee. History, memory, philosophy. Wrong every time. Responsibility. Wrong. Continuity. Wrong. Sacred trust. Wrong. Free of the past, free of the future. Guiltless, blameless, free to do as we please.

	Right here. Right now. For all time. Until we end time, too. *(Pause)* Wrong, Hazel. You and Del are so goddamn wrong you can hardly walk. *(He exits)*
DEL:	A house isn't much. Some 2 x 4's, a window to look out of, a roof for the snow and a door to—
EDNA:	Slam on a shyster's face.
DEL:	—a door to lock behind you when you leave. You take the family pictures and you find a new wall to hang 'em on. *(He removes the photograph* EDNA *has just hung. He puts it in the trunk.* EDNA *re-hangs the photo)*
EDNA:	Can't you hear it?
DEL:	What?
EDNA:	You're deaf, dumb and blind.
DEL:	Hear what? The mice in the walls?
EDNA:	There's no mice in this house.
DEL:	Rats then.
EDNA:	Should have drowned you.
DEL:	You missed your chance. You won't find a sack big enough for me now.
EDNA:	The house talks, Del.
DEL:	Jesus! Lock her up. Talking doorknobs.
EDNA:	Don't be so goddamned literal-minded. Not voices.
DEL:	You said the house talks.
EDNA:	Sometimes this house gives me a little nudge.
DEL:	The foundation is cracking.
EDNA:	The day your father went missing, I was sitting at the table, right where you're sitting now. I felt a tap on my shoulder. The telegram came three days later. Two weeks ago, the same thing. The letter from Cyrus at the bank came a day later. We've been here so long the house knows bad news is coming long before it gets here. It knows.
DEL:	Do you know how crazy that sounds?
EDNA:	I'd be crazy if I ignored the signs.
DEL:	Close your mouth, the neighbours will hear.
EDNA:	Ask Mrs. Goldstein. She knows.
DEL:	She believes you?
EDNA:	She knows. Listen. She looked after the house one January

when we were at your aunt's. A blowy cold night. She was worried about the furnace going out and the water freezing up. She stoked the furnace, then made herself a cup of tea, you know, just to sit for a moment till the kitchen warmed up a little. She was hardly finished her cup when the creaking started on the stairs, like someone was coming down. The creaking stopped about halfway.

DEL: Frost.

EDNA: Someone came down. Looked over the banister and saw a friend of the family sitting drinking tea in the kitchen. It turned back upstairs. Then went to bed, I guess.

DEL: Mrs. Goldstein makes a lot of dandelion wine for a widow.

EDNA: Don't judge other people by your own mirror, boy. Especially one as cracked and black as yours. *(Long pause)* Some nights I hear him breathe.

DEL: Who?

EDNA: Your old man.

DEL: Dreams.

EDNA: No. It's him that's dreaming. Sometimes he snores. Like he's been drinking heavy, maybe even poisoned himself. His breath catches in the back of his throat, that's what wakes me up, that catch and the sudden silence. I lie awake waiting for his breath and his heart to start again. He starts to breathe. Then I can sleep.

DEL: It's a dream.

EDNA: Sometimes I know... I know that he's still alive.

DEL: Fifteen years.

EDNA: You hear stories of men wandering around with amnesia, drifting after the war. Living alone when they have a wife and kids, pets even, a house and job waiting for them maybe just over in the next town. But they don't know. They can't remember. But your old man isn't like that. I see him getting off the train, looking up the street, looking down the street, then flagging a ride for anywhere but here. Maybe for the sandy, sunny south.

DEL: I don't think so, Ma. Fifteen years.

EDNA: Missing in action. No casket. No funeral. He could be anywhere.

DEL: He's dead.

EDNA: You haven't heard him snore.

DEL: If I lived in a haunted house I'd leave.

EDNA: Would you?

DEL: Oh yeah.

EDNA: You might get lonesome for your ghosts.

DEL: They'd have to find me and they'd have to stop me.

EDNA: You don't know ghosts.

DEL: Maybe you know them too well.

EDNA: I'd be lost without them.

DEL: No.

EDNA: I would.

DEL: You've never tried. You haul them around like old trunks. Busting your back moving them from room to room, stubbing your toes. You should think about travelling light for a change.

EDNA: Travelling light. I'm not 20 any more. *(Pause)* And I don't think I'd want to be.

DEL: Ghosts. Jesus.

EDNA: You've never felt anything here?

DEL: I liked living here. But the house never talked to me.

EDNA: That's too bad.

DEL: Maybe.

EDNA: If a house doesn't talk to you then it's not your home.

DEL: Maybe I haven't found my home yet. We're all going somewhere. You, too. That's what the letter says. P.S. Goodbye.
He exits. EDNA *watches* BUTCH *drag* HAZEL *in by the arm— an excited child trying to inspire a skeptic.* EDNA *exits when the skepticism gets too much for her.* BUTCH *puts the second wall up in the following scene*

BUTCH: You're standing on Main Street. It's 1967. What's at the west end of the street?

HAZEL: Christ, I don't know.

BUTCH: Close your eyes. You are 12 years old. Standing on Main

Street. Facing the river. Turn to your left. What do you see at the end of the street?

HAZEL: Nothing.

BUTCH: Snow. September. Baseball uniforms. The sand pit. Clothes on the line. Walking to school, creosote on the ties.

HAZEL: No. Nothing.

BUTCH: People then. Think of the people you liked. Who's on the street?

HAZEL: All the people I liked lived somewhere else.

BUTCH: Pick a day you liked in '67.

HAZEL: I prefer anything after 1986.

BUTCH: There was no town by '86.

HAZEL: Exactly.

BUTCH: They didn't even leave a ghost town. It's buried. Here. As if an earthquake took it. A mud slide. An ICBM.

HAZEL: Pretty thorough, I'd say.

BUTCH: Don't you dream of where everything started? Don't you dream of home?

HAZEL: I have a home. 500 miles south of here.

BUTCH: South, that fucking borderland? It's a picture ripped out of a cheap cookbook, it's a grainy newspaper photo. Your home is here.

HAZEL: And you have a home, too.

BUTCH: They tore up the mainline, they knocked the buildings over. They buried it 20 feet down!

HAZEL: Most people leave home, Butch. It's called growing up.

BUTCH: But we didn't leave. It was taken. We had no say.

HAZEL: So?

BUTCH: A home is everyone's right.

HAZEL: You have one.

BUTCH: It's been faked.

HAZEL: You want the world.

BUTCH: I want what's mine.

HAZEL: It wasn't yours.

BUTCH: We built it with our sweat and our blood.

HAZEL: *(laughs)* You were a kid.

BUTCH: We cleared the land and we put the railroad through and we dug the mines and we hauled ore by hand. Our ancestors are buried here. Pioneers.

HAZEL: You were a kid.

BUTCH: *(showing his wrists)* This is the same blood.

HAZEL: Watered down Kool-Aid. If you were a hardy-assed old pioneer you wouldn't be whining like this. They went where they had to go.

BUTCH: Before the CPR said thanks for everything and started running freight through the northern States. Before then. When we had a mainline here. A place to live. You remember.

HAZEL: No.

BUTCH: There was no movie on Wednesdays. One played Thursday to Saturday. A new movie Sunday to Tuesday. Every week for years, you'd see the film cans on the sidewalk, going to the train. Until the show closed down cause everybody was sitting at home with their VCR's and cable and dishes. And sometime after that they killed the passenger trains. And sometime after that they killed the freights, too. But the show was the first thing those bastards killed.

HAZEL: The show.

BUTCH: We called it the show. 'Goin' to the show tonight?' 'Yeah.' 'Wanna go to the Redwood for a pop, first?' You remember.

HAZEL: You're whistling through your ass.

BUTCH: You remember the parades on the first of July.

HAZEL: No.

BUTCH: We dressed the dog in baby clothes and pushed him around in the carriage. In '67 we dressed up as *coureurs de bois*. We had a canoe. Moccasins. Leg-hold traps. We won a prize. It was the Centennial year. It was a big deal. We won first prize in 1967. Remember? *(sings)* 'One little, two little, three little provinces, we love —'

HAZEL: Don't be such a goddamn retard.

BUTCH: Ha! You see? Retard. No one uses that word any more. Retard. 'What are ya, some kinda retard?' That's history. History, Hazel. History!

HAZEL: Oh, Jesus H. Christ!

BUTCH: Mom used that expression.

HAZEL: So does half the western world.

BUTCH: You heard it from her. Potlicker.

HAZEL: What?

BUTCH: 'How ya doin, ya old potlicker?' Del used that one. Do you even remember Del? Tall guy, big goofy smile, lost his job when the diesels came in, started into the booze —

HAZEL: Shut up.

BUTCH: You can't re-invent him, you can't pretty him up, he was a goddamn drunk.

HAZEL: Shut your fucking yap about Del.

BUTCH *has found something here, but doesn't follow it up.*

BUTCH: What's a lard sandwich? Depression food, from the '30s. Ask me what's for dinner. *(HAZEL ignores him)* 'What's for dinner?' Potatoes and point. Then you eat your fried baloney and point at a picture of roast beef, say 'mm good roast,' yeah, you remember. What was the Legion? The beer parlour. What happened Wednesday afternoons? The stores closed. And Andy from the hardware went to the beer parlour and got pissed. No. Not pissed. Half cut. And you remember.

HAZEL: What would I win, the fucking lottery?

BUTCH: There was a forest fire. The town was evacuated. We loaded up the station wagon. The cat hid under the wood pile, we were going to leave her behind. Socks. Yes. At the gas station three drops of rain landed on the windshield. We went back to the house. Did we unpack the car? *(HAZEL doesn't answer)* We drove around that night. All the houses were dark. It was scary, eh Hazel. Mom talked to the chief of police. We went home. We were the only ones on our street. It was quiet. Like in a horror film. Did you sleep that night? Everybody we knew got to go away for a few days. Not us. We sat in that empty town until the fire stopped moving towards us and everybody came home telling great stories. You hated mom for depriving you of that trip. You said she was nuts. For trying to save the house with a garden hose. Like pissing on a volcano, you said. But she was born there, raised there, worked there, married there, raised us there.

HAZEL: The town was gonna burn to the ground.

BUTCH: Only if she let it.

❡

Lesley Battler
from *Walking the Line*, 1993

Almost Familiar

I.

TWO WEEKS AFTER HER MOTHER DIED, Eva returned to work, walking down to the bus stop with Richard, as she did every morning, dodging road repair pits, gravel mounds and the slalom course of orange and black warning signs. She had to cross the service road of a highway, and the bus stop shimmered at the other end, in a cloud of road and truck dust. A worker did up the zipper of his coveralls in front of Eva, looking brashly at her as he tugged. She felt light-headed and overwhelmed and she turned her head, looking carefully in all directions, as if she was a small child who had to be led by Richard across the street. Beyond the traffic flow, Eva could see only an empty grey-white sky. This area of the city was always busy, but now she felt if something happened to her she would not be able to shout for help. Or even if she did cry out, the words would remain in the back of her throat and no one would be able to hear her.

She walked gingerly down the stairs at Berri Métro station, joining the sound of nine o'clock people clip-clopping down to the track, turnstiles popping like distant gunshot. This station was like an airport with its long passages, yet another corner to turn, another escalator to ascend or descend, signs she had to read again as if she hadn't seen them before, even though it had only been two weeks since she had last seen them. She had to stop herself from following the stream of people heading in the opposite direction.

She and Richard stood in their usual place by the door, facing each other, protected from the crowd by a pole. Eva started to mock-rant at Richard, as she did every morning, assuming her dictator's voice. "Where *is* the state limousine? I should not be inflicted with the ghastly sight of people *working* before I've had my morning champagne and caviar, or had a chance to peruse my *Daily Tyranny*. How can I enforce Total Quality Management in my labour camps now?"

A long time ago, Eva and Richard decided they were both dictators in their relationship. The dictator game started during a fight. They had reached an impasse about something or other, probably money, and Eva had brought home a picture of Napoleon she found at work and wrote out, "As I, the maniacal tyrant look down upon my pathetic peons, I reflect on how their puny lives mean nothing to me except as the brute labour necessary to execute my mad desires." She had taped this to Richard's computer screen, and when he saw it he laughed. The impasse was broken, and they had been playing the dictator game ever since.

On the Métro, Richard pretended to slump and said, "Oh no. I hear a speech coming on. I guess that means I can get some extra sleep. No wonder everyone in your country takes such long siestas, the way you jam the broadcast system with your speeches. All these poor people on the train are pretending to be asleep, hoping they can forget about your nightmare regime."

Eva laughed, but there was one big difference now though. She had lost her sense of humour. Her morning Métro routines weren't funny any more, but she couldn't help it. It was as if she was compelled to make these morning speeches, and the only thing that saved her neck, was that most of the people on the train spoke French. She gestured at the people and said to Richard in her dictator's voice, "They all get vacations. What more can they ask for? Being leader of a country is an awe-inspiring responsibility. I don't get vacations."

Then she felt her dictator's voice slip and she was speaking in a half-normal tone. "I haven't had a vacation in five years. Unless you count my trip with Club Dead. It was such a treat I didn't even accept any pay for it. A week of lying on the beach, surrounded by all those black umbrellas and beach towels and that undertaker who served the black gins with the sprig of nightshade. I thought the whole place would die laughing."

"Everyone in your country should be given nightshade," said Richard. "Or cyanide."

"Cyanide is banned in my country," Eva said, firmly in her dictator's voice again. "People must die properly—blindfolded in the courtyard."

Usually the game would stop at this point, but she couldn't stop herself, nor could she stop her voice from sliding between her dictator's voice and her normal voice, so that it ended up sounding like the painful cracking voice of a teenaged boy. "The best part of the vacation was kicking back and visiting the family. My dad's a little mossy, but mom's there now too. Why can't some people take better care of themselves? Dying young is so déclassé, so un-middleclass. I say, make all those people buy Stairmasters. In my country, I send Fitness Cops to the rural areas. Don't get me wrong though. I enjoyed Club Dead immensely. I'm back now, truly regenerated. There's nothing like having your whole life rendered utterly meaningless to get you back in the swing of things."

Eva suddenly stopped speaking.

Lately, she had been lingering downtown after work to attend comedy shows, without telling Richard what she was doing. For all she knew, he could be imagining her having an affair, although she was really sitting by herself in Club Soda or The Comedy Nest, waiting for another stand-up comic to appear on stage. She was fascinated by them. To Eva, there was something incredibly brave about a comic appearing on stage, singled out in light. It was like seeing someone walking a tightrope and she sat on the edge of her seat, afraid the comic would slip up, afraid the audience wouldn't laugh, or worse, start heckling and fleeing for the parking lot. On the Métro these mornings, she had a hint of what it must feel like to be on stage, walking that line between wanting to keep it funny and being capsized by the undertow of what went into that humour, all in front of people who went to comedy clubs to laugh.

Richard placed his hands on her shoulders and made her look at him. "We're taking a vacation," he said.

"You know I can't afford it," she said quietly. "I won't get paid and if I take too much time, they'll bring someone else in to do my job. That means Club UIC. UIC's a nightmare these days. If I go on a vacation and I lose my contract, that'll be a 'quit for unjust cause.'"

"Unjust cause!" said Richard. "That's ridiculous. Your mother has just died. You've worked for five years without taking a break, and a funeral is not a break. That's not unjust cause. You can appeal that."

Eva smiled. "You're so cute—naïve but cute. I've already checked with the Labour Board, with the Minimum Wage Commission, and with UIC. Basically, I'm screwed."

"Well forget about the job then," said Richard. "I make enough, and if I can't even help out, what kind of person am I? We'll go on a vacation, anywhere you want."

"Is this what things are going to be like from here on in?" said Eva. "Me having nothing and depending on you?"

"Well that's how it works in my country," said Richard in his dictator's voice. "The peons have nothing, and I have everything. It works for me."

"Look over there," said Eva, pointing.

Richard turned his head and Eva said, "There's a coup going on in your country right now and I'm making a grab for your treasury. I don't really feel like heading into an abyss of anonymous failure just yet, so I think pistol-whipping you up a City Hall aisle is a good plan. I'll spend all the holidays sucking up to your family and forget it's because I have nowhere else in the world to go. I'll plunge myself into your career. I won't say a word about my childhood because no one is around to re-member it anyway. We'll have kids and then I'll throw all my frustrations into being a perfect mother and then, conscious of how my own life as an independent human being failed, make damn sure that kid gets into medical school. That's how it works isn't it? This is what happens to people like me."

"We'll look at the atlas tonight," said Richard.

When they got off the Métro, Richard linked his arm around Eva's, but she felt embarrassed, as if she had been on stage and the light had been turned on her at the wrong time and she was standing in front of an audience with tears streaking down her cheeks. Her mother died, she had no family, she was someone who had been working for six years in one place as casual labour. She was someone who had become what she most feared, a shadowy, weightless, useless half of a couple, and it was as if Richard had just seen her fall.

2.

Eva resented the way Audis and BMWs owned the autobahn, the way they expected tourists, lesser cars and particularly the Eastern European "peanut cars" to keep their places in the right lane. She wondered how the East Germans and Czechs felt, crunched up in their Trabants, Skodas and Moskvitches, pausing for frequent breakdowns and overheated engines, seeing the sleek Western cars sailing by them.

She had a good idea by the way they always deferred, pulling over to the shoulders for Westerners, and she felt dismayed, jolted when the cars pulled over for her and Richard.

Richard received an angry blast from someone's high beams when he had the temerity to actually slow down to allow a Skoda to rejoin the traffic. Eva hated passing the little cars. Richard was right, they really were terrible cars with blackened exhaust pipes, and they smelled like naphtha. But she liked them, the way their shades of blue, green and yellow gave them a foolhardy, festive quality. Eva cheered whenever she saw a peanut car pull into the left lane, challenging an Audi's divine right. She would have been happier if they could have stayed in the right lane, keeping pace with them, or poking along behind them, but it didn't seem to be possible, either by the rules of the road, or the design of the cars. A rented Opel wasn't an Audi but it couldn't sit behind a Skoda either, and Eva kept wanting to apologize every time they passed one.

The border crossing between West and East Germany was as eerie as Eva imagined, with all the state apparatus still in place, but deserted. Watchtower windows were broken. Vines twisted around searchlights, turning them into maypoles. Signs instructing people to slow down and stop had been painted over, so spectral achtungs floated above cars flying past them as fast as possible, fading into the forlorn grey-blue of the sky. Eva had wanted an East German stamp on her passport, but there was no one in the booth to ask. All gone, thought Eva. With only hints it had ever once existed. She shivered, not knowing if it was miraculous or a frightening emptiness. She was sure she could hear the sound of speeding cars echoing for miles.

At the border crossing between East Germany and Czechoslovakia, on the German side, two guards stood by a painted line on the highway, and Richard pulled up to them. A man in a booth neither had noticed, barked "Halt!" and ordered them over to the booth. "Don't shoot!" Eva cried, imagining the guards raising their guns. The poker-faced man examined their passports, then looked out the window at Richard and Eva, then at the Opel Richard had rented in Amsterdam with the Netherlands sticker on it. "Kanada!" he stated in a voice implying they had pulled a fast one on him. Eva heard the "K" in the word.

As soon as they felt they had passed the border, and were definitely in Czechoslovakia, Richard pulled over.

"You realize we don't have any Czech money and neither of us knows the word for bank?" said Richard.

He looked alarmed, but Eva couldn't stop herself from feeling pleased at his discomfort. She had hoped travelling like this, absorbed in momentary impressions and encounters would make her feel she and Richard were on equal footing. She had chosen Prague because she had always wanted to go there, but Richard had been unnerved by her choice.

"Aww," she said. "Don't tell me the poor dictator is scared. Prague-ophobia can be cured with help. Don't you have support groups for overthrown despots in your country?"

Richard puffed out his chest. "I am not scared. I am merely concerned about my people."

They laughed and embraced, then Eva couldn't stop herself from saying in her normal voice, "Now you know how I've been feeling in Montreal these days."

Huge single family houses and old churches marked the countryside, looking like abandoned barns on the outskirts of Montreal. Walled villages gave Eva the feeling she was at a cold, off-season beach. The walls, which were the colour of wet sand, blended into an enflamed sky and burnished leaves, all blanketed by the haze of soft coal, burning wood, and scrub fires, until Eva had the impression the whole country was smouldering. A teenager, without jacket or helmet, shot by them on an antique motorbike, his long blond hair washed in diesel oil and dust. Eva held her breath, imagining how unprotected he was, and how nothing would cushion his fall.

They passed hundreds of Liaz trucks, all smelling like Coleman stoves, and a massive industrial site, which looked to Eva like the ones featured in PBS documentaries about Eastern Europe, appeared out of nowhere. She thought of the refineries out past Pointe-aux-Trembles, the oil storage tanks painted in bright primary colours, pipes that snapped together, looking as cheery and harmless as if they had been designed by Fisher Price. Here, the statues of workers at the entrance were so coated with oil, coal and car exhaust, she could hardly tell what they originally depicted. They were honest if nothing else, she thought, these statues of workers reduced to shapes made of the substances that were killing them.

"God, the pollution," said Richard. "My eyes are stinging."

"Well why don't you march in and tell them they're offending your delicate sensibilities," snapped Eva. "There's plenty of pollution at home, you know. I can smell this walking to the bus stop every morning."

She knew she was reacting as if he had made a personal criticism, and she hadn't been thinking anything much different from what he had said. She saw Richard looking at the countryside, with a detached, almost smug look on his face, and she imagined him looking at her that way. Shaven hills swelled, advanced and receded, completely unlike the ones in West Germany, which were so defined and anchored by their miles of forests and endless vertical rows of corn. The countryside looked bare naked, she thought suddenly. The villages made her think of camouflaged villages in wartime, designed to disappear into their surroundings, the family treasures covered in plain brown wrapping. The roadside shrines they passed cheered her a little. She was unable to imagine the shrines had all been removed, placed in some sort of storage, and then reinstated after December 1989. Maybe the churches were all abandoned, but someone had been carefully tending to the saints all along, and she liked that thought.

When they reached Karlovy-Vary and parked the car, Eva felt as if she had somehow gone back in time to the early sixties, but instead of seeing it as a young child, she had gone back with the eyes of an adult. Faded signs in store windows, resembling good-life 1960s "Drink Coca Cola" billboards advertised Russian vodka. The signs reminded her it was a resort town, but couldn't help noticing it was inextricably mixed with poverty. The wide boulevard, grand hotel on the corner, casual clusters of people gave her a familiar holiday feeling, an echo of the feeling she had when her parents took her on trips when she was young, but mixed with the feeling it was an illusion. This must have been what things really looked like as a child, she thought. Everything she couldn't remember, or purposefully left out of the childhood stories she told Richard. The ragged patches of paint on the walls of buildings, the cardboard replacing window panes seemed very familiar to Eva. She almost stumbled over a mound of coal at a chute and watched, trying to be unobtrusive, as two elderly people loaded coal into two buckets on a wagon, then scuttled off with their booty. Her family had once had their electricity cut off, and she had never wondered what would happen if her parents simply could not have paid to have it reinstated.

She and Richard were relieved the hotel on the corner could change money. The woman at the desk spoke some English, and Eva was touched by how proud the woman was about speaking English and having this job. Richard pulled out two hundred Deutschmarks and passed them to her. The woman blanched.

"This—you want changed?"

Eva and Richard nodded.

"Czech money you want?"

They nodded again.

"Currency regulations are—no more," the woman said carefully. "Spending in the country—you no longer have to do."

Eva and Richard looked at each other.

"We weren't sure about that," said Richard. "We have an old guide book."

"You still need?"

Richard nodded. The woman reached into a drawer and pulled out a wad of Czech crowns, peeling off what seemed endless bills.

"Here," said the woman. "A receipt I'll give you. Proof that you changed money at respectable place. You can change back into Deutschmarks anywhere, anytime. A guarantee."

Eva was glad to have the receipt, but she wanted to spend all the money in Czechoslovakia. She didn't want to know that two hundred Deutschmarks equalled that many Czech *koruna*. "Thank you very much," said Eva and Richard together, but Eva almost felt as if she and Richard were accomplices committing a bank robbery. She wanted to break away from Richard and tell the woman the money was all his.

Their pockets were now stuffed with koruna, stiff greenish bills with a man's portrait on them. Eva remembered reading somewhere, probably at work, that the new currency was issued just before the change of government, and the pictured man was an old-guard Stalinist.

"Since we're here," said Eva, "let's go into the restaurant and get some swill. Ministry of Swill, there's no caffeine in my system. This outrage can't be allowed to continue."

In the restaurant, Eva half-expected women from the pages of old *Life* magazines to enter, dressed in slim suits and pink pillbox hats. Instead, a waiter tossed two badly typed menus on the table.

"Hmm," said Eva. "My guess is 'káva.' "

She made a stab at pronouncing the word, then pointed to it on the menu. The waiter disappeared. Half an hour later a small cup of coffee appeared on the table. Grains swirled from the bed of grounds at the bottom of the cup.

"Bubble bubble toil and trouble," said Eva. "I wonder if there's some way of reading coffee grounds."

"That really looks foul."

"Tastes like French coffee, only a little chewy. We coffee drinkers are a hardy breed."

"You've got some grounds caught between your front teeth," said Richard.

Eva started picking her teeth and Richard cleaned his glasses. He had only recently started wearing glasses and she thought he cleaned them obsessively.

"You look like a raccoon, constantly cleaning those things," she said.

"She says, picking her teeth in public," said Richard.

When Eva put on Richard's glasses so everything was just a little blurred and distorted, the hotel did look grand and resort-like with high ceilings and huge windows, people grouped leisurely at tables, but when she took them off again, she could see the dining hall was as austere as a church hall, overheated and drafty at the same time, permeated by the same smell of coffee. A creaking echoing building that seemed as if the wind could unfasten from its foundation, and it would go sailing down the boulevard. It reminded Eva of her mother's house after she had moved all the furniture out of the living room. She had stripped the old rug off the floor, shocked by how bare and strange the room had become, and how the layout of the rooms, without furniture, did not look like any house she could ever have lived in. The house was for sale, but Eva's mother hadn't wanted to let anyone in to see it, and had dreaded people seeing her so shrunken and diminished, with no more substance to her than a tiny bird, her skin frighteningly transparent with a faded greenish tint from the radiation treatments.

At night, Eva slept in her old bedroom which had become the spare room, and the rain echoed all over the house, and tree branches brushing against the windows sounded like townspeople in the bushes, villagers from old movies with torches and pitchforks, trying to peer in through the window at them. Eva understood only too well why her mother didn't want anyone to come inside, even if it was to help. She shuddered, trying to imagine what her mother would have done, or not done, if she hadn't had a daughter.

"What is it sweetie?" Richard asked.

His expression was so tender, almost beseeching, that Eva couldn't make a joke. She didn't know whether she wanted to cry or leave the table, or what she wanted from him. His sympathy was unbearable to her, but she knew she didn't want him not to care.

"Just thinking," said Eva.

The waiter finally returned, with a price scribbled on a scrap of paper.

"I don't know if we can keep squandering our money like this," said Richard. "Know how much that coffee cost you in Canadian?"

"No clue," said Eva.

"Somewhere between five and ten cents."

"Are you serious?"

"I think I understand why that woman at the counter reacted like that," said Richard.

"What should we do about tipping?"

"I think they add the tip on," said Richard. "I saw him write something down, then he erased it and wrote that. But it doesn't seem right not to leave a tip."

"But if we do aren't we sort of flaunting something? Here my good man, we're rich tourists, here's a penny for your trouble."

"It's such a little bit of money. He can use it, so who cares," said Richard.

"That's not the point," said Eva, surprised by the edge in her voice. "Maybe he's a proud man, doing his job, getting by the best way he knows how and he's sick to death of people coming in with money and throwing it around as if it could help, as if it could do anything for his life and the way things really are, simply because they can, because they have power and he doesn't...."

"Whoa," said Richard. "You were once a waitress. What did you call people who didn't leave you a tip?"

"Scum-sucking leeches," said Eva.

"Well there you go. I think our basic choice is we can be rich North Americans and leave a tip, or be rich North American cheapskates."

"Yeah but—there's no way around that is there?" It was the most complicated coffee Eva had ever ordered.

Outside the hotel, pairs of men Eva couldn't decide were policemen or soldiers strolled down the boulevard, their faces reminding her of soldiers' faces in World War II photos, achingly young and unformed in their olive uniforms. A white palace at the centre of a park made her feel chilled and lonely, although there was no particular reason for it. It was at the centre of a pleasant park where people sat on the benches, not as grandiose and authoritarian as many in Paris with their dictator balconies. The palace did not jar Eva with the collision of cultures like some of the buildings in Strasbourg, the way warm peach and pink walls would be weighed down with Germanic falcon crests or ebony-coloured beams. She couldn't understand her discomfort, or why every snapshot she took felt like something she was stealing from the city. It was a strange feeling of being in surroundings that looked a little familiar, but changed so they were not quite the way she remembered them. Like the way she might feel if she returned to see her mother's house, even though it was only a month after her death.

"I think we should go on to Prague," she said, keeping her voice light. "Either that or I really need the spa that's supposed to be here."

"Yeah, those cops are giving me the creeps," said Richard.

3.

She and Richard plummeted into a dark area of Prague where the buildings, as massive and impregnable as cliffs, overlooked long blocks without streetlights. There were very few cars on the road, and Eva thought it looked like an occupied city after curfew. She could imagine people sequestered in secret annexes. Streets circled and zigzagged, cut to fit around great buildings, some as narrow and treacherous with as little margin for error as mountain passes. Richard guided the car into shadow-warped alleys, past tall silent buildings with their windows blanched bright in the moonlight. They seemed to stare out at Eva with the eyes of the blind. Looking down at her hands, she saw every vein and wrinkle stand out, and outside the car window, every leaf, brick and shadow stood out too, limned like a photograph in silver and black clarity. A large motionless merry-go-round in a public square made Eva think this could be a real Pinocchio city, one that could be severe and foreboding. She could imagine Pinocchio and his friend Lampwick being changed into donkeys because they were bad at their lessons.

After spending what seemed hours driving back and forth over every one of Prague's sixteen bridges, they found the tourist bureau, only to be confronted by a scrawled sign taped over the wicket which said, "No rooms." When Richard was almost ready to give up and was trying to resign himself to parking somewhere and sleeping in the car, they finally found the Hotel Savoy. Eva thought it looked and smelled like a post office. and it was so inexpensive, she again had the feeling she and Richard were committing a crime. She tuned an old white radio on the cabinet and found only one music station, playing soft stately classical music. Eva supposed it was meant to be soothing, but she found it accentuated the strange mixture of the familiar and completely unknown, the sense she couldn't shake of being in the past, her own past but rearranged and with something missing. Many weary tourists had found the Savoy and it made her think of a dorm, the way the doors constantly banged, the way groups seemed interconnected with other groups in associations formed long before Eva's arrival. Police cars, visible from the window, barreled down the empty streets, conjuring up all the police state associations her imagination could generate.

"Maybe they don't do much any more," said Richard. "Maybe they just drive around like cowboys now."

"I heard a lot of sirens in Paris," said Eva. "They weren't scary though. They were just part of the street noise and it almost sounded like party time, not this one drawn-out sound echoing through the night."

She was conscious of her own voice making conversation. It felt as if she had brought someone back to a dorm room after a dance, and they were tentatively sounding each other out. She thought she should be making coffee or offering him a beer or something, a few rounds of backgammon.

"Why do you love me?" she asked him suddenly. Richard looked surprised, because she didn't usually ask questions like this.

"Because I have to," he said. "I've been ordered to by the Great Dictator."

"No, seriously."

Richard paused, and Eva was aware of how silent the streets were. She thought of how quiet everyone had been around her at work, after she returned from her mother's funeral. She could describe to Richard the murmurs and rustles of uneasy condolence from her co-workers, and how the floor seemed to shimmer beneath her feet until she wanted to break a window and wave an SOS flag. But she couldn't make him feel the complete unreality, the way she would see someone on the street who looked like her mother, or father for that matter, how her heart would start pounding as if it could be possible. But it came down to the fact she would never ever see them on a street anywhere, and while Richard was surrounded by flesh and blood family members, she could only see phantoms and touch photographs. Eva supposed she asked the question, hoping his answer would make her feel real.

He finally said, "Well you're sweet and cuddly."

"Yeah yeah, so are hundreds of people."

Richard drew back. He looked at her with the confused, tender expression which hurt Eva because he couldn't know what she wanted from him, when she herself didn't know.

"You see things differently than anyone else. You give me a conscience. You make me *think* about things."

It was the answer she always thought she wanted to hear from Richard, but she herself could no longer believe it was true. Or that it mattered even if it was true.

"I'm just really worried," she said. "I can't see any reason on earth why you would want to love me. It seems like I get by because of your support, your generosity, and I just plain don't have anything to offer."

"I think of us as a couple," said Richard. "When you're upset, so am I. I don't keep tabs on whose money is whose, how much I'm putting into this or how much you're putting into it. I'm being honest when I say what's mine is yours."

"That's kind of my point," said Eva. "You're even a better *person* than I am."

"Do you want me not to help out?"

"Of course not," said Eva. She was back to square one again. Of course she wanted him with her. Of course she didn't want him to be indifferent or callous.

They sat down on opposite ends of the bed. Richard started

changing into his pyjamas and Eva looked at his body as if seeing it for the first time, as if she had never felt his fine dryish skin before, or connected his moles with a felt pen, or felt his jaw bone pressed ardently against her cheeks or breasts.

"I'm feeling really inhibited," said Eva. "Strange, like I want to change in the bathroom."

"Yeah," said Richard. "I know what you mean."

He started cleaning his glasses.

"Oh no," said Eva in her dictator's voice. "It's the ritual cleaning of the glasses. Every night after you polish all your medals and have some peon lick your boots clean."

"I can't appear from my balcony unpolished," said Richard.

They looked at each other and started laughing. Their laughter sounded hollow to Eva though, as if they really were two strangers in a hotel room, or two old friends who were about to have sex for the first time.

The door handle rattled in the night. Any time someone on the floor stumbled to the w.c., their door shook. Richard stirred. "Weird dreams," he mumbled. "I keep hearing those sirens. The S.Q. was in my dream. They stopped me on some trumped-up charge somewhere outside of Quebec City, and I had no recourse." He wrapped his arms around her and drew himself close. She lay awake, feeling his heart beating like a little animal, and she held him, thinking of being in the hospital holding her mother, wondering why it had to be that the only times she experienced this kind of power, it had to be tinged with despair, the sense of holding someone's fragile life in her hands, feeling if she moved the wrong way or said the wrong thing, she could destroy someone. She wondered why it had to be that when she was strong, someone else had to be weak.

In the Málá Straná district, Eva passed an old house with a star-shaped plaque above the entrance in Czech, German, French and English, describing it as the house where Goethe might have lived if he had he ever lived in Prague. In one morning she had been confronted by palaces and consulates with carved portals, tiptoeing to see high proud windows and cornices glistening like ice, eye-level with lions' heads and heavy bronze door knockers, and then passing tiny houses she almost had to bend over to look at, tiny houses so old they were rounded at the edges: the plaster covering their brick or stone seeming to frost them. Eva consulted the book on Prague she carried in her bag and was delighted to discover people had given them names like, "At the Golden Star," or "Golden Tree."

Before coming to Prague, she read the story of John Nepomuk who refused to betray the Queen's confidences to King Wenceslas and was thrown off the Charles Bridge one night in 1393, into the dark waters of the Vlatav. The King's henchmen pushed back the people with their spears, but when the holy man disappeared into the waves, five small blue flames appeared on top of the water as a sign to the people. Statues of John Nepomuk presided over every dark corner where time had stopped, and Eva was excited to see the same story she had read, repeated on a plaque. These were exactly the kinds of stories, the kind of history she had hoped to find in Prague. It was a sly, miraculous and very human history, of an occupied people defying various forms of authority, from John Nepomuk right on down to the poor people naming their cottages, people holding on to their own in the best ways they knew how, and these were the stories that were passed on through the centuries so Eva could hear them too, whimsical defiance coming down the years and into the streets, working their way between the bricks and into the stone poetry of the architecture. Eva didn't know very much about Czech history but she thought she understood the stories better than she understood the grandeur in Paris, great deeds that might have been, great people adopted by the city whether or not they had ever even visited Prague.

While Eva was resting in a square a ragtag parade wended its way past her, a merry collection of jesters and minstrels, a man beating a big bass drum in a brightly coloured patchwork suit, and best of all an elephant that looked like Topo Gigio, distributing flyers advertising a brand new performance theatre. This seemed to Eva to be so connected with the stories she had read and the history all around her, she applauded. One of the jesters bowed, kissed her hand and gave her a flyer. She felt happier than she had in months, as if she herself was part of, and even contributing to the history of Prague. It finally felt as if something was right.

Wenceslas Square was vast, a boulevard rather than a square, and Eva imagined what it must have looked like in December during the Velvet Revolution. She was delighted to discover the King Wenceslas of the statue was the hero of the Christmas song. She had always been fascinated by that song, able to picture the king on horseback, the snow lying deep and crisp and even all around him, the poor man gathering winter fuel the same way that little couple in Karlovy-Vary had scooped up the coal. A woman tending a memorial at the statue, placed fresh flowers in the jars, wiped the plastic-wrapped photographs of people who had been killed in 1968, and straightened the vivid little shrines.

Eva wished she could do that for her mother. A photograph and a handmade cross were so much more poignant than straight rows of tombstones, a handful of wildflowers instead of decorously planted geraniums and shrubs. She supposed nothing short of a procession along a windswept field, mountains glooming in the distance, a holy man in ceremonial robe carrying a mysterious symbol, handfuls of earth, dirges and head-to-toe black would have satisfied her. When her time came, it was either that or to just walk into the river like Claude Jutra. She detested the stuffy little rooms full of polite chatter in funeral homes, more comfortable and sterilely middle class than anything she or her parents had ever lived in, with carpets muffling any sound of grief, the Kleenex box always at hand to absorb the pain.

She found Richard near the statue of King Wenceslas, taking pictures.

"There you are," he said. "I was a little worried you got lost."

"Like I can't walk across the street without you?" said Eva. She immediately regretted saying that and added, "Oh I did get lost, you know me. This street map I got at work is five years old and all the names have changed, which made everything fun."

"I got into a conversation with a German tourist about cameras. He had an old Leica, just like my father's," said Richard. "You didn't come across any postcard or souvenir shops in your wanderings, did you? I promised to send my parents and my grandmother postcards from Prague."

"I didn't see any," said Eva. "But I didn't even look. I don't have to send postcards any more. I could send some to friends, but it doesn't matter whether or not I do. I don't have to go to my hometown ever again, I don't have to remember anyone's birthday, I don't have to buy souvenirs, I don't have to do anything any more."

She hadn't meant to sound as if she was wallowing in self-pity. The thoughts had just come to her mind and she was sounding them out, feeling her way around them, trying to get used to the whole idea of living without mattering to someone else, to not have to take care of anyone simply because they were there, of not having anyone who *needed* her.

Richard kneaded her shoulder blades and although it felt good, she suddenly felt stifled, as if he had been sensing her thoughts and had come to stop them, to prevent any sort of release. She drew away from him sharply, almost able to hear a tearing sound, and headed blindly down the boulevard, knowing how hurt he must be, and that he didn't deserve this treatment, yet she was unable to stop herself. She noticed how the faded glory of the art deco "Hotel Europa" existing beside dingy department stores, more 1960s-style vodka advertisements, and the mood she had been in while looking at the statue and the shrines vanished, leaving her confused, disoriented. It was as if she couldn't reconcile the two sides of Prague. She didn't know if the glory of the Old Town disguised the bleak, uncertain present, or whether the Old Town was the real, true Prague, and the rest was temporarily imposed on it. It also felt to her as if Richard's sympathy had caused the great emotion she had felt in Old Prague to give way to a feeling of loss, of being trapped in a grey uncertain present. She couldn't even pretend to be a shadow of her old self if he was constantly pitying her.

Richard had been in an odd formal, even courtly mood since Wenceslas Square.

"I should have known you were upset," he said.

"You did nothing wrong," said Eva. "You never do. You were sweet—like you always are. I was mean to you—big surprise."

"I don't know what it's like. I've never lost anyone close. My grandmother is ninety-two."

She looked at his face. He had filled out since she first met him ten years ago. There was now a network of faint lines around his eyes, and the two lines extending from his nose to his chin were becoming ever deeper and more indelible, just as hers were. She had to think he looked happier, more content since they had become a couple. Ten years ago, she had advertised for a third roommate and he had shown up on her doorstep, thin and hungry-looking, his hair practically shoulder-length, wearing a jean jacket which was at least two sizes too large for him. She thought it must have taken her all of five minutes to fall in love with him. They moved eight times in ten years—together. For five years they both worked contract office jobs. Times were good when they both had high-paying contracts. Times were bad when they were both out of work, the lowest point coming when she had goaded him into chasing her around Place Ville Marie, and they had thrown the bank books at each other, neither wanting to take responsibility for their bleak financial state.

Then Richard got his MBA, became an associate professor in a management faculty, finally getting his PhD so he would be assured of being able to rise through the ranks. He had changed so much in ten years, thought Eva, and they were good changes. Friends often told her they had never seen a man who had flourished so completely being part of a relationship. But sometimes she found herself missing the old hungry Richard, and found the successful Richard oppressive. Her life hadn't changed in the slightest, she thought, except get worse.

"I can't take being nothing but a pathetic wretch any more. I just live on your charity and I can't stand it any more."

"You are not living on my charity."

She thought she detected a smug look to the set of his lips. He was developing a detached, above-it-all expression, and she felt an urge to hurt him, to wipe that look off his face.

"You've never thought of me as your equal, have you? I've always been your own private charity case, haven't I? Just someone to bug your mother, or give you comic relief from your stuffy professor friends. Maybe you figure you can score big points in the next life by being a saint to this big loser. I bet deep down, you secretly love this."

He placed his hands on her shoulders, and Eva found herself excited and aroused by the passion which appeared on his face, and in his voice.

"What brought this on? Just what crime against humanity have I committed anyway?"

"I'd rather live in a cardboard box in a park making speeches to innocent passersby than go on like this. I think we should split up. We're not a couple—just a host and a parasite. I'm leaving this hotel. I'm staying here in Prague. I could teach English. Yes, that is something I could actually do without your help."

She knew she had hurt Richard. The worst thing she could do was tell him their relationship was worthless. The biggest difference between them was, she thought, that he loved being part of a couple, and she loved Richard. If she ceased loving Richard, the relationship would end. Sometimes she suspected he could go on forever without ever wondering if he still loved her, Eva. His face became cold and he said, "Now you're just being silly."

"I've got news for you—people are silly. I'm leaving."

"There's an empty threat."

The door slammed when she left. She looked behind her and saw Richard following her. She started to run. Gradually he dropped back, then disappeared. The absurdity of it all finally hit her full force, and she wondered what the police would say if she flagged one down to complain about being pursued by a good man who wanted to help her. She could see it being a comedy in Paris, a farce with a happy ending, Eva knowing exactly how she felt and what she wanted from Richard, Richard understanding, and the two of them falling into each other's arms in the hazy twilight commotion at the Eiffel Tower. Here, she knew no one would understand her rejecting a man like Richard.

Eva felt watched as she made her way into the Old Town. The statues were more numerous than the people walking the streets. They stood on top of the highest buildings, lay down on the stone tombs, sat on horseback, adorned cornices like the figureheads of old ships. They stood in the hearts of fountains, glistening with water. Granite eye sockets shed tears of soot. She strolled down mysterious boulevards in the dusk, looking up at the narrow crooked houses with their charmed entrances, wishing she knew the word that would open the wooden doors and latched gates to her. Cobblestones shone as if they had risen from the sea. The moon came rolling out from behind the clouds and a golden weathercock pecked at the few small revealed stars. The rising moon filled the streets with a snowy light. Medallions above doors contained women's portraits and the moonlight brought them to life, their stone faces becoming tender to Eva, almost real flesh and blood.

Everything people had ever dreamed was right there in Prague, on buildings, in public squares; angels, demons, mystic rabbis, holy saints, every vision of heaven and hell was painted or carved or sculpted, and right in front of Eva's eyes, depending on which corner she turned. She knew she had walked around in circles when she again passed the statue of the crouching man whose hunted face looked exactly like Kafka's. He was frightening enough at noon, she thought. White lettering on a garage door "Garaz Neparkovat!" floated in front of her, looking like mirror writing. She thought of the first day when she returned to work after her mother's death, coming up from the depths of the Métro and noticing, as if for the first time, the office building she came out of was called "Aetna," a word that looked vaguely Greek, and that it might mean something if she could only find the right way of rearranging the letters. Feeling that way in Montreal had been alarming to her, yet in Prague it seemed natural.

Eva strolled down the Charles Bridge. There were plenty of tourists, but the crowds were not overwhelming, and Eva wasn't used to seeing so much space between groups. She stood in front of a black Christ with a sign saying "INRI," and some Hebrew words in gold hanging around the statue's neck like a Christmas garland. Eva had read the Jews had been forced to erect the statue and renounce their faith, but had slipped in some Hebrew words to the effect of "not really." She stood, thinking how it summed up everything she had seen in Prague.

It grew darker. Only a few vendors remained on the bridge, flicking matches and lighters to show their wares, one burning his hands while she selected an ink drawing. Making her way across the bridge, she passed some Czechs playing frisbee with Russian army hats. Someone tossed a hat to Eva, and she held it, unable to believe she could actually join in. Another Czech pretended to set his hat on fire and everyone roared with laughter. Without Richard, Eva suddenly felt free, as if she had emerged from a long convalescence. She pretended to stamp on her hat. She pounded her chest and strutted around, curling her finger under her nose as a moustache.

"Charlie Chaplin!" someone called out.

Someone flung her a general's hat with gold braid, and she put it on and postured, really imitating Charlie Chaplin. The Czechs couldn't stop laughing and neither could Eva. She thought of how this would probably not be happening if Richard were with her, and she laughed even harder as they did a Charlie Chaplin conga line down the bridge.

Some of the Czechs were calling things out, and Eva called out in English, in her dictator's voice, "Hell with the Russians! Hell with the Germans! Hell with Richard!" She didn't have to worry about slipping into her normal voice, or saying anything that could wound another person, or revealing too much, or appearing as if she was falling. She knew the Czechs couldn't understand her, and she didn't know exactly what they were calling out, but she felt they were united, and she could go on being Charlie Chaplin forever.

Lights switched off, the river flowed into history, jazz bands on the bridge continued to play softly in the dark. Eva stopped. Nowhere else had she ever felt such a feeling of transition, of sheer open vulnerability, uncertain celebration; emotions mingling the way darkness mingled with light. Pain and joy on the verge of turning into each other, it was that precarious, and it hurt that much. She continued walking toward the castle, past boutiques, antique and china shops. A group of Czechs just ahead of her suddenly, spontaneously started singing, in parts and harmonies, walking toward the castle, blazing against the black sky. She wanted to believe the poverty and scavenging she had seen was the illusion, and this beauty was what was real. She wanted to believe it was possible there would be a place in the world, where people could just start singing like this, and she could follow them to the ends of the earth, with tears streaming down her face, as if this was the most reasonable and natural thing in the world to be doing. She wanted to believe in the stories of resistance, of underdogs rewriting their own history, and it was exactly how she wanted to rewrite her own history, the difference she wanted to maintain between herself and Richard. As if just by playing Charlie Chaplin, or hearing the singing, she could believe in the validity of her own life. That her circumstances truly did not matter, but that she could, really could see, hear, touch, taste, and this could be enough. Just to exist could be enough.

Completely exhausted, she found the same restaurant where she and Richard had had morning coffee and afternoon lunch. Restaurants were still scarce enough that this one had become a real meeting place, although tourists sat on one side and Czechs on the other. She hesitated. After her experience on the Charles Bridge, she did not want to sit on the tourist side, but the Czechs were sitting in large interconnected groups, already deep in their own conversations. The tourists sat spaced apart from each other, and Eva felt she didn't have a choice.

The staff worked long hours. She was served by the same waitress she and Richard had this morning, and the same man was sitting in the bathroom, collecting his two crowns and handing out generous sections of toilet paper. Earlier at lunch, she and Richard had entered into a conversation with a jovial German man about the food and bathrooms. Eva's initial response to the man in the bathroom must have been quite visible, for the German man laughed and said, "That was my wife's reaction exactly." Now the man in the bathroom seemed as familiar to Eva as a co-worker. She thought of how the German man had saved the table for her and Richard, and in spite of his complaints, left an enormous tip without having to think about it.

A group of British students sitting near Eva compared records they had bought, rare albums at incredible bargain prices, by the sounds of it. Eva examined the menu. Dinner was a choice between goulash and steak. She chose the goulash. The British students all ordered ice cream desserts, which all of a sudden looked unbelievably enticing, and Eva requested the same. The waitress very apologetically told her the restaurant had run out of ice cream. "Sorry. No more. Gone," she said. Her expression was so much one of "I can't do anything" that Eva longed to tell the waitress, "No, you shouldn't be apologizing to me. I'm the one with the gargantuan North American appetite."

The waitress brightened up when Eva ordered a beer. "Now that's something I can provide," her face expressed. Eva was given an enormous pitcher for what would have been something like twenty cents, and the look of relief on the waitress's face made Eva ache. No wonder all the tables were laden with these pitchers. She was overcome by the same feeling she had in the mornings when every day it seemed as if there was another homeless person standing at the top of the escalator with his hand out, or bundled up on fetal position on the floor, and even if she gave them everything she had in her pocket every morning, it would not do a damn thing. She thought of Richard and wondered if there was really any difference between his kind fumbling attempts to help her, and the way she had been loving and pitying a poor but proud country, imposing her own self onto someone else's brave, creative underdog history. She was afraid she had made a terrible mistake, when Richard came in through the restaurant door.

To Eva, he looked just like he did the first time he had come to her apartment, his movements swift and direct, his black trenchcoat looking exactly like something he would have worn in the old days, even though she had picked it out herself.

"I was hoping you'd come back here," said Richard.

"I'm sorry," said Eva. "For all those things I said."

She saw his face soften, and she had always loved the way his face could almost imperceptibly change from being cool and distant to soft and tender, and how little it took to make it change. She remembered the way his heart had beat, how he had curled up as close to her as possible, how she had held him on that first night in the Savoy.

"Why the change of heart?"

"It's being here," said Eva. "The waitress's face, the police even—I can't explain it."

She started to tell Richard about her walk down the Charles Bridge, then picked up the hat from her lap and put it on her head.

Richard laughed. "Hah! They know a dictator when they see one."

"It has real gold braid."

"If you think I'm going to polish that every night…"

"No no no," said Eva. "You've got it all wrong. It's got your name inside it. They gave it to me to return to you. It must have fallen off your head in '68. That was before your head swelled to the size it is now."

They walked back to the hotel, placing the hat on each other's head, taking turns posturing and strutting. But Eva was almost in tears, because of how much she really wanted him, how much she needed him, how much she loved him. She also couldn't help being aware that they were the only two people who could afford to goose-step down a boulevard in Prague, wearing a dictator's hat.

¶

Stephen Henighan
from *Deserters*, 1985

The Border

FLASHLIGHT BEAMS SWAYED through the undergrowth like giddy signposts. Edward wavered, dropped to the ground. The beams yawed, then steadied, probing the foliage above Edward's head like long, diffuse fingers. Supple leaves and smooth bark turned waxen in the white light. Edward listened, trying to catch some sound of the men who were carrying the flashlights. He heard the whirring and chirping of insects, disruptions in the foliage, the unsteady rhythm of his own breath.

His hands sweated against the AK-47. The flashlight beams cut back and forth, back and forth. Edward, tensed, lifted the butt of the gun snug against his shoulder. His eyes strained. How many of them were out there?

He glanced around him. The men and women in his patrol were scarcely breathing. Many of them were adolescents; none was over twenty. He thought of Norma, who sat in his math class during the long hot days, completing her exercises faster than anyone else in the dirt-floored room and peppering him with questions about the world beyond Nicaragua: "Why don't they have a revolution in the United States, Don Eduardo?...What kind of car do you drive?...Are North American students fighting to end imperialism?" At night Norma, Javier and the rest would go to the outskirts of Latargo to do armed vigilance, waiting for the contras to come through the bush. Edward's students were at home with guns, had buried murdered classmates; they worked in their parents' houses, gave up schooldays to work in the fields; the girls slept with their boyfriends from their early teens and often had two or three children before they turned twenty. They all, constantly, asked Edward questions about *capacitación*—about improving themselves and learning new skills. After more than a year in Latargo, Edward still tried to regard these youngsters with detachment. He had come to Nicaragua to escape a collapsing marriage: fleeing commitment rather than seeking it. When visiting foreigners asked him why he was here, he would shrug his shoulders and say: "Look, I'm just here. It's no big deal, OK?"

On Edward's right the bush twitched. Edward pivoted, bringing around the levelled barrel of the AK-47. Then he lowered the gun. He could see the man who had moved. It was Javier, in whose mother's house Edward was living. Javier picked his way through the undergrowth, padding forward in a crouch, his lips pursed. Shadow lacquered Javier's Mayan face so that when he stopped, poised, scanning the night, Edward saw him as a mask, a hunter from another era incongruously outfitted in fatigues, digital watch and thick black hair that pushed from under his military cap and hooked around his ears.

Edward held his breath, watching the flashlight beams sawing through the humid darkness. Only a few minutes had passed since they had been jerked awake, scooped up their AK-47s and begun to creep quickly up the rough path leading from their encampment through the coffee plantation and on into the bush that ranged up to the Honduran border. The contras had turned on high-powered flashlights and waved the beams around, as Javier had warned Edward they might. It was a trick they used to give an exaggerated impression of their numbers; they would try to deter attack with a confusion of swinging beams until they had doused the coffee plants with gasoline and were ready to retreat behind a wall of flames. Edward remembered something else Javier had told him: one person in three turns and runs at the first sight of combat. Edward had never before been this close to battle. He looked across at Javier, but Javier had disappeared. Edward lowered himself into a duck-walk crouch and peered through the leaves, his AK-47 pointed into the darkness.

¶

Javier's mother's house was built of splintered grey boards that ran vertically from floor to ceiling; the front door closed in two wooden leaves, as did the shutters of the lone window. One of the shutters hung slightly askew, so that even when they were closed a crack of light crept in. A partition of pitted concrete ran three-quarters of the way across the floor, dividing the house into two rooms. Edward slept in a corner of the front room, his cot veiled by a sheet draped over a length of string. The floor was hardbeaten black earth, interrupted by the crowns of a few large boulders. The smaller back room gave onto a tiny yard where Javier's mother, Luisa, cooked on an open fire under a lean-to surrounded by unkempt grass. Luisa was a dark-skinned middle-aged woman who wore threadbare dresses hung over a bony frame. She could silence her family—she had two sons and a daughter at home in addition to Javier—without raising her voice above a whisper. Luisa's husband had been a heavy drinker; five years ago, shortly after beginning to work as an organizer for a newly formed women's cooperative, she had chased him out of the house with a smoldering stick from her cooking fire. She spoke of her victory over her husband and the revolution's victory over the dictatorship in the same breath, frequently in the same words, as *el triunfo*. "Since the triumph many things have changed," she would say, and Edward never knew whether she was describing her private life, or the world around her.

❡

Edward stopped short. A flashlight beam had snapped to life directly in front of him. This shaft of light was much closer than the others. He could see the glare diffusing through the dank night, the humidity picking the beam apart particle by particle. A mistiness wrapped the limbs of the trees. For a moment Edward was dazed. He dropped to his knees, lifted the AK-47 to his shoulder and reached his finger around the trigger. The weapon's unremembered weight made Edward's shoulders ache.

On his right, Edward half-heard half-saw Javier sliding, rolling, stealthy as an uncoiling snake, toward him. Javier covered the half-dozen paces that separated them without making a sound. Arriving alongside Edward in a deep crouch, he pressed his mouth to Edward's ear and whispered in a barrage of hot breath: "We can surround this one, cut him off from the others."

Edward shook his head. He whispered into Javier's ear: "Won't that scare them? They'll start burning the coffee, no?"

"They'll do that anyway." Javier paused. "OK, let's wait a minute."

Javier slid away through the leaves. Edward released a long, half-smothered sigh: he had bought himself a few seconds. He breathed greedily, his finger balanced against the trigger of the AK-47.

When he looked up a second flashlight beam had joined the beam closest to him. He watched the two fraying channels of light dousing the bush; the other beams remained farther back, a glowing haze deep in the undergrowth. Two beams, Edward thought. Did that mean two contras or twenty? Should he wait or attack? He sat breathing in a deep crouch. The men and women in his patrol seemed to be drawing closer together. On his left, amid shadow made denser by contrast with the sweeping flashlight beams, Edward could make out Norma's silhouette, her peaked cap and heavy curls. He had seen that silhouette one evening in the window of the house—recently overhauled by a government home improvement project—where Norma lived with her mother. The project was taking a long time to reach Luisa's end of the street. Luisa was outspokenly, cuttingly, envious of Norma's mother's good fortune: brick walls, a stone tile floor, steel sheet roofing, even a battered television set that Norma and her mother had somehow saved the money to buy; on the wall above the television hung a garish plastic bust of Jesus Christ and a somber red and black portrait of Sandino, Nicaragua's national hero, wearing the inevitable broad-brimmed hat. In the house, Norma helped her mother with her younger brothers and sisters, looked after a child of her own by a boy who had died the year before in a contra mortar attack, and convened meetings of the local Sandinista Youth. Now her silhouette dissolved, bowed low, disappeared. She pulled herself alongside him, her eyes liquid in the darkness. "What d'we do?" she hissed, her mouth close to Edward's ear.

"Wait," Edward mouthed. Drawing his face close to Norma's hair, he whispered: "Wait till others join these two. Unless they start burning the coffee."

Norma slipped away. She knew infinitely more about fighting than Edward did, but because he was her teacher, her *profe*, she came to him for advice. Norma, like his other students, conceived learning as part of the revolutionary process; as their *profe*, Edward found himself accorded a kind of mystical authority that was completely foreign to him. He watched Norma's shadow slowly sliding from view. Her profile popped into sight a short distance away, then melded into the night. The smell of her body lingered in the humid air. It was the smell of crowded Nicaraguan country buses: the musty, almost honey-like odor of poverty, unwashed flesh, caked sweat and dust-impacted clothing. Ahead of

Edward, the flashlight beams continued to swivel silently. Edward shuffled three half-steps toward the source of the light, keeping his head low, achingly conscious of each tiny scuff of sound that his boots pawed from the earth. The humid night air insinuated itself like oil between Edward's hands and the AK-47: his palm slipped on the barrel, the trigger grew slick beneath his finger. The silence was unbearable. He could feel his testicles contracting until they were as small and hard as acorns. He padded forward on hands and knees, brought himself to a crouch and waited.

¶

The year before, a few weeks after his arrival in Latargo, Edward had worked in the coffee harvest for the first time. The harvest was grueling. The people around Edward worked with a stamina he could not hope to match. They seemed impervious to the staggering heat, oblivious to the weight of the sun and the pricking, buzzing and biting of a multitude of insects. Edward slogged through each day, determined not to quit before the week was up. The fiery pesticides with which Nicaraguan farmers drenched their crops made Edward's head spin and put him off his food. Each night two or three members of the harvest crew would do vigilance, everyone else's safety depending on the ability of these two or three individuals to remain awake and alert through the night after spending the day in the fields. Edward, who had no militia training, was excluded from this duty. To compensate, Javier did double vigilance, going an extra night without sleep. After the harvest had ended and Luisa had dispatched the lice from his hair by shaving his skull almost bald, Edward enrolled in a militia training course. He spent three weeks waking early, hiking up and down hillsides in the heat, taking apart, reassembling and firing AK-47s, practicing hand-to-hand combat with peasant women and students. Edward's instructor in the course, a stocky young man in combat fatigues, reinforced his lectures by flourishing an instruction manual which, it soon emerged, he could barely read. But at the end of the three weeks Edward felt at home with a gun in his hands. This year, during his second January in Latargo, Edward was again working in the coffee harvest in the hills above the town. The hand-over-hand movement required to pick the beans still wore him down; his sole attempt to heft a full bag of undried coffee beans ended in back-straining failure. This year, though, he would be able to take his turn doing vigilance.

¶

The humidity was suffocating him. He faltered forward, his back hunched. The flashlight beams seemed only inches away.

He was knocked off his feet. A detonation lifted the earth around Edward's boots: his ears stung, wet foliage slapped him in the face. He lay on the ground, winded, his cheeks stiff with pain from the fall. A volley of shots erupted, like the beating of a jackhammer; Edward's eardrums recoiled. More shots exploded: there was a cry, then another and a prolonged moan that rose to a whimper. More shots: one of the two flashlight beams in front of Edward toppled like a felled tree. The haze of beams farther back in the bush was extinguished: the contras were no longer trying to ward off attack. Now they were shooting to kill. Edward felt his flanks, clapped his hands over his forehead, touched his face anxiously until he was certain that he had not been wounded by the grenade explosion that had knocked him off his feet. He slithered forward, poking the AK-47 awkwardly in front of him. More gunfire: he could hear the bullets tearing through the leaves above his head. He had lost his sense of direction, didn't know where the contras' flashlights had been or where the men and women in his patrol had gone. Then, off to his right, he saw a crouched figure that looked like Javier. He heard Javier's AK-47 unleash a whining barrage of shots, setting off a chaotic, earsplitting response. The bush resounded with a furious, confused pounding. Edward ducked through a veil of leaves and staggered as automatic rifle fire exploded around him. He dropped to the ground, clapped the butt of the AK-47 against his shoulder and squeezed the trigger. The gun buckled against his shirt. Edward kept shooting until the gunfire around him began to subside; a moment later it kicked into life again, harsher and angrier, deeper in the bush.

Keeping his body low, Edward stumbled forward. He tripped over something heavy and soft, and forced himself to keep moving through the dark wet foliage. He stumbled against Javier, who sat crouched over another stretched body. He stopped.

It was Norma. She lay on her side, twisting in pain.

"*Profe*," she moaned. "*Mi profe.*"

Javier, crying, turned toward Edward.

"*Profe.*..." Norma murmured, her black curls darker than the ground beneath her.

"I'm here," Edward said. "Look, I'm right here." He crouched beside her, shaking his head. Only a few minutes ago he had been asleep. Now he was wide awake. A spasm of pain wrenched Norma's body away from him; she ground her face against the earth. The sprig of a coffee plant overhung her shoulders and head, veiling her with long, ruffled-edged leaves flowering from soft bark. Edward laid his hand on Norma's shoulder, steadying her. He felt her muscles knotting with pain beneath his palm; the musty smell of her body enveloped him. She blinked, her eyes suddenly clear in the darkness. "*Mi profe*," she said.

Gunfire hacked through the matted branches, cutting closer. Edward strained to locate the path over which they would have to carry Norma, down through the coffee plantation to the encampment. But the undergrowth had folded shut behind him in a wall of silent leaves; the way back had disappeared.

¶

Hugh Hazelton
from *Crossing the Chaco*, 1981

Serra do Roncador

I am coming to you
  down from the mountains
  mist rising in myriad
  pillars from the jungle

I am coming to you
  the bridge is washed out
  we all get down from the truck
  and rebuild it with loose rock

I am coming to you
  through tall, cooling palms
  and giant ferns
  smelling fresh with rain

I am coming to you
  the trucker's helper is chanting to him
  "don't go to sleep, don't go to sleep"

I am coming to you
  waiting in a river port
  playing poker with the hotel keeper and his cronies

I am coming to you
  on a boat's tin roof
  the smokestack deafening
  lying staring up at the Amazon sky
  next to the carcass of a wild hog
  drying in the sun

I am coming to you
  five days hitching and on mud-covered buses
  watching them chop down the forest
  daydreaming, dozing off

I am coming to you
  with an aging face and hands of failure
  filled with plans and impossible desires
  and a battered, resurgent faith

I am coming to you
  because you love
    and demand justice and love for others
  because you spend hours wading in tidal pools
    watching the forms of life
  because making love we cease to exist
  because you exist
I am coming to you

Sertão ou Selva

dawn
filters through
the boards of the truck

your face
turned toward me
in a slat of faint light
sleeping

I don't know where we are

¶

Ann Lambert
from *Parallel Lines*, 1991

Act One, Scene Six

Spot on RAMON.

RAMON: *(To audience)* I came to America. I came to America when there was nothing left for me in Salvador. I left the university to teach at a tiny school in a tiny village. Teaching is a very...suspicious occupation in my country. *(Beat)* One day, the soldiers came, and they took me back to the capital, San Salvador. *(Beat)* I denounced them all...all the names...even the ones I didn't know. *(Pause)* When I came to America, there was nothing left for me in Salvador. My world was brand new, like the hundreds of shiny cars I see everywhere here. *(Beat)* But it is different to arrive when you have no choice. I am not an immigrant, with big eyes and an open heart. I am a refugee. I washed dishes until I could only dream about dishes, higher and higher mountains of them, never finished, never clean. I scraped enough food off those plates every day to feed that village for a month. *(Beat)* One day, I went to drink in the bar next door to the restaurant. I wanted to drink until I couldn't see those dishes any more. I found her there. She had the look of someone who looks for her soul in a bottle. I recognized that look.

Spot fades on RAMON.

Lights up on RAMON *and* LINDA. *They are sitting on two stools, facing the audience. She's not drunk yet, but well on her way.*

LINDA: I mean, do you *know* how many people in this city...no...this *planet* make a living *serving* people? It's scary...Not *doing* anything, not *producing* anything useful, not *creating* something...except enough money to claw their way to another day. Claw their way to another day...I like that! *(Beat)* It's not like those suits on Wall Street *do* anything either. They just chase bits of paper around, and make a fortune. Go figure. And...and...when they get nervous?

When they panic, cause they're like sheep, they all scare at the same time…the rest of the world has to pay for it. I know…my Dad was in the business. Drank himself to the Big Stock Exchange in the Sky. *(Beat)* Us…service people have got to organize. Everyone else is…*organized.* That bastard has fired an army since I worked there. No job security. No benefits. You break a leg and they may as well shoot you. It's just such a *piss-off.*… *(Beat) (Leans on* RAMON *'s shoulder)* Listen to me. Do you even know what "piss-off" *means?*

RAMON: Not the words exactly, but the feeling is clear.

LINDA: I'm surprised to see you here. Thought you turned into a pumpkin at five o'clock. You're always racing outa the restaurant before anyone sees you go. Can't say I blame you. You want another beer? Frank! Ramon, this is Frank. Best bartender in the city. No, I mean it. I don't say that for nothing. Frank, this is Ramon, our dishwasher. Ramon's from…Where're you from again?

RAMON: El Salvador—

LINDA: Right! Nor…tega's your President?

RAMON: No. You confuse us with Nicaragua and…Panama.

LINDA: And you guys are the Communists?

RAMON: Nicaragua is Communist. Well, what Americans call Communist. Salvador is Fascist.

LINDA: It's a real mess down there, isn't it? I mean, they shoot you for looking the wrong way.

RAMON: Some are killed for their ideas. Some for nothing at all.

LINDA: At least you die for…something there. Here we die for… Leather jackets—

RAMON: And I read…for these…high-heel sneakers?

LINDA: High tops! Yeah! *(Beat)* I wonder what I would die for.…If I'd die for…*anything.* I guess if I fought for something for a long, long time…and someone wanted to take it away. It's hard to imagine…I never fought for anything—

RAMON: This…I don't believe.

LINDA: No…never. I've never wanted something badly enough. It's a waste of time. Waste of energy.

RAMON: Sometimes you have no choice.

LINDA: You know, I'd *love* to have no choice. You know what I mean? I'd love to be...forced to fight for something I could *die* for. Nobody here cares enough. I mean you *see* things right in front of your nose, but it feels like it's happening far, far away. It's like your life just follows this...track, just follows these lines...parallel to everything else. But you don't touch. *(Beat)* Maybe I'd die for my kids. Yeah.

RAMON: You have children?

LINDA: Are you kidding? No, no, no...Jesus. That's all I need. I just got rid of a deadbeat boyfriend. Well, not just. A year ago. A musician. Too sensitive to find a job. Christ, they attract me like flies to shit. *(Beat)* You have kids?

RAMON: *(Beat)* No.

LINDA: Married? Girlfriend?

RAMON: No.

    Lights face on RAMON *and* LINDA. RAMON *to audience.*

RAMON: We drank and talked, drank and talked, the alcohol working like the oil in an engine. Everything coming smoother. *(Beat)* She was the first...American who really looked at me. I told her the iguana story. The iguana and Jacobo. Jacobo was my best friend, and godfather to my children. Yes, I had three children. Two of them is still alive.

    Lights back up on RAMON *and* LINDA. *She is drunker.*

LINDA: So I quit college and started out on my own. *(Beat)* My parents never got over it. I mean, they *did* everything right. I wasn't supposed to end up a waitress.

RAMON: What were you supposed to be?

LINDA: Oh, Christ, Anything but *that.* I tried a few things. I could never...finish what I started. Now, I just don't...start any more.

RAMON: A waitress is so bad?

LINDA: My mother still pretends it isn't true. When her friends ask her what I'm doing, she says I'm finishing my studies. They must wonder. I guess, in a way, it's true though. I study. *(Beat)* I can't talk to them any more. My brother's a born-again Christian. You know, they take the Bible seriously. Jesus is gonna float back down here with a big sword and kill all us pagans. Then all the true believers will get yanked from their cars on the freeway, or wherever they are, and get sucked up to heaven. They believe this. I mean, *you* try to reason with them. Oh, shit. You religious?

RAMON: At one time. I have seen on the subway…advertisements that say the Madonna appeared to a young boy in…Queens? I thought she came to me once. But she disappeared when I stopped drinking.

LINDA: *(Laughing)* Oh, yeah. You got to be careful with hallucinations. *(Beat)* God's on T.V. everyday, if you want to watch—

RAMON: On these talking programs? I saw the eyes of God, once. In the face of a soldier. They were eyes with no history, no memory. *(Beat)* I didn't like his eyes. *(Beat)* My neighbors here watch T.V. all day. They don't *do* anything, they just watch. I don't like these shows that tell you when to laugh—

LINDA: Sitcoms. You don't have the same thing at home?

RAMON: Oh yes…Stupidity is universal.

LINDA: *(Beat)* Why did you leave? Never mind. Dumb question. Cause you had to, I guess.

RAMON: *(Beat)* There was an…offensive. Army offensive against our town. To…clean it up. The soldiers chased us from one side, and the helicopters waited on the other. It is called a hammer and…anvil operation. We were chased to a river, hundreds of us, terrified, mortars dropping around us. I ran and I ran and I found a tree to hide under. It was so loud. I thought my head would explode. Then I felt a terrible pain in my back and I screamed, "I am shot, I am shot! "My friend Jacobo was behind me, and I hear him laughing, like a crazy man. The helicopters had scared an iguana from the tree, and it was hanging from my back, its claws ripping into my skin. *(RAMON starts to laugh)* A stupid iguana! *(LINDA laughs)* We laughed about that for many weeks after. *(Beat)* We shit our pants laughing. *(Beat)* It's a long time since I think of this.

LINDA: *(They look long and hard at each other.)* Do you want more? Beer?

RAMON: Yes. I buy.

Lights fade on bar. Over, a pulsing sound. Louder and louder a helicopter. Lights up on RAMON *and* LINDA *at her apartment. There is a bed, scattered beer bottles. Lights are very low, so they are seen in shadow. They start to kiss, then grab at each other, very hungry, tearing each others' clothes off. They fumble around drunkenly. Then, they are making love.*

RAMON: *(Voice over. Throughout lovemaking)* Dear Carmen…I am having trouble to think tonight. You cannot imagine the noise here…louder than the market on Saturday afternoon. Remember our demented roosters? How they would crow in the middle of the night and drive me crazy? Here it is the scream of ambulances, the voices of cars. Are the children all right? Do you understand why I had to leave? It was the shame I felt when I looked into their eyes. The shame that made me question what I did. Even the good things. *(Beat)* There is so much here! If you spent all day dreaming of all the things you could ever want, you could not begin to fill the stores. Everything is so clean. It is like big MacDonald's like we saw in Mexico. Blue eyes and blond hair. But, underneath, much is very…dirty. Here, it is not a crime to be poor. But it is a disgrace. Something you have brought upon yourself. I try not to think of Tono. I know Juan said it was God's will, and we cannot blame Him. Blaming God takes the guilt away from those who should be punished. Sometimes I dream of having another baby to take his place. Forgive me. I could not live with the fear any more. I am not courageous like you. *(Beat)* I told them…things. I told them. Jacobo is *dead* because of me. You can't cry in front of them. You can't cry because…frailty gives them courage. It nourishes them. They are empowered by it. *(Beat)* She is the first woman I have touched since you. I need to touch someone so much it frightens me. Tell the children. Tell them I am still their father. I miss you, Carmen. Your husband. Your compañero. Your husband, Ramon.

Lights dim, then rise up. LINDA *stumbles to her feet.*

LINDA: I know I 've got one beer left in the fridge. Share? *(She sits by*

RAMON. *Strokes him.)* How did you get these scars? What happened to you?

RAMON: *(Beat)* I have a wife. I have two children.

¶

Kathleen McHale

from *Description of Light*, 1991

Sunset's veil falls on desert colors,
charcoals, red and yellow ochres,
buff-colored sand and sage.
Grey green trees, pinyon pines briefly
wear muted tones, then
full bright again beneath sheer
billowing curtains of light and dark;
a shifting palette.
Every window frames
a deliberate composition.

I take off my dress and lie
on the hot sand when
no one is near; I
try to press myself
into it. I hold the sand
in my hands,
use a mortar and pestle to grind soil and
then mix it with linseed oil
and try to paint with it.
Colors here have settled
behind my eyes;
wind has driven them
through my skin, into
my joints;
brushstrokes as close
as my lips forming sound.

Hills sleep
around my adobe home;

umbers, greys and shadowy blues lie
lightly on waves of sand. They seem…
to draw close then
fall away.
Silence breathes evenly in
silken domain; a vast sea of stillness.

I'll be with you again soon
Alfred.
I imagine you
reading my letters
in the study at
the farmhouse. Your day's traces
echo even here.
I move with care through my hours
confident now
that the chords of my days
vibrate
in your inner ear.

1945
I watch the world
through holes in desert bones;
sky, mountains, fabric flowers and the moon
appear in my telescope
of pelvic bones. Animal bones I have found.
I fix images
one by one
in lasting frames.
My artifacts have visited death
and returned to sandy bloom.
Sky seen through this aperture
is a fragile blue sapphire.

Gas is rationed, butter too.
Los Alamos is forty miles away but
sifts like black ash
into shop counter conversations.
The world beyond me
is visiting death.

I scrape my palette clean,
take pigment from new tubes and
wash my brushes twice.
The weight of my task sleeps like lead
behind my ribs.
I paint a flaming red sky seen
through gold bones.
Maria turns on the radio;
flesh is falling off
burning bones
somewhere in Japan.

¶

Nino Ricci
from *Rita*, 1987

Snake

EXCEPT FOR A NEW COAT OF PAINT here and there on a door or window frame, via San Giuseppe had probably not changed much in over a century, the same shadows shrinking and stretching with the movement of the sun, the same cobblestoned quiet hedged in by balconies and thick stone walls and resting its sleepy head against the doorway to history. On a summer day, with the sun just past its apex, you would find the street almost deserted, all the villagers either comfortably snoozing in their homes after their noonday meal or stretched out in some shady bower in the fields, munching on bread and provolone. On July the fifteenth, though, in the year 1956, one small boy had ventured into the sun and was sitting cross-legged now on the stone bench in front of his grandfather's house, a book called *Principi Matematici* open in his lap to page 3.

I had not done well on my grade one exams. The teacher had sent me home with a note:

Vittorio Innocente è intelligente ma falso. *Pero, se la signora non si interesse alla sua educazione, non ce niente a fare.*

'*Falso*' was the dialect word for 'lazy.' I was lazy but showed some potential. The teacher blamed my mother for failing to rein me in. She was still sore about the smoking incident.

My mother shook her head and laughed when she read the letter.

"Well, next year we're going to show la maestra, eh, signor Innocente? When you grow up you're going to be a pope, so I can live like a queen in my old age. This summer you can catch up on all the lessons you missed while you were out chasing sheep with Fabrizio."

Hence the *Principi Matematici*. Which, however, I was not attending to. I had slipped into one of those states of passive indolence which were very common at that time of year, especially when it was one o'clock and the sun was shining and the whole world seemed wrapped in a warm, yellow dream. My grandfather had gone up to Di Lucci's for a digestif— Di Lucci, a true entrepreneur, must have been the only person in Italy who didn't close up shop during siesta, and would take his own lunch downstairs in his back room instead of upstairs with his family to make sure he didn't miss any customers. His initiative had paid off—Di Lucci owned the only car in Valle del Sole, a somewhat battered 1952 Fiat Cinquecento, which he had bought used in Rocca Secca and which he parked prominently next to his bar, not heeding the warnings of his wife about the *invidia* it was likely to inspire there.

My mother had received a letter that morning from the *postino.* I had gotten a look at the envelope—neat, legible script in bright blue ink, and Italian stamps. But when my grandfather had asked her who it was from, my mother had said that it was from my father. Who else ever sent letters to my mother? After lunch, my mother had slipped out of the house, making me promise to sit still in the kitchen and study my books.

"Where are you going?" I asked.

"I have an appointment."

"With who?"

"With the man who cuts the birdies off of boys who ask too many questions."

Always joking, my mother.

After trying unsuccessfully to study in the kitchen, I had come out finally to my place on the stone bench. My attention was now fixed on a cluster of goat droppings. A swarm of flies hovered around it, the braver ones alighting and calling out to their friends, "It's goat, but it's not bad!" They rubbed their hands together the way my uncle Pasquale did when he sat down to a plate of pasta al' uovo.

A flock of sheep came around the corner from the direction of the square. Behind them walked old Angelo Danello—The Red, we called him, because his father had once been to Russia; though many years of faithful drinking had helped him conform to his name, for his face and nose were bright with broken blood vessels. He moved with the measured nonchalance of someone who had nowhere special to go, slapping his sheep stick against a loose pant leg as he walked. The horde of flies around the goat droppings rose in unison as the sheep approached.

"Ho, Vittó," Luigi called out as he passed. "*Ma che fai, dormi o vivi?*"

"I'm studying my mathematics," I said, opening my eyes wide and flipping a page. "I'm going to be a pope."

"A pope! Why settle for a pope? Why not Jesus Christ himself?"

This possibility had never occurred to me.

I stared after Angelo as he ushered his flock up the street. Not far beyond my grandfather's house the cobblestones ended and the road deteriorated into a dirt path. A thin cloud of brown dust rose up from the ground as the sheep moved onto the dirt, and the sheep's bleating turned hoarse, as if they were choking. At the Fonte di Colle di Papa, Angelo stopped for a moment, cupped his hand under the spout, and brought some water to his mouth.

As the bleating of Luigi's sheep grew distant and small, I turned my eyes back towards the black and white silence of my book. I turned another page, relieved for a moment by the taut crinkling of paper, but found myself confronted again by another page of odd pictures and symbols. One black apple plus one black apple equals two black apples. Then, underneath, these strange markings: $1 + 1 = 2$. The book seemed to be arguing that I make some connection between the apples and the markings underneath them, but the sun, reflecting off the white page and filling my eyes with sleep, was arguing otherwise. Slowly my eyelids drooped and closed, while a happy host of apples and numbers, freed from the tyranny of the book, danced in my head in wild combinations.

I was awakened by a muffled shout.

The shout—it sounded like a man's—had seemed to come from the stable. I set down my books and started down the steps at the side of the house—the house had been cut into a slope, so that the stable, which lay underneath the kitchen, was buried on the street side but opened out at ground level in back. But when I rounded the corner at the bottom of the steps I stopped short. The stable door was closed, but through a crack at the bottom of it, a small, tapered head was flicking its tongue—a snake. I had seen it just in time, and now I stood frozen as it slithered long and slim through the crack in the door and down a row of tomatoes in my grandfather's garden. I stared after it, watching the tomato vines rustle in its wake, until sound and motion disappeared, finally, into the ravine at the edge of the garden.

Snakes, in Valle del Sole, had long been imbued with special meaning. You could hear any number of snake stories around the village, Snake and the Maiden, Snake and the Frog, Snake and Umberto Lotto, a nineteenth-century *padrone* who had no sooner raped his young daughter than he was bitten by a snake and dropped dead. There was a saying in Valle del Sole, "*Dove l'orgoglio se ne va, la serpe sta.*" Snake comes before a fall. It was pro forma in Valle del Sole to make a sign of the cross whenever a snake crossed your path.

But the villagers' views on snakes were not completely consistent. No doubt if they had been pressed most of them would have cited the Bible as their authority, not realizing that even the Bible was not entirely clear on this point: after all there were two versions of creation in the opening chapters of Genesis, two origins, different worlds which parted, perhaps, forever, one fallen but one still serpentless and sublime. And then there were traces in the villagers' beliefs that stood outside biblical tradition, predated it. There were those, for instance, who saw the snake not as a symbol of evil but as a fertility figure, and who refused to kill snakes, fearing it would ruin their harvest. They believed the snake's ability to shed its skin was proof of its immortality, and sometimes bought old snake skins from *la strega* in Rocca Secca, which they ground into powder and spread over their fields. There were other variations, more complex, those who thought a snake crossing you from the right brought good fortune, from the left, bad; others who saw two snakes, the evil brown and the sacred green. There were even a few heretics who thought that a snake was just a snake. But the orthodox view held that Snake was a direct agent of the evil eye.

The snake that had crossed my path had been green, but it had come from the left. In my excitement I forgot to cross myself, and it was a moment too before I remembered the strange shout that had aroused me from my sleep. Now when I turned back to the stable door I saw that it had been opened slightly, and that two dark eyes were staring down at me from the shadows. I could make out no features of the figure they belonged to—only those two eyes, drinking up the darkness around them and concentrating their energies on me as if to make me disappear by sheer force of will. I was just about to turn and run when the stable door opened a few inches further, and the two eyes suddenly swooped out of the stables like swallows, rushing towards me. But as they caught the sunlight they underwent a magical transformation: they turned suddenly a sharp sky blue, like two bright flames, and the sight of them filled my head, burning away all the other features of the figure that was bearing down on me.

My only thought now was escape. But as I turned to run my legs got tangled together and I fell to the stony ground. I lay still for a moment on my stomach, waiting in terror for whatever had come out of the stable to pounce on me, my arms crossed over my head to shield me. But the blow did not come; and a moment later the sound of cracking twigs and moving branches behind me told me that something had followed the snake into the ravine.

For a moment I sat where I had fallen, waiting for the pounding in my head to subside and rubbing my scraped palms to ease their pain. Then I went up to the stable door and cautiously pulled it fully open, not daring yet to step inside. As the door opened, a shaft of sunlight gradually stretched into the stable, coming to rest at my mother's sandalled feet. She was standing over the low wall of the pig pen, pouring a bucket of water into the pig's trough, a lantern burning pale blue beside her. Her dress was wrinkled, and I noticed a piece of straw hanging in her hair. She turned as I came in.

"Vittorio," she said casually, setting her bucket on the ground. "I thought you were studying your mathematics."

"I heard someone shouting," I said.

"Oh, that was nothing. I saw a snake."

"It was a man's shout."

My mother fixed her eyes on me and made a characteristic movement with her lips, a pursing together and a drawing to one side.

"What did you see when you came down here?" she said. Something in her tone told me that I should think carefully before answering her question.

"I saw a snake coming out of the stable," I said cautiously.

My mother smiled and crouched down beside me.

"Don't be afraid," she said. "Maybe other people will ask you what you saw, too. What will you tell them?"

I stared down at the ground. Question and answer: so much of my world was formed this way, from grade one catechism forward, the orderly arrangement of facts, the suppression of some, the bringing into prominence of others. My mother now was asking me to pick and choose, to tell a story that began with a snake, but ended with her standing calmly before me, as if nothing had happened.

"Only a snake," I said, still not looking at her. "That's all I saw."

My mother stood over me a moment, then bent to plant a kiss on my forehead. I had said the right thing, then. And now that I had said it I began to wonder if I really *had* seen anything more, if the afternoon sun had not simply been playing tricks on me. It had all happened so quickly that for a moment it was just possible to believe that those blue eyes had been some strange aberration that could not be explained through any of the usual rules by which things happened, like a miracle. It would not be until the next day, when I came down to take out the sheep, that I would find the pair of tinted glasses in the straw, the same kind that I had lost in the river the year before.

But now something else had caught my attention.

"Mamma," I said, "there's some blood on your foot." I had noticed two small red spots, like pin pricks, on her ankle.

My mother bent down and passed a finger over the little drops, smearing them across her skin.

"Oh, Christ," she said, taking a deep breath. "Vittorio, run up quickly to Di Lucci's and get him to bring his car. Tell him I've been bitten by a snake."

¶

Daniel McBain
from *Art Roebuck Comes To Born With A Tooth*, 1987

Chapters 4, 5

IDA MISSED TALKING WITH SARAH the way she had with Hartland at age four. She did not explain about the dead battery as she backed the truck up the grain elevator ramp, how the engine would not turn over unless popped into gear while the truck was rolling. It would have seemed pointless to comment on the heavy snow, the cold, the darkness, or the new white colour of the elevator, which used to be orange. She recalled mentioning similar trivialities before Hartland was able to engage in proper conversation; she had since grown used to remarking these kinds of details alone in her mind.

Sarah stood quietly on the truck running board while her mother dug a cookied Kleenex from her windbreaker and wiped the girl's nose. Ida wound the child's soft blue scarf around her face and throat, pulled her parka hood over the matching wool toque and led her by the hand down the steps from the elevator and along the train tracks. All without saying a word.

Ida stopped on the train platform. She set her parcel of paperback books on the bench armrest, opened her purse and took out a mirror and lipstick. The round mirror, reflecting the Via Rail clock light, cast a pale moon on her face. As she rubbed on the lipstick something caught her eye in the mirror. A man was jogging down Main street. He was lugging something over his shoulder that resembled a huge gray potato. Ida turned and stared at the running figure while Sarah shuffled around the platform, collecting wet March snow on the toes of her boots. The man disappeared behind the elevator. Sarah stooped for a mittful of snow and put it to her mouth.

The boxcars were unfamiliar to Ida. Neither cocoa-coloured grain cars nor heavy equipment flatbeds, these cars were brightly painted murals: dancing poodles dressed in tutus and hats; a bald man in leopard skin holding a barbell suspending a pair of Shetland ponies; an adult-looking boy, eyes closed, touching the forehead of a man on crutches; and a two-headed calf whose four eyes stared sympathetically at Ida and Sarah. Glittering blue firework-stars sparkled throughout the designs, trailed by red and white streamers.

A sign on the front car read:

COLONEL WINCHESTER'S TRAVELLING CARNIVAL
ANIMAL ACTS
GAMES OF CHANCE
FEATS OF STRENGTH
LITTLE DOTHAN, CHILD HEALER OF SICK, LAME

Ida took Sarah's hand and trotted briskly toward the gray hump of the Centennial Arena. An auto-repair lantern faintly illuminated a sign of which Ida could discern,

ring Ag cul l air

the other letters splattered with sticky snow. Now and then the door opened and a thin light ushered in a few silhouettes.

Just then the man with the large—duffel bag?—scooted under the lavender beam of a mercury vapour streetlight, flung wide the rink door and backed into the cold light inside.

At the rink Myrtle de Havilland took Ida's three dollar admission and stamped a bird's footprint on the back of her hand. "It's all the Co-op Store had in the way of rubber stamps," she explained, pulling off Sarah's mittens and letting them dangle from their idiot-string while she printed a meandering trail of bird tracks across her knuckles. Sarah examined the tracks while the women chatted. She flattened her thumb over one of the marks and inspected the purple rings in her thumbprint, then put the berry-purple ink to her tongue. She did not grimace, as though she had known all along it would taste awful.

Ida pretended, for the moment, not to notice Louise Bronfman and Margaret Rose who were working at the food counter. Each time Ida encountered these two women she was grilled endlessly about James: Had there been any improvement? Had he shown any sign of recognizing Ida or Hartland? There was always an oblique reference to Warren, asking if he was still helping out with the farm work, conspicuously forgetting he was the father of Ida's daughter. Though they always spoke sweetly to Sarah.

A flea market had been set up in the refreshment area. Ida strolled through the picnic-style tables, looking at the mishmash of goods people had brought to get rid of: a French-English dictionary, a Wheat

Pool rain gauge, real Down East maple syrup, a dozen Petro-Canada Prairie Lily tumblers, a clothes-pinned wad of crossword puzzles clipped from the *Leader Post.* Proceeds went to the Buffalo Plains Blues for uniforms.

As well there were hand-knit toques and socks and mitts, a pair of toddler's bob skates, moccasins from the Indian Reserve, a speckled graniteware bedpan housing a family of slightly pruned cactuses, a Labatt rumpus room mirror, an Ookpik doll and a stack of records beginning with the 1812 *Overture.* Then Ida felt a stab of nostalgia.

Beyond a model railroad and a set of Barbie doll wigs were a white hat and cane. The hat was flat-topped, made of stiff compressed straw. The cane was spindly and brittle; it would be unable to support any weight.

It was not the first time Ida had scrutinized the party cane—just a few years ago she had unloaded it at a similar junk depot. One day when Hartland was five months old James arrived home from an auction sale at Phil Springhill's. He burst into the house, twirling this very cane and dancing around, making such silly faces and singing so foolishly that Hartland, laughing uncontrollably, filled his diaper. Ida had never before (or since) seen James act with such abandon, and she liked it. Four years later, the day of James's ... accident, the only handy crutch was the useless vaudeville cane. Her husband's arm around her shoulder, Ida stumbled him to the living room rocking chair where he remained, the rocker runners carving ski-tracks into the braided rug.

Ida shook off those thoughts and chose a handful of used romance books to trade for the ones she had brought. Margaret and Louise were waiting with fat grins. "Well," said Margaret, "lookit what the cat dragged in!"

"Here comes trouble," chimed in Louise. Hefty arms crossed under their bosoms, the two women formed a fleshy-smelling bar solid as a grain-truck bumper.

"Look what the cat dragged in!" repeated Margaret.

The women inquired about life on the farm, fussed over Sarah, commented sagely on the rigours of raising two children as a single parent (tickling the subject of Warren Putnam without mentioning his name) then, "How's James doon?" boomed Louise.

Almost imperceptibly, Ida nodded her head. She stared, eyes unfixed, at the armoured chest in front of her. Had there ever, she wondered, been any space where the two breasts did not press together like sacks of flour?

"He earns his keep."

Louise chuckled. "Hey?"

"Sure, we dress him in castoffs and prop him up in the field. It's better than a scarecrow." Unwavering, she clipped her gaze first on Louise, then on Margaret. The women eyed her, unsmiling, until she lifted her upper lip into a cold smile, pulling taut the cheeks of her tired face.

The two wives began cautiously to cough up bits of Snickers and soon they were roaring loud as horses. Crowned with back-combed waves of mannish hair, the large heads shook heavily until finally their laughter abruptly died and was replaced by businesslike speech as the books were bartered.

Barnyard smells wafted sweetly into Ida's nostrils as she stepped into the rink. Sheets of plywood lay over the ice and a layer of moist sawdust covered the plywood. In the centre of the rink two rows of stalls and pens were occupied by livestock. The rink's perimeter was flanked by a camp of roofless tents held taut by guy ropes roofing-tacked onto the plywood sheeting. One or two languid people sat on plastic pop-crates outside each tent. A hundred or more people milled about, adding to the low din of moos and baas and oinks; more voices, and some other unrecognizable sounds, could be heard inside the tents. Ida began to wish she'd curled her hair.

A young man dressed in a siwash sweater and designer blue jeans stopped in front of Ida, dropped a paper plate to the ground as he took the last bite of a piece of pie and, casually lifting one foot and then the other, chiselled a keel of wet sawdust from the soles of his cowboy boots with the handle of a plastic fork. Ida decided he must be a Selkirk because of a peculiar, not unattractive overbite which the mother had given the six children. Beside him was a tall, neatly dressed man whom Ida recognized as a Born With a Tooth Métis, Paul Brulé, who had come to take away the telephone when Ida's debt to Sasktel grew too large. The Indian man winked at her as he ate from a bag of Humpty Dumpty potato chips.

Ida strolled over to the first animal pen, tugging Sarah by the hand. Inside was a less than year-old billy goat whose two horns had sprouted so close together they were fused into one unicorn horn. He nudged his head through the fence toward Sarah. The girl reached between the wooden rails, trying to grab hold of the horn, but the goat twisted his head around so he could lick her fingers. He singled out her thumb and began to suck.

"Looks like he still needs his mom, eh?" The voice was a resonant hoot that sounded like it came through a long pipe.

Ida turned to see Reginald Fort, the square bruise-nailed fingers of his right hand stuffed through the handle of a rooster cage. A crew of other farmers stood nearby with more roosters in cages. Bud Mackenzie, who each summer custom-mowed Ida's hay sloughs, had set his cage by his side and was masterfully rolling a cigarette in corded hands missing the right index finger, the left pinkie and half of the left ring finger. Mike Batoche, an old bachelor with thin white hair and a tree of tiny red veins on his nose, smiled a shy, toothless smile while young Lance Richard, a swaggerer in a hockey jacket who had caused a scandal with a young teacher while her husband was up north working on his sod farm, gave Ida an insolent smirk.

Bud Mackenzie smiled devilishly at Sarah and gestured with a gnarled hand. "Nice-looking boy, eh? Isn't that a fine-looking little boy?" This was the only technique Ida had seen Bud Mackenzie use with children: telling girls they were boys and boys they were girls. Boys, if taunted to the point of rage, would respond with kicks to the shins, girls with a hammered fist to the thigh. Little girls sometimes insisted tenaciously, "I am *not* a boy," while both boys and girls often burst into tears.

Sarah showed no reaction whatsoever, merely stared at the deformed hand holding the rolled cigarette and watched the inverted V of smoke flow from the man's nostrils each time he took a puff.

"What are you going to do with the roosters?" asked Ida. The question made the men kick at the sawdust and look at each other for answers.

"Contest."

"Judging, y'know."

A man, one of the carnival people, waited anxiously outside one of the tents. Occasionally one or two men entered, many carrying roosters in cages.

"We best get in there," said Bud Mackenzie, taking a wooden match from his pocket. He struck the match on his fingernail and relit the burnt-out cigarette in his mouth. He rubbed out the match flame on his pant leg as another cloud of smoke veed from his nostrils. "Sorry you and your little boy couldn't come. Just us and the judges are allowed." He picked up his rooster cage. The rooster, at eye level with Sarah, let out an ear-splitting squawk.

"Cack-ca-caw-CRAW!"

In the pen next to the unicorn-goat, a single chicken picked at kernels of grain in a tinfoil pie plate, making the sound of a child's drum. A newspaper photograph stapled to the front rail of the stall showed a ruffled hen who squinted quizzically at two eggs, one round, the other bowling pin-shaped. The caption under the picture, clipped from the Buffalo Plains *Bi-Weekly*, identified the hen as "Bowling Betty."

Ida looked tiredly about the place. A barker outside a tent hooked her glance, pointing at her and Sarah as he recited, "Bring the kids, bring grandma and grandpa, bring yourself, see the impossible, experience the inexplicable, be amazed by the amazing—*witness the horrendous realities of the savage world...*" Meanwhile, a great hubbub had erupted in the tent where Bud Mackenzie and the others had entered with their roosters.

In a nearby stall a boy posed beside a young black bull while his mother snapped a Polaroid picture. The mother looked around for a place to set her cigarette and finally gave it to the boy's younger sister to hold. After the flash the boy, wearing a white Stetson and western shirt, hopped over the stall and stood for another photo as he was awarded a blue ribbon by the mayor, Bill Seagram. A group of the boy's friends teased him as he wriggled his shivering arms into a parka. Other cattle-men stood smoking and talking with the boy's father. One of the boy's friends Frisbeed a paper pieplate at the hockey time clock, hitting the "Visitors" sign.

A long rubbery man with skin the colour of old moss stood in the shadow of a tent flap. His black eyes darted from one person to the next while he fingered the slender blade of a sword like the stops of a wind instrument. Eventually he sidled up to the cattle group, leaned his head back, exposing a lean, snakelike neck, and was about to slide the sword down his throat when a short stocky man in a cowboy hat took one long stride forward and stamped his foot. "You git on outta here!" he growled.

Ida wished Hartland could have had the chance to do the things that required a father, like 4-H. In the few short years that James had actually been a father to Hartland he had taught the boy a lot about plants and animals and the weather. He used to tell Ida how when Hartland grew bigger he would teach him to break horses as he had done as a boy, how to make shelter in the wild, how to snare rabbits. Now and then, against Ida's wishes, he took the boy over to the reserve for an afternoon visit with old Pa Lacasse, who had taught James to fish with a gunnysack and how to distinguish edible berries from poisonous ones.

It was painfully comical now for Ida to remember her hopes that Warren Putnam would be a father to Hartland. It was funny to think of Warren doing anything. Apart from playing darts with her beer buddies.

Seven years ago the municipal grader had come scraping down the valley hill road of the Cole farm. Ida watched the grader shave the short stretch of road past the yard gate then, through the trees behind the house-trailer, she heard the diesel engine labour as the grader continued, trying to climb the scrap of a trail that dribbled off into rock and prairie wool on the back hillside. With a gnashing of gears the grader retreated down the hill and in a few minutes Ida spotted Warren at the well, pumping water into his cupped hand. She invited him in for a glass of iced tea. Two months later when a new municipal counsellor was elected and gave his son the grading job, Ida hired Warren to work in the vegetable fields she was struggling to cultivate on her own. He ended up staying.

Ida's hopes that Warren might play a fatherly role were quashed the first winter. When the willow-banked river froze hard enough to sustain weight, Hartland shyly brought out the old hockey sticks, skates and gloves that had been his father's and asked Warren if he'd like to come play on the ice. Warren responded with a quick snort which seemed to indicate he understood the joke and found it a funny one too.

As a boy Hartland had stood longingly by his father's rocking chair, trying to imagine the gray-faced man active in the leather-smelling hockey gear, trying to remember him as joyful as he had been, quiet eyes full of light instead of staring perpetually at nothing. In recent years his sadness about his father had hardened into a bitter stone of hatred for Warren and, Ida felt, for her too. Everything he said now had a sharp edge to it. A couple of days ago she had asked him to go prime the water pump and he had snapped back, "Why don't you get your *lover* to do it?" making the word sound as thick and greasy as possible.

Ida continued her way around the rink. She was uninterested in the agricultural exhibits and wasn't curious enough to enter one of the carnival tents. She didn't even like having to say hello to the people she knew.

An albino standing outside a tent calmly inserted a flaming stick into his mouth and closed his lips then held a second torch near his mouth and exhaled, causing a yellow gob of flame to leap out. Behind him passed a gray-haired man in tight paisley trunks who was tattooed everywhere Ida could see except his eyelids. Across the man's back, over one shoulder, down under the opposite arm and around his chest, a faded blue panther chased its own tail in the blue jungle covering the man's torso. The man draped a raincoat over the shoulders of a woman dressed only in a tiger-stripe bikini. The woman had dark brown eyes, pencilled-in auburn eyebrows and long hair the colour of ripe wheat. They looked road-worn.

Ida pulled Sarah through a clog of people gawking into a tent doorway where an animal act was taking place. In front of the next tent a young man clad in black tights and top hat, wearing white pancake makeup over his entire face, performed magical illusions in mime. He pinned his dark eyes on Sarah, theatrically pressed his right thumb and forefinger into a pair of tweezers, tilted his head sideways and poked the finger-tweezers into his eye. Slowly at first, then faster, in mock alarm, he reeled out a string of finely knotted silk scarves: coral-lime-fuchsia-banana-orchid.

Sarah pressed her fists to her mouth and grinned as the mime stared in bewilderment at the tropical rainbow of silk dangling from his head. He looked sadly to Sarah for help, then his face brightened, he held his left fore-finger aloft—even to Ida a comic-book light bulb seemed to appear over his head—the long slender fingers probed into his left ear and tugged out, first the stems, then the only slightly rumpled heads of a bouquet of white carnations, the coloured scarves sucking back into his opposite ear like a long wet noodle.

The mime passed the flowers among the ladies of the applauding crowd and reached casually behind Sarah's ear where he found a white dove; he placed the bird in Sarah's small white hands. She allowed it to peck gently at the tip of her nose until the man lifted his hat and the bird flew to the top of his head.

The crowd chuckled as the magician bowed low, elegantly ran his hand along the brim of his hat and placed it squarely over the top dove on his head. Then, with a grandiloquence of facial and corporeal gesticulation, he turned to Ida and silently beseeched the company of her daughter. Soft eyes wide and asking, he tilted his head and held forth his open palm as if offering the girl candy. Sarah pulled away from her mother, entranced by the kindred mute. The magician took her by the hands and studied her, fixing his eyes on her back boots, her brown parka, the blue knit scarf hanging loosely from her neck, her open child's face. Everyone eyed the pair curiously as the young man stared into the girl's blue eyes, she returning the gaze.

"POOF!" The magician reached into a chalice by his side and dashed a pellet into a pewter dish; a smoky cloud smudged the air. Seconds passed in gray opacity as the ring of spectators waited for the anemic white light to filter down from the fluorescent tubes, slowly swallowing up the black motes.

The audience gasped as the two fingers took shape amid the smoke.

There before them were not Sarah and the magician but an adult woman with Sarah's blue eyes and yellow hair standing in a black mime-suit beside a fine, dark-haired boy in snow boots and a blue scarf. The boy stood expressionless, quietly waiting. The woman, at first leaning indolently on one leg, pulled herself to her full height. Blue eyes experienced, lips curved, softly mocking: it was a face of quiet power. Sarah, fully grown, turned and gave her mother an enigmatic smile until Ida was forced to look away.

All noise in the rink ceased as a pounding filled Ida's head. A black midget clown, weaving through the crowd with a tray, held a paper horn of pink snow under Ida's nose. She closed her eyes until he had gone.

As the next puff of smoke cleared Ida felt Sarah's child fist curl around her thumb and squeeze. The magician doffed his black hat, spun it, and bowed.

THE SNOW CRUNCHED UNDER THE CAR TIRES like the grinding of Hartland's molars as he pulled into the lot behind Hank Best's Fivepin Palace. A faded collage of rusty tin signs—the red Daily Mail airplane, the Scottish-looking Export A lady, the Player's sailor—came weakly to life in the glow of the headlights. Hartland opened the tailgate, wrapped his father's head well in the blanket and carried him toward the rink.

He had parked in the blind alley to avoid anyone spotting Warren's station wagon—he knew he had beaten his mother to town because he'd glimpsed her backing up a blocked side road—but when he walked by the hotel beer parlour he had to pass three of the McLuhan pickups idling line-abreast with the McLuhan brothers and their wives inside. A sedan with Manitoba license plates stopped across from the elevator and a gang of Indians inside asked where they could buy gas. As Hartland directed them a handful of kids ran by, chasing a volleyball in a game of broomball shinny. Finally the Indians thanked him and drove away, the undercarriage of their car scraping bottom as it rumbled over the level crossing.

Hartland pulled his toque-mask over his face and ran. James's body, flopped over Hartland's back, jounced with the chugging motion; each step made him grunt, breaking a dry grumble that rattled in his throat. The noises—James's closest sounds to speech since the day of the accident in the chicken coop—faded as Hartland weaved through the cars parked at the arena.

Inside, he gaped at the camp of black tents, dazed by the crowd and the noise. He grabbed the sleeve of a man carrying an armful of batons and tennis balls. "Where's Little Dothan?" he demanded. The man, dressed in tights and an open parka, lithely raised a runnered foot and pointed to a long tent halfway down the rink.

"Little Dothan'll be on after the animals," he drawled.

Hartland made a beeline for the tent. He backed into the tent-flap doorway and let the flap fall shut. A narrow pathway led past a small stage and through the penalty exit to the bleachers where a dozen people watched a muzzled bear cub waddle after a fish on a stick held by an acne-scarred blonde. Presently the woman led the bear to a small cage, undid the leather muzzle and flung in the fish. She closed the door after the bear and draped a purple tie-dyed sheet over top the cage.

The next performer was a green parrot who warbled scattered, halting lines from "Dixie" and "Swanee River," then flew back and forth between two open cages at opposite ends of the stage, making a dramatic dive through a hula-hoop in the centre. A crew of gawkers, led by a stooped man with long ears and a rubberish face, clodded together in the doorway. For the show's finale the bird perched on a mini-trapeze, held a doll's baby bottle to its beak with one foot and toppled over as though drunk. The trainer milked nervous applause from the audience, allowing "Magnum" to cling upside down until everyone was clapping loudly.

"That's all, folks!" croaked the parrot.

A pair of overalled men hauled away the bear cage on a dolly. White flames of frost had formed on the dark sheet from the bear's breath. Next, the man who had directed Hartland climbed onto the stage, took off his parka and began juggling firesticks. The carnival manager, dressed in a gray, wide-lapelled suit, came and broke up the crowd blocking the doorway. Only the big-eared man entered, the others moving on. The juggler tossed more and more items into the air while another man hopped onto a unicycle and wheeled back and forth. A paper plate struck the cyclist on the ear.

When the show finished, Jonathan York, the Presbyterian minister, stepped onto the stage. He introduced Little Dothan as a big little evangelist where he comes from, an inspiration and a young go-getter, then he led the crowd in applauding the pre-adolescent boy who bounded onto the stage.

The evangelist stared at the audience as if memorizing faces. He wore a navy blue suit, white shirt and black tie; his buckskin hair was brilliantined back, exposing a large clear forehead. A pair of quick brown eyes poked out of the pudgy cheeks like cloves in a ham. Finally he spoke. "Ah know what yore thinkin'.... Right about now, yore mind's askin' you a few tough questions an' yore haffin' to do some fancy footwork just to come up with the answers.... Who is this guy anyway? Isn't he just another one of those preachers that spews off a lot about the word o' God, throwing out big words like salvation an' heavenly ree-wards? Furthermore, this one ain't even a man, he's just a punky kid."

Little Dothan's family watched proudly from the side of the stage. The mother sat at a portable electric organ; the father stood at her side, petting the long blond braid of Little Dothan's older sister.

Little Dothan pointed to a barrel-chested man sitting with his wife and two daughters. "Is thet what yore thenkin'?"

The man smiled reverently. "Yes sir," he crooned.

"Well I'm gonna let you in on a little secret," said Little Dothan in a confidential tone. "If I was you settin' there an' listenin' to some knee-high ramble on, I'd be wonderin' too!" He let out a round jovial laugh echoed by a spatter of nervous titters from the audience.

"I won't bore you with how the Lord chose me for to be his spokesman an' how empty my life was before an' all o' that stuff ... but I will tell yew this: that I ain't got no more choice in the matter than any one other of God's chosen speakers. Whatever words thet come out," he slapped his chest with a hand puffy as a pincushion, "are the words God put there. Could be that's why I don't tell such good jokes!" He flashed a polished smile then suddenly became serious.

"But I ain't here for to tell no jokes. I'm here to tell you it's time." He gave a hard stare. "Time ... that you threw off them old shackles keepin' you out of God's house. Shackles of sin, of hate and selfishness and greed... and of lust. Because, brother, there ain't much time left."

Hartland leaned forward, his neck tight as fence wire. His head bobbed in a continuous nod as he mouthed Little Dothan's words, repeating aloud the ends of sentences: "...much time left." There was a slight rasp to his breathing.

"We are livin' in the End-days, my friends. *Verily I say unto yew, this generation shall not pass.* We are witnessin' the end of Satan's free ride on Earth and I know and you know it cain't go on much longer. *The day of the Lord cometh, cruel both with wrath and fierce anger, to lay the land desolate: and He shall destroy—the—sinners."*

Hartland turned excitedly to his father. The man's eyes remained as empty as they had been at home in the valley.

"I bin hearin' lots about drought in these parts, 'bout how the ground's all dried up and there's no grass in the pastures. 'Almost seems like the heavens have forsook us and the world's comin' to an end.' I heared one farmer say over to yore little Chinese restaurant right here in Buffalo Plains, Canada. But I wanna tell you that you ain't seen nothin' like what's gonna happen come the last days on this here Earth. Isaiah seen it far off in the distance: *Suddenly, in an instant, the Lord Almighty will come with thunder and earthquake and great noise, with windstorm and tempest and flames of a devouring fire.* You talk about yore wrath of God—there's gonna be some spankings all right!

"*The stars of heaven and their constellations will not show their light. I will punish the world for its evil, the wicked for their sins....* And yew better pray, like Luke says, *that you may be able to escape* All that's gonna happen, 'cause what's gonna happen's conflagration and perdition right here on this Earth. If you-all wanna end up crispy critters you know exactly what road to follow. The road of avarice, the road of sensuality and vile acts, the road of baseness and cruelty and falseness and excess!"

"Excess," repeated Hartland hotly. Little Dothan dabbed his boyish brow with a gray silk handkerchief.

"He blasted the Sodomites one time, right offen the map, and now he's started up toilet-cleanin' again. Just take a drive through San Francisco once, they're dropping like flies. An' it's not just the homos, the fornicators'll be next.

"I seen in one o' yore farm newspapers here, *The Western Producer.* 'Farmers. Condominium co-op offers two weeks annually in tropical paradise.' " He gave a sneering smile. "Well I hain't been around long as most of yew folks but even I know *eternity* in paradise sounds a darn sight longer than *two weeks!*"

Little Dothan's mother broke into the opening chords of "Christ Whose Glory Fills the Skies," while Little Dothan's sister held up cardboard cue cards. Silver braces glinted as she sang. Little Dothan's father mopped his son's face with a towel and handed him a large Coke in a waxed cup. The plump boy slurped through the straw, took a deep breath and took over holding the cue cards for his sister, overpowering the other voices with an unbroken soprano—"Dark and cheerless is the morn..." The blue-eyed girl squeezed up and down the bleachers collecting money in a tambourine. She smiled sweetly at Hartland as he dropped in a couple of quarters, the tambourine making a "zlissle" sound.

Little Dothan warned of the threat of nuclear warfare. He stressed the necessity for Western nations to stand together against the Red Menace, fortifying their resolve in fulfilling their NATO commitments. He cited scripture, he cited John F. Kennedy. He shouted and whispered and raised his chubby fists in the air.

Fiery red fever splotches kindled the boy's cheeks; he slipped off his blazer, rolled up his shirt-sleeves and loosened his tie.

"Ladies 'n' gennlemen, I hope 'atcherall here with a open heart tonight," drawled Little Dothan, " 'cause we just might see some miracles happen. *Fill* yoreself with the *al*mighty *Lord*," he shouted, sweeping a stubby forefinger across the bunch, "and you fill yoreself with the protector of good and the avenger of evil."

"...venger of evil," said Hartland.

"I wanna tell you people that you got to have *faith*, you got to believe, and not only that, you got to believe in belief. I'm askin' you to have faith in faith, belief in belief and trust in God. Place yourself in the hands of the Lord Almighty, let yourself go, feel yourself melting back into your chair and know that the good Lord is there with a giant catcher's mitt to hold on tight. He won't let you down. What I say is true, it is the truth, the Lord will *not* let you down. See yourself floating through the air and coming to a big woolly cloud. Just ease yourself back into that old fluffy white cloud."

Organ tones hummed, soft as fuzzy bowstrings, as Little Dothan's mother toed the lowest notes. Little Dothan soothed and consoled in a voice warm as felt.

"What I say is true, it is the truth. Yore a child o' God. Faith in faith, belief in belief, trust in the Father, He won't let you down, *He will not let you down*." Hartland's head spun. Happily numb, he watched the blonde girl float like a white-robed angel between the rows. The tambourine in her hand was padded with blue and purple bills. Hartland grubbed euphorically in his empty pockets, jostling the body of his dozing father while the girl smiled and waited, her blue eyes placid and cool.

A rooster crow broke the calm.

Abruptly Hartland's father's weight left his shoulder. Hartland cranked his head to the right and watched as the man straightened from his slouch. He blinked, squinted, wiped his eyes, picked his teeth, rubbed his nose, scratched his ear. Somewhere amid the whirling eddies of sound reeling through Hartland's brain he heard bits of phrases in a strong high voice: "reach out...heart in your hands...and ye shall find..." James Cole slapped his knees. Slowly he rose to his full height—his spine giving out a series of pops and cracks as he arched his back and stretched—smeared an enormous yawn-tear across his cheek, dug deep in the pockets of the trousers Hartland had crammed him and his pyjamas into, and dropped a wadded five dollar bill onto the pile.

Little Dothan stopped speaking. He looked puzzled, watching Hartland's father who stood examining his own white breath. "OK, you're blockin' the view, sir. You'll hafta sit down now."

Hartland jumped to his feet, a smile peeled across his face.

"He's *saved!*" he shouted.

"It's James Cole," said someone.

"This kid's better'n Kreskin."

Little Dothan stood stunned for an instant.

"Yea-ess!" he exclaimed. "Yea-ess! Hold the phone folks, we have a miracle. Yea-ess! The hand of God. The blind shall see and the cripples shall get up and ..." He stopped stared, speechless, at James Cole. Little Dothan's mother tore a camera from a vinyl bag and started flashing pictures.

Little Dothan was standing next to Hartland's father now. *Flash.* Jonathan York stepped in beside Little Dothan. *Flash.* Someone had an arm around Hartland's shoulder, but he didn't know who—everything was disappearing around him: sounds, sights, smells. Everything except... a hand.

Hartland, eyes glued to the hand extended warmly between his father and him, afraid to look up, afraid not to, slowly, as if in a dream, raised his right hand—not feeling a part of his own body: an offering—and allowed it to be squeezed, his ears full of distant ebbing sounds as he swallowed hard and forced his head to tilt upwards and meet the friendly, cheerful face of his father, the man who hadn't looked at anybody since Hartland was four years old, hadn't spoken—hadn't so much as quivered his lips or turned his eyes in their sockets—giving his son a radiant grin, eyes crinkling sunnily at the edges.

"Hey, Buddy," said his father. "I'm Art Roebuck."

⁋

BIOGRAPHICAL NOTES

Lesley Battler is the author of *The Polar Bear Express*, published by NuAge Editions. She lives in Montreal.

Cormorant Books published **Roma Gelblum Bross**'s *To Samarkand and Back* in 1988. She brought out the second edition on her own in 1992, and is working on a second, related set of short stories. "The Stepmother" also appeared in P. Scott Lawrence's anthology, *Souvenirs: New English Fiction from Quebec* (Cormorant, 1987). She lives in Westmount, Quebec.

"Eddy Goss" and "Angels" were published in **April Bulmer**'s collection of poetry, *A Salve for Every Sore*, by Cormorant Books in 1991. She is working on a collection of prose poems under the working title of *Sisters of the Sacred Heart*, about an order of Prairie nuns talking about their spiritual lives. She lives in Toronto.

Jennifer Clark is part of an experimental theatre collective in Montreal, where she writes poetry and drama. She is a freelance commercial writer. "this is a story" is her first published work. She lives in Montreal.

Portions of **Mark Cochrane**'s thesis have appeared in *Prism International, Malahat, Poetry Canada Review*, the *Moosehead Anthology, Fiddlehead, CV2* and *Canadian Literature*. He is working on two volumes of poetry, one of which concerns the "W.J.M." to whom "Three Years from Long Beach" is dedicated. He lives in Vancouver.

Su Croll's *Worlda Mirth* (Kalamalka Press, 1992) was nominated for the Gerald Lampert Memorial Award of the League of Canadian Poets for first book of poetry. She is at work on another book of prose poems, and lives in Vancouver.

"Then" was published in *Poetry Canada Review;* a different version of "Mother" appeared in *A Room of One's Own.* **Jill Dalibard** is working on several poem series, including one on the death of her father called *The Lost Meadows,* and one on returning to her roots called *Home Journey.* She lives in Montreal.

Ken Decker's "Molecularclockevaluation" was part of the collection *Backyard Gene Pool* published by Quadrant Books in 1982. He lives in Vancouver.

Richard Harrison's *Recovering the Naked Man* was published by Walsak & Wynn in 1991. Near completion is another collection of poetry, *Hero of the Play,* about men, women and hockey. He lives in Scarborough, Ontario.

Elisabeth Harvor is the author of several books of poetry and fiction, the latest of which is *Fortress of Chairs* (Signal Editions, Véhicule Press, 1992), for which she shared the 1993 Gerald Lampert Memorial Award from the League of Canadian Poets for first book of poetry. "A Sweetheart" appeared in *If Only We Could Drive Like This Forever* (Penguin, 1988). She lives in Toronto.

Crossing the Chaco was published in 1982 by White Dwarf Editions of Montreal. **Hugh Hazelton** is co-editor of *Compañeros: An Anthology of Writings About Latin America* (Cormorant Books, 1992). He is translating a book of Salvadoran short stories, and editing a bilingual (French/Spanish) anthology of Latin American writing in Québec for Editions Hexagone. He lives in Montreal.

Stephen Henighan is the author of *Other Americas* (Simon & Pierre, 1990). A version of "The Border" appeared in *Nights in the Yungas* (Thistledown Press, 1992). He is studying for a doctorate at Oxford University in England.

Teresa Jurkowski is working on a collection of short stories for which she won a Canada Council Explorations grant in 1993. "Bread" is her first published work. She lives in Montreal.

"Falling" has appeared in *Fiddlehead* magazine and in the anthology *Souvenirs* edited by P. Scott Lawrence. **Julie H.P. Keith**, of Westmount, Quebec, is working on another collection of short stories.

Parallel Lines was given a reading by the Playwrights' Workshop in Montreal in 1992. **Ann Lambert**'s *Self-Offense* was produced off-off-Broadway at the Cucaracha Theater in 1993. She has had several radio dramas produced by the CBC, the latest of which was *Welcome Chez Ray* in May 1993. She lives in Montreal.

Stacey Larin's "Tense" was published in Lawrence's *Souvenirs* in 1987. She is working on fiction that crosses "spiritual, scientific and literary truth" and lives in Hamilton, Ontario.

"When the Elections Came to Town" appeared in **P. Scott Lawrence**'s short story collection *Around the Mulberry Tree*, a version of his thesis (Exile Editions, 1985). *Missing Fred Astaire*, a second collection, was published by Véhicule Press in 1993. Scott is working on a novel. He lives in LaSalle, Quebec.

Grant Loewen's *Brick* was published by DC Books in 1992 under the title *Brick, Looking Up*. A version of this selection was read in the Literature Montreal summer reading series in 1992. He is working on a novel *The Glass Bottom* and lives in Montreal.

Prodigal Son was given a dramatic reading by the Playwrights' Workshop in Montreal in 1989. Under the title *This Night the Kapo*, it won the Dorothy Silver award in Cleveland, Ohio, in 1991. A novel, *Hellman's Scrapbook*, was published by Cormorant Books in 1992. **Robert Majzels**, of Montreal, is writing another play.

Art Roebuck Comes To Born With A Tooth was published by Oberon Press in 1991. **Daniel McBain**, of Montreal, won the John Glassco Award of the Literary Translators Association of Canada as the best first literary translation in 1990 for the Costa Rican children's novel *Cocori*. He is working on a new novel.

David McGimpsey's "The Trip" is published for the first time here. Another poem from his thesis, "Babe Ruth," was published in *Rampike*. David is finishing his doctorate at Dalhousie University, studying American literature. His thesis concerns baseball novels. He lives in Halifax.

The selections from **Kathleen McHale** were included in the published version of her thesis under the title *The Intimate Alphabet* (Cormorant Books, 1993), a poetic exploration of Georgia O'Keefe's life and work. She lives in Acton Vale, Quebec.

Jennifer Price, of Mount Uniacke, Nova Scotia, writes for a radio station. She is working on poems about her mother and other women in her family, looking at the personal experience of being connected to the past, present and future through filaments of likeness.

Nino Ricci's *Lives of the Saints* (Cormorant Books, 1990), the first book in the trilogy *Rita,* won the Governor-General's Award for Fiction in 1991, the W.H. Smith/Books in Canada first novel award, and the F.G. Brassani Award. It has gone through ten printings. *In a Glass House*, the second book, was published by McClelland & Stewart in September 1993. He is working on the concluding novel and lives in Toronto.

Colonial Tongues is scheduled for production in the fall of 1993 by the 25th Street Theatre in Saskatoon. **Mansel Robinson** is working on *Standing With the Children*, a five-part radio drama about J.S. Woodsworth, founder of the CCF, for CBC's Morningside program. He lives in Regina.

Three prose poems from **Bryan Sentes**'s thesis were published in *Zymergy*. One, "Homo Omnibus," won first prize in the Saskatchewan Writers Guild annual literary competition in 1985. He has just finished the first of three volumes of poetry. He lives in Montreal.

"A Final Vision" appeared in **James Smith**'s *Translating Sleep: A Serial Meditation by and about Alexander Graham Bell* (Walsak & Wynn, 1991). Thanks to an Ontario Arts Council works-in-progress grant, he is finishing another poetry manuscript, *Leonel/Roque ¡Presente!* He lives in Toronto.

"The Princess, The Boeing and The Hot Pastrami Sandwich" was included in **Ray Smith**'s *Century* (General, 1986), *The New Press Anthology #1: Best Canadian Short Fiction* (General, 1984) and *Canadian Classics*, published in 1993. He won QSPELL's Hugh MacLennan fiction award for *A Night at the Opera* (Porcupine's Quill) in 1992. He lives in Westmount.

The Glass Mountain was published by Doubleday (Canada and U.S.) in 1985 and in the United Kingdom by Michael O'Mara. **Sharon Sparling**'s subsequent novels are *The Nest Egg* (Macmillan of Canada, 1991) and *Homing Instinct* (HarperCollins, 1993). She lives in Westmount.

"Close Calls" was one of ten stories published by Cormorant Books in 1991 under the title *Close Calls*. **Patricia Stone** has finished a second collection of stories, *Mixed Company*, which is being considered for publication. She is at work on a third collection, *A Special Place*, and on a novel. She lives in Peterborough, Ontario.

Ruth Taylor's reworked version of her thesis, *The Dragon Papers*, is scheduled for publication in the fall of 1993 by The Muses' Co., which in 1988 published her book *The Drawing Board*. She lives in Montreal and working on another collection of poetry.

Sandy Wing's fiction has previously appeared in the anthologies *Matinees Daily, Saturday Night at the Forum* and *Souvenirs: New English Writing from Quebec*. She lives in Etobicoke, Ontario.

32 Degrees editor **Raymond Beauchemin** of Montreal graduated from Concordia University's Master's program in Creative Writing in 1992. His thesis comprised two short stories, "The Corvette" and "No

Small Thing," and a novella, *Hardraw Scar,* which, completed as a novel, is being considered for publication. A journalist with ten years' editing experience, he works at *The Gazette* of Montreal. He teaches creative writing at Concordia's Centre for Continuing Education.

¶